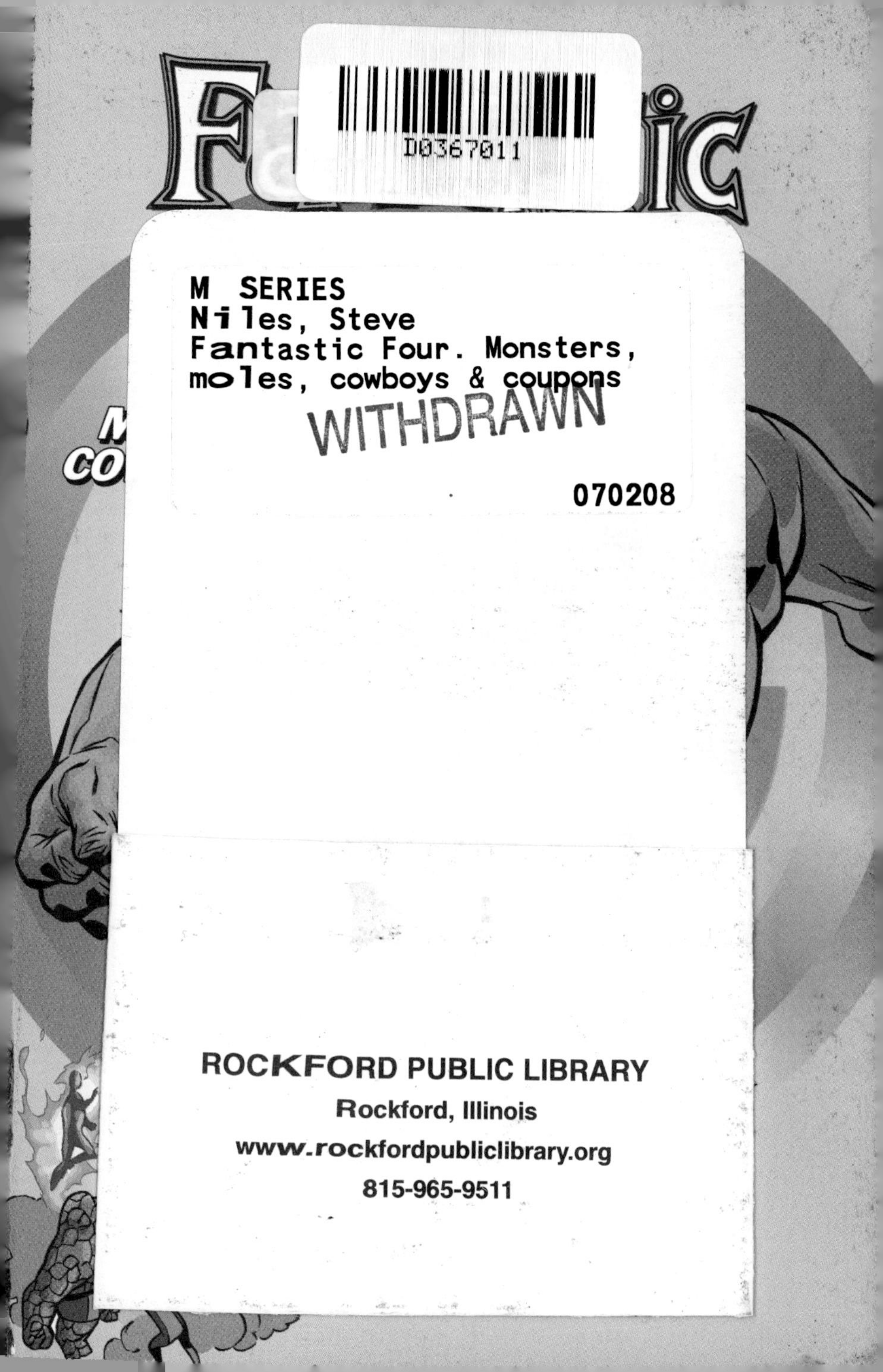

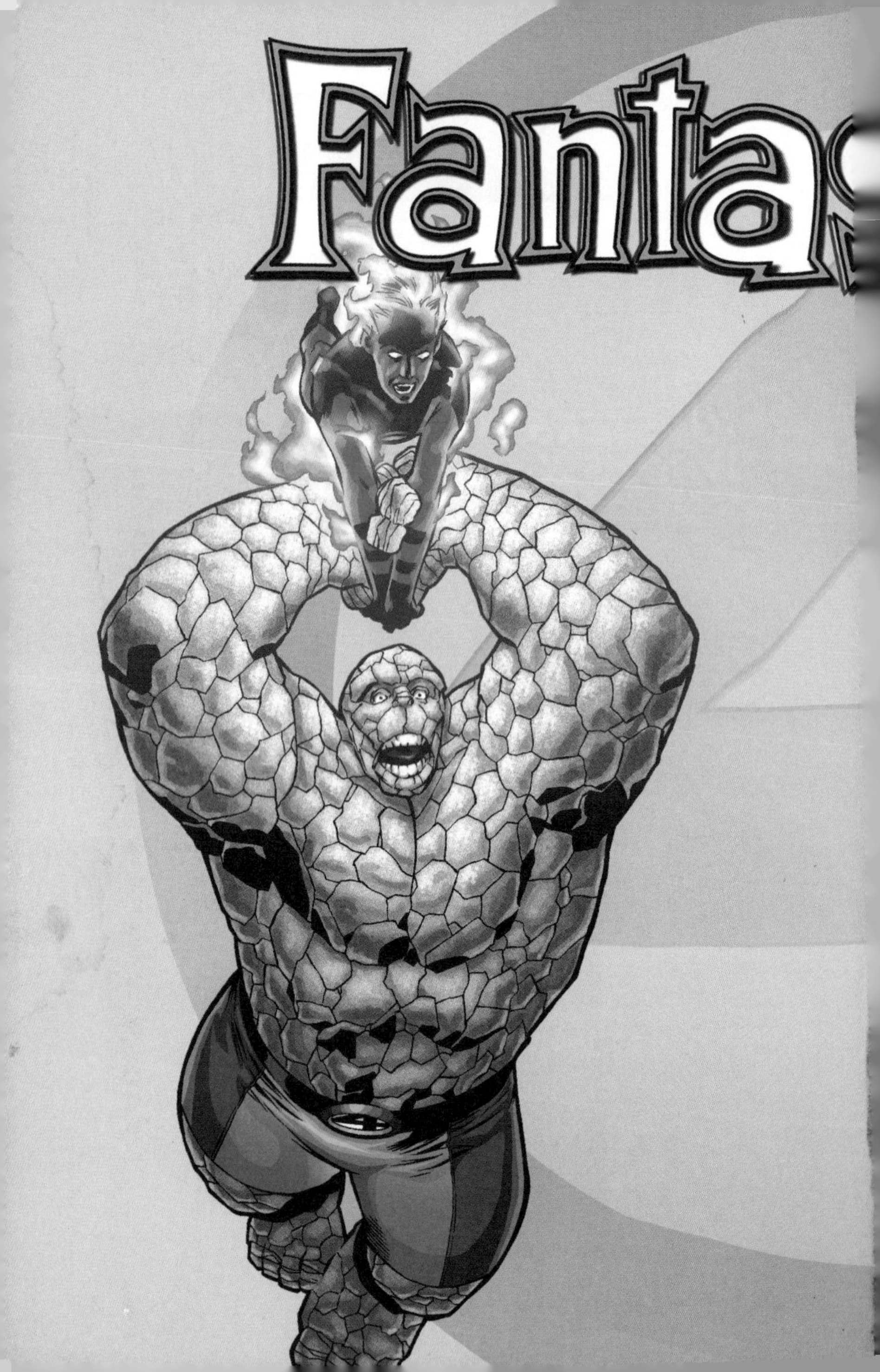
Fantas

tic Four

MONSTERS, MOLES, COWBOYS & COUPONS

Writers:
**Steve Niles, Daniel Way, Kirsten Sinclair
& Joe R. Lansdale**
Pencilers:
**Leonard Kirk, Steve Scott, David Hahn
& Ronan Cliquet**
Inkers:
Kris Justice, David Hahn & Amilton Santos

Colorist: **Lee Loughridge**
Letterer: **Blambot's Nate Piekos**
Cover Art: **Leonard Kirk with Terry Pallot,
Lee Loughridge & Brad Anderson**
Editors: **Nathan Cosby & Mark Paniccia**
Special Thanks to MacKenzie Cadenhead

Collection Editor: **Jennifer Grünwald**
Assistant Editors: **Cory Levine & John Denning**
Editor, Special Projects: **Mark D. Beazley**
Senior Editor, Special Projects: **Jeff Youngquist**
Senior Vice President of Sales: **David Gabriel**
Vice President of Creative: **Tom Marvelli**

Editor in Chief: **Joe Quesada**
Publisher: **Dan Buckley**

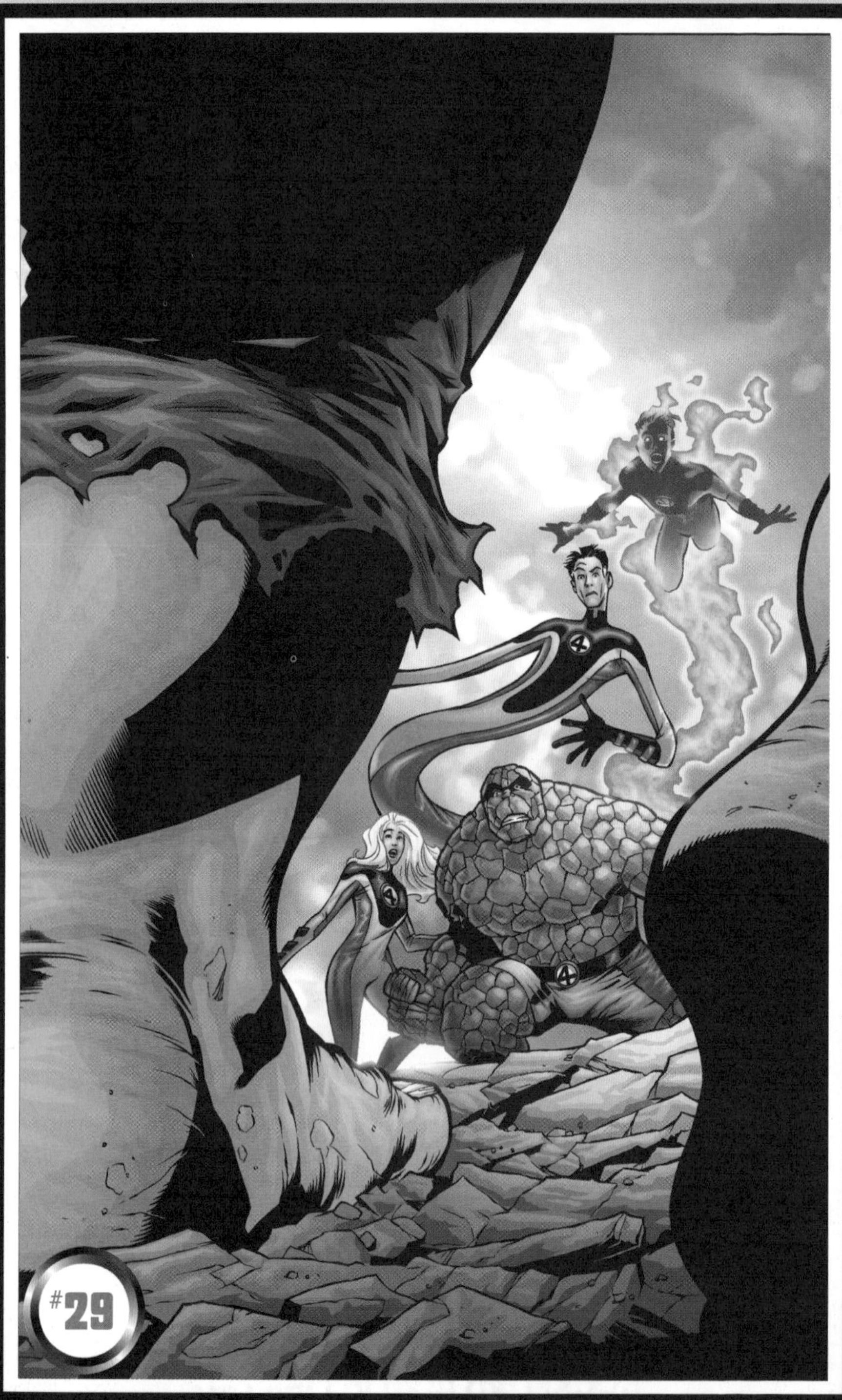
#29

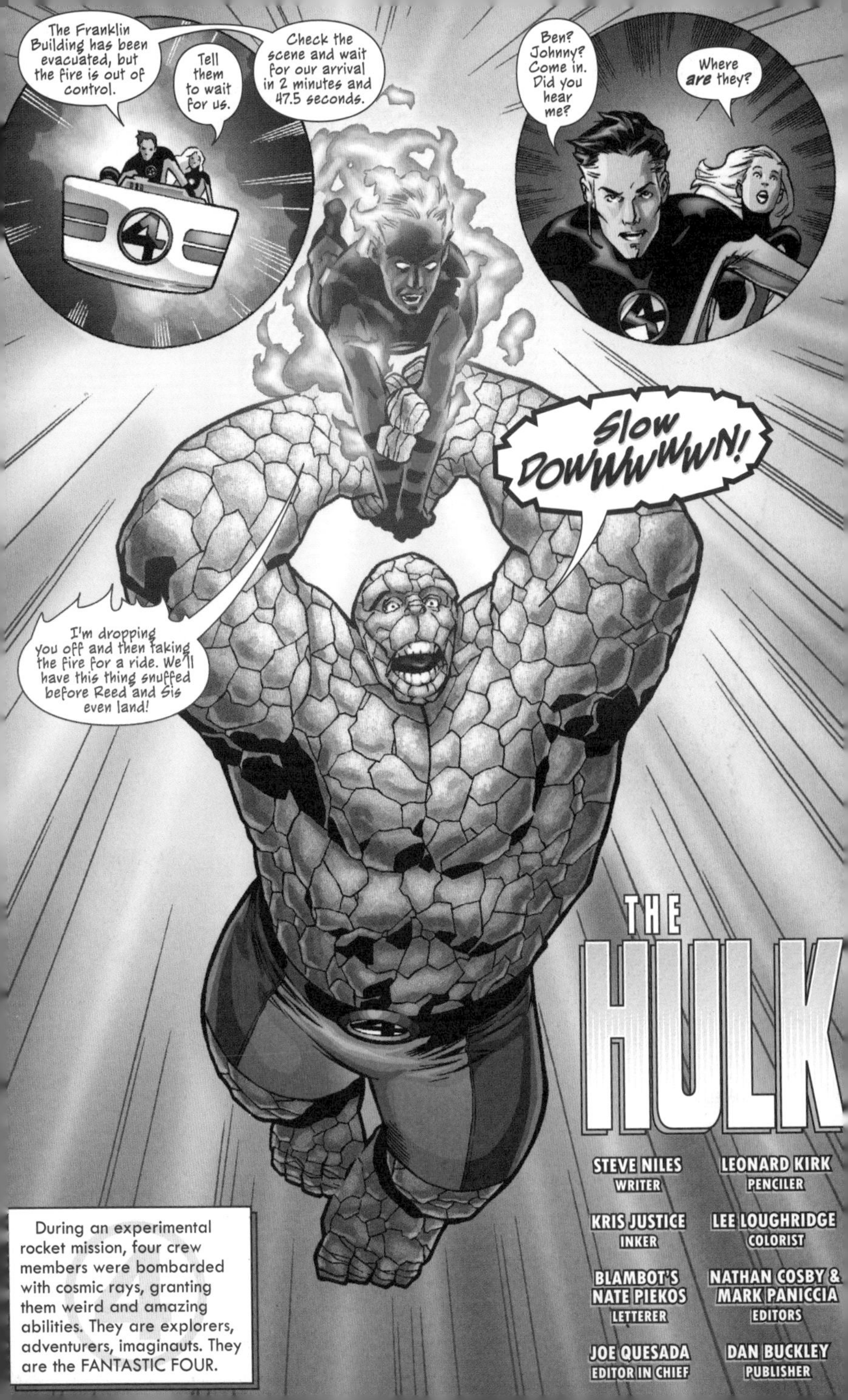
The Franklin Building has been evacuated, but the fire is out of control.
Tell them to wait for us.
Check the scene and wait for our arrival in 2 minutes and 47.5 seconds.
Ben? Johnny? Come in. Did you hear me?
Where *are* they?
Slow DOWWWWWN!
I'm dropping you off and then taking the fire for a ride. We'll have this thing snuffed before Reed and Sis even land!
THE HULK
STEVE NILES WRITER
LEONARD KIRK PENCILER
KRIS JUSTICE INKER
LEE LOUGHRIDGE COLORIST
BLAMBOT'S NATE PIEKOS LETTERER
NATHAN COSBY & MARK PANICCIA EDITORS
JOE QUESADA EDITOR IN CHIEF
DAN BUCKLEY PUBLISHER
During an experimental rocket mission, four crew members were bombarded with cosmic rays, granting them weird and amazing abilities. They are explorers, adventurers, imaginauts. They are the FANTASTIC FOUR.

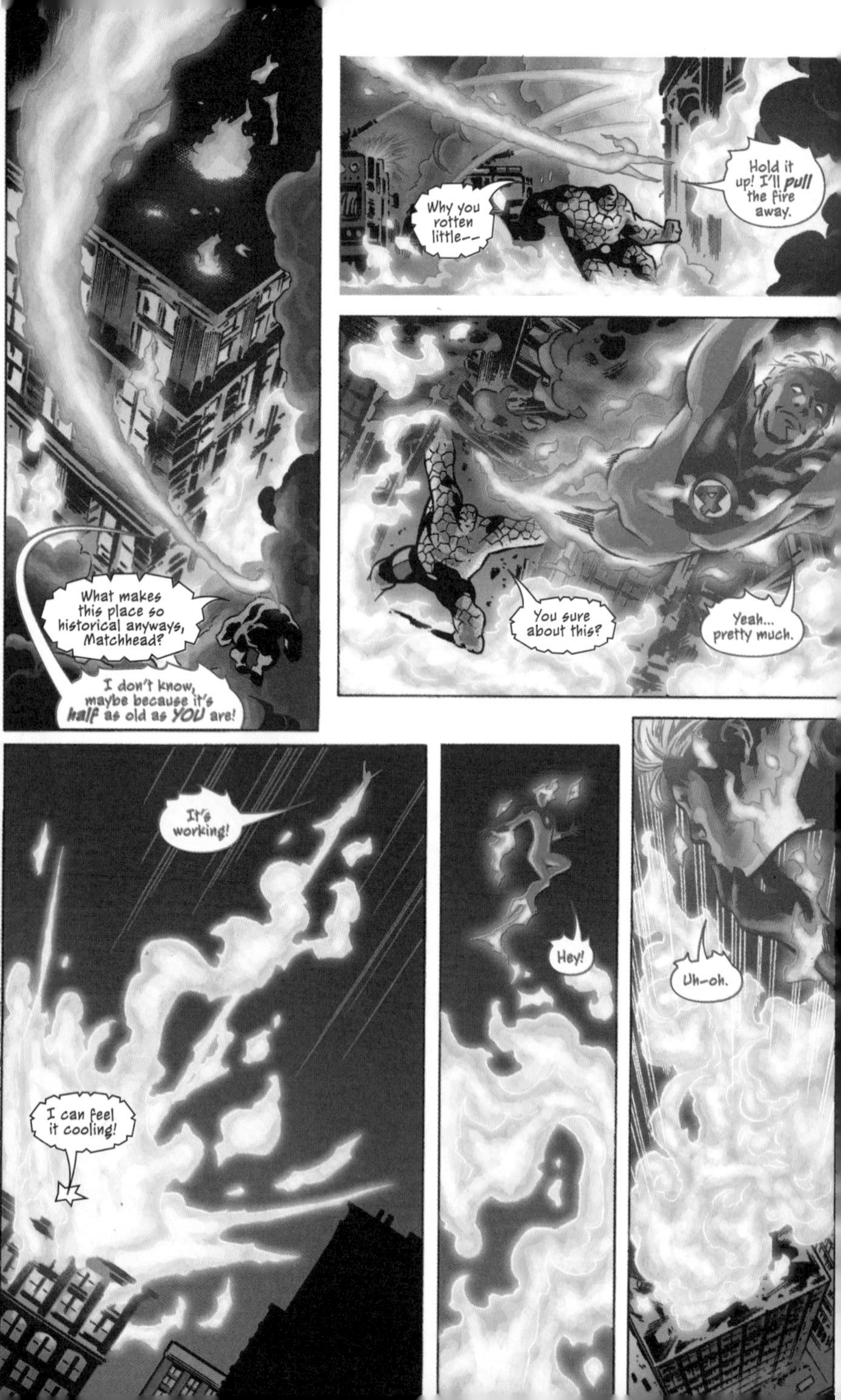
What makes this place so historical anyways, Matchhead?
I don't know, maybe because it's half as old as YOU are!
Why you rotten little--
Hold it up! I'll pull the fire away.
You sure about this?
Yeah... pretty much.
It's working!
I can feel it cooling!
Hey!
Uh-oh.

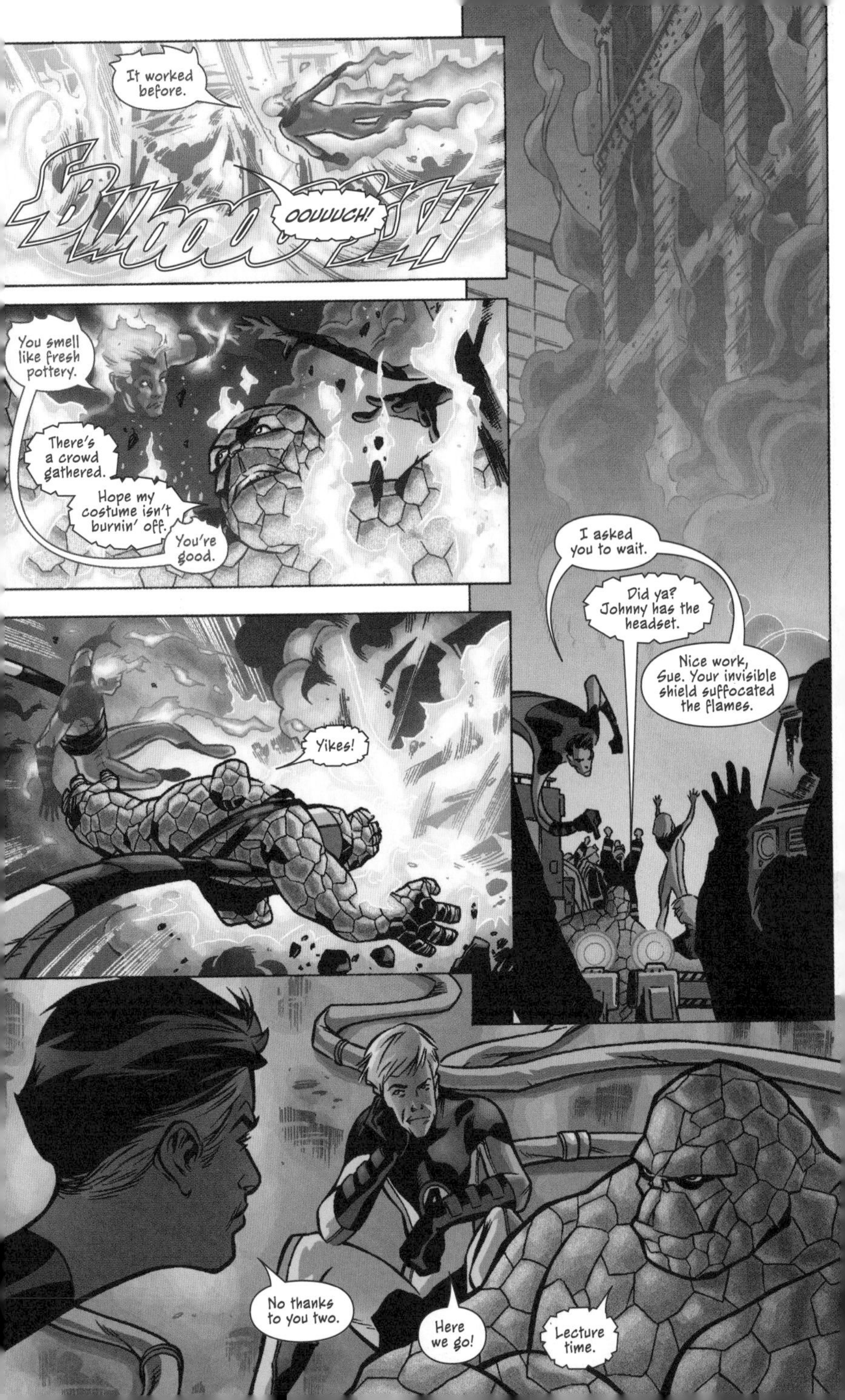
It worked before.
BLOOOSH
OOUUUCH!
You smell like fresh pottery.
There's a crowd gathered.
Hope my costume isn't burnin' off.
You're good.
Yikes!
I asked you to wait.
Did ya? Johnny has the headset.
Nice work, Sue. Your invisible shield suffocated the flames.
No thanks to you two.
Here we go!
Lecture time.

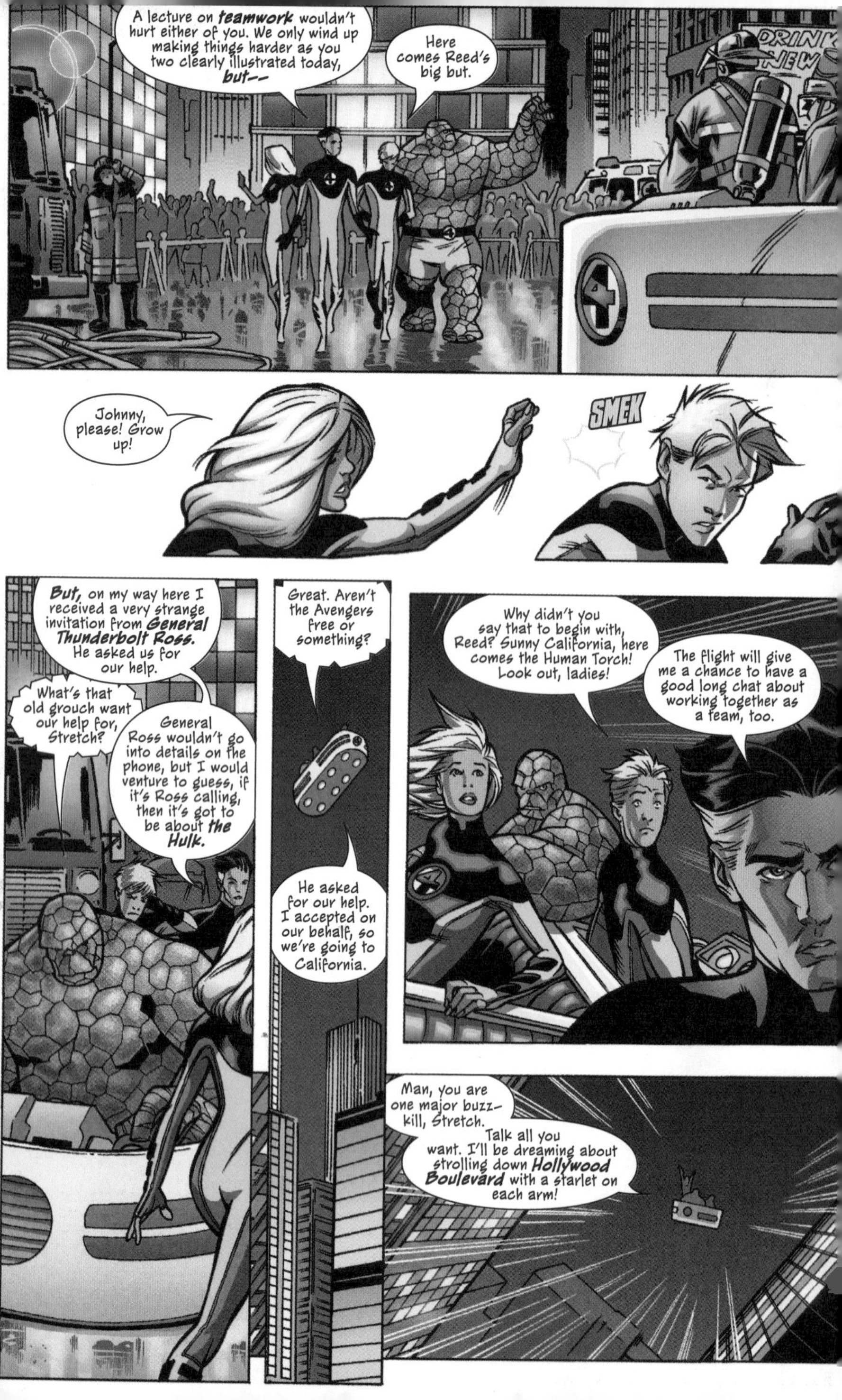
A lecture on teamwork wouldn't hurt either of you. We only wind up making things harder as you two clearly illustrated today, but--
Here comes Reed's big but.
Johnny, please! Grow up!
SMEK
But, on my way here I received a very strange invitation from General Thunderbolt Ross. He asked us for our help.
What's that old grouch want our help for, Stretch?
General Ross wouldn't go into details on the phone, but I would venture to guess, if it's Ross calling, then it's got to be about the Hulk.
Great. Aren't the Avengers free or something?
He asked for our help. I accepted on our behalf, so we're going to California.
Why didn't you say that to begin with, Reed? Sunny California, here comes the Human Torch! Look out, ladies!
The flight will give me a chance to have a good long chat about working together as a team, too.
Man, you are one major buzz-kill, Stretch.
Talk all you want. I'll be dreaming about strolling down Hollywood Boulevard with a starlet on each arm!

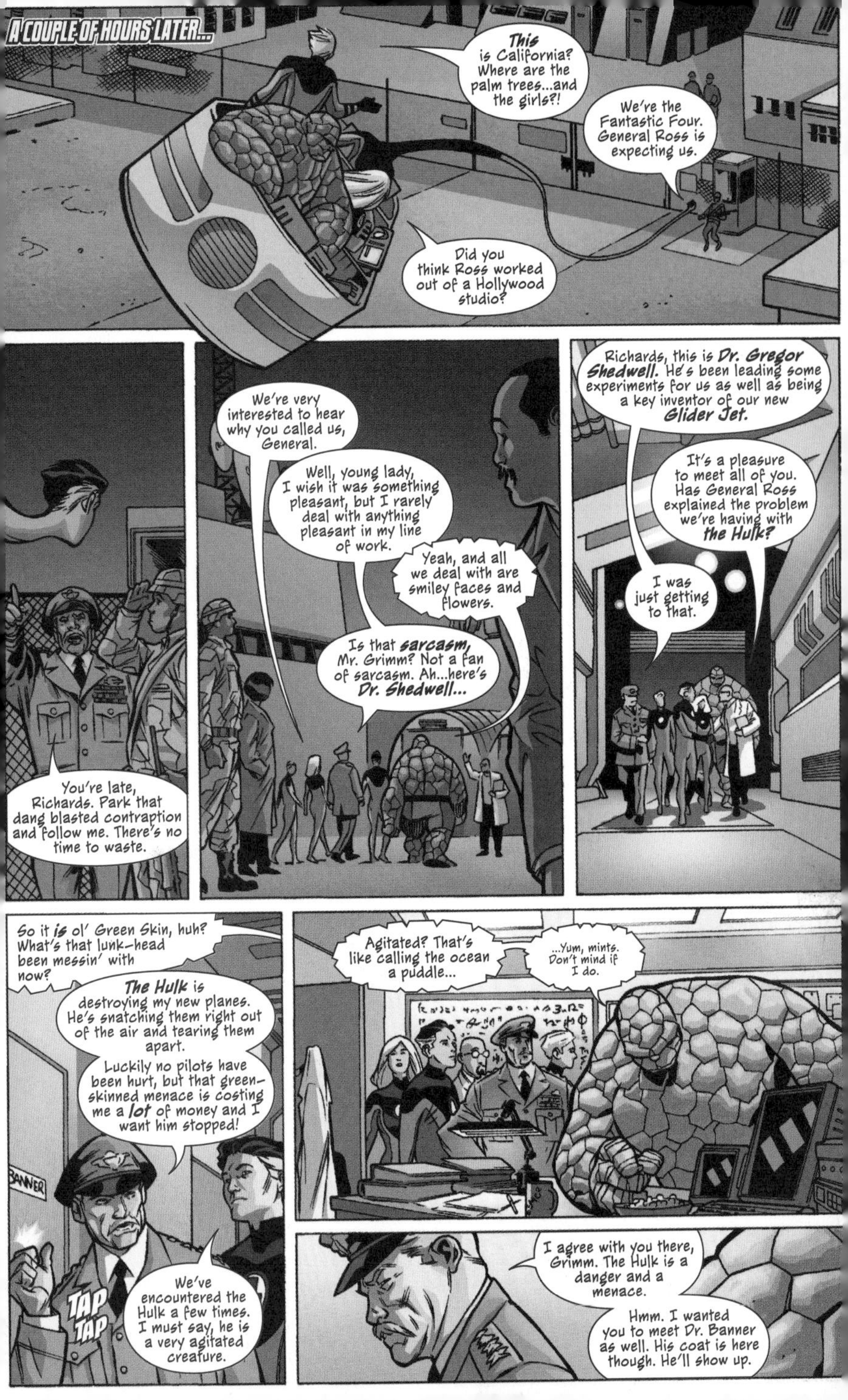

A COUPLE OF HOURS LATER...
This is California? Where are the palm trees...and the girls?!
We're the Fantastic Four. General Ross is expecting us.
Did you think Ross worked out of a Hollywood studio?
You're late, Richards. Park that dang blasted contraption and follow me. There's no time to waste.
We're very interested to hear why you called us, General.
Well, young lady, I wish it was something pleasant, but I rarely deal with anything pleasant in my line of work.
Yeah, and all we deal with are smiley faces and flowers.
Is that sarcasm, Mr. Grimm? Not a fan of sarcasm. Ah...here's Dr. Shedwell...
Richards, this is Dr. Gregor Shedwell. He's been leading some experiments for us as well as being a key inventor of our new Glider Jet.
It's a pleasure to meet all of you. Has General Ross explained the problem we're having with the Hulk?
I was just getting to that.
So it is ol' Green Skin, huh? What's that lunk-head been messin' with now?
The Hulk is destroying my new planes. He's snatching them right out of the air and tearing them apart.
Luckily no pilots have been hurt, but that green-skinned menace is costing me a lot of money and I want him stopped!
BANNER
TAP TAP
We've encountered the Hulk a few times. I must say, he is a very agitated creature.
Agitated? That's like calling the ocean a puddle...
...Yum, mints. Don't mind if I do.
I agree with you there, Grimm. The Hulk is a danger and a menace.
Hmm. I wanted you to meet Dr. Banner as well. His coat is here though. He'll show up.

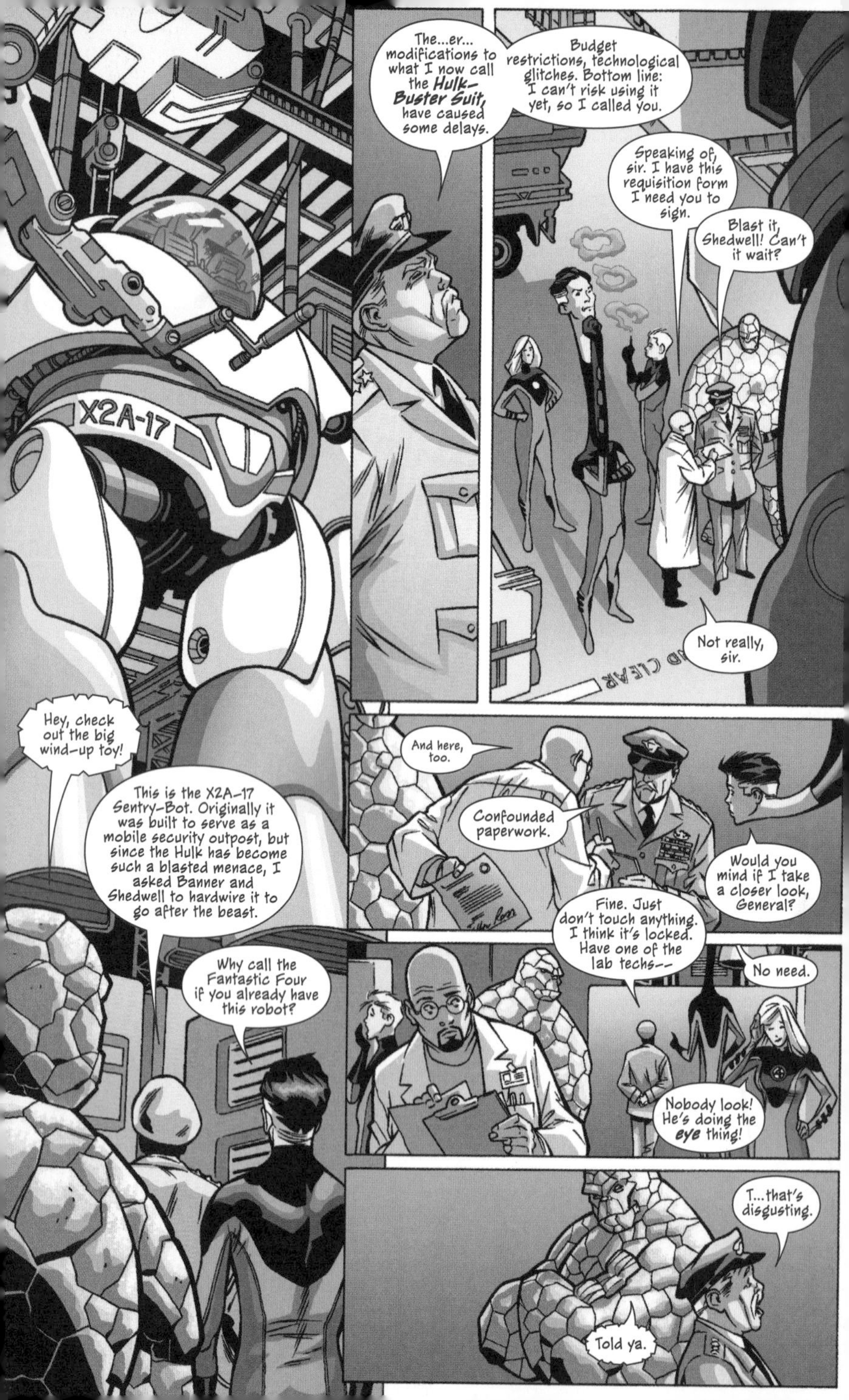
X2A-17
The...er... modifications to what I now call the Hulk-Buster Suit, have caused some delays.
Budget restrictions, technological glitches. Bottom line: I can't risk using it yet, so I called you.
Speaking of, sir. I have this requisition form I need you to sign.
Blast it, Shedwell! Can't it wait?
Not really, sir.
Hey, check out the big wind-up toy!
This is the X2A-17 Sentry-Bot. Originally it was built to serve as a mobile security outpost, but since the Hulk has become such a blasted menace, I asked Banner and Shedwell to hardwire it to go after the beast.
Why call the Fantastic Four if you already have this robot?
And here, too.
Confounded paperwork.
Would you mind if I take a closer look, General?
Fine. Just don't touch anything. I think it's locked. Have one of the lab techs--
No need.
Nobody look! He's doing the eye thing!
T...that's disgusting.
Told ya.

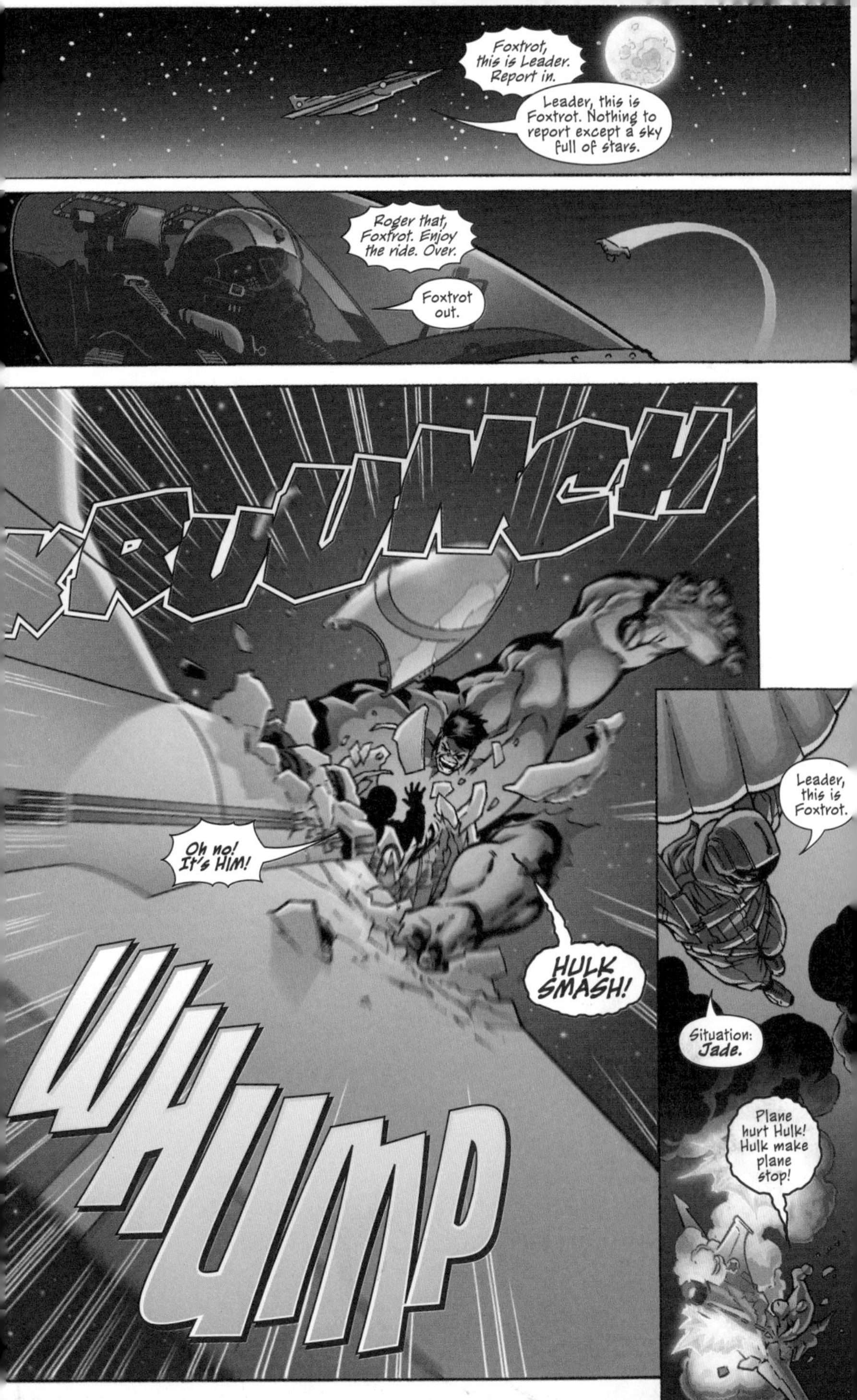
Foxtrot, this is Leader. Report in.
Leader, this is Foxtrot. Nothing to report except a sky full of stars.
Roger that, Foxtrot. Enjoy the ride. Over.
Foxtrot out.
KRUUNCH
Oh no! It's HIM!
HULK SMASH!
WHUMP
Leader, this is Foxtrot.
Situation: Jade.
Plane hurt Hulk! Hulk make plane stop!

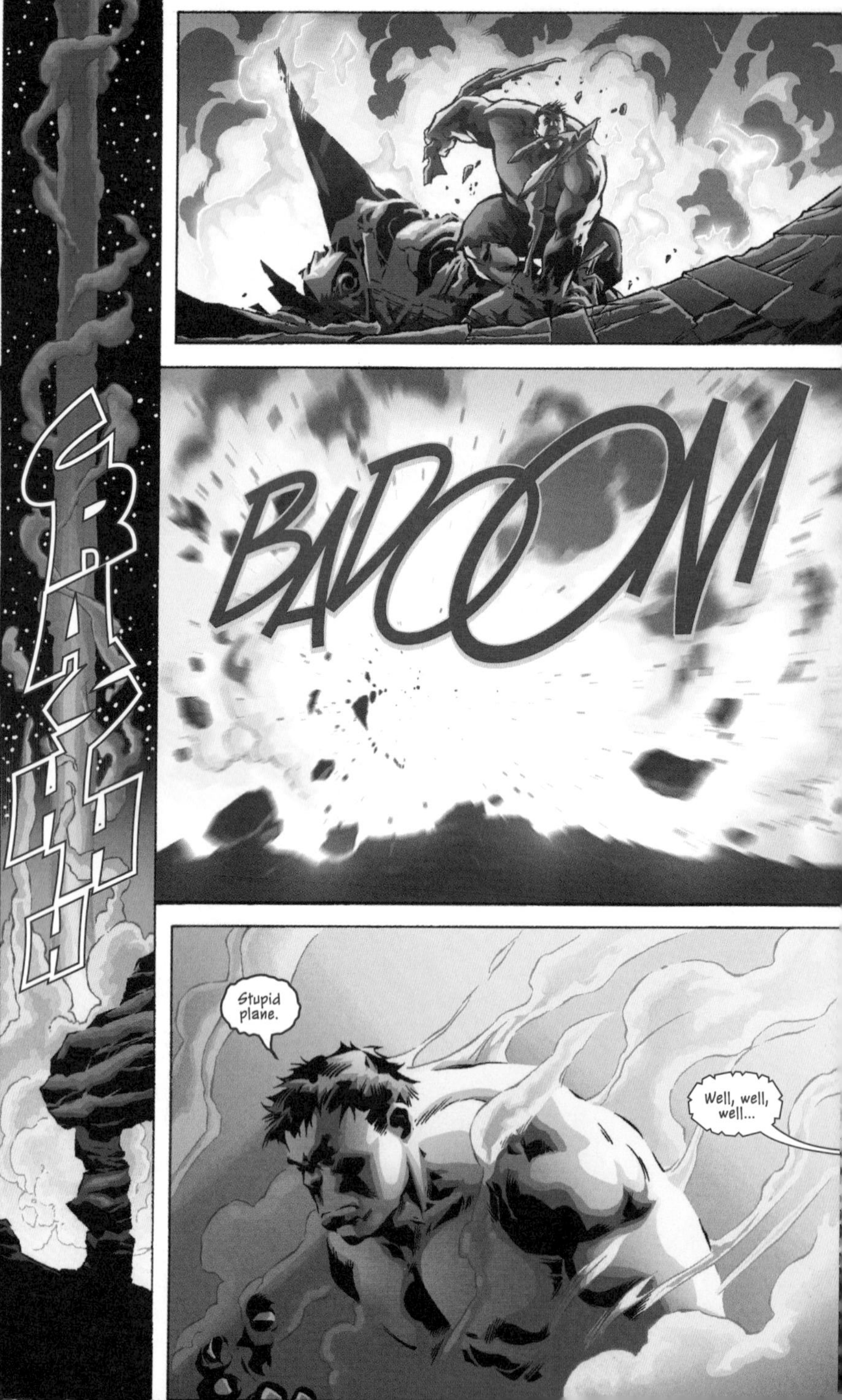
BADOOM
Stupid plane.
Well, well, well...

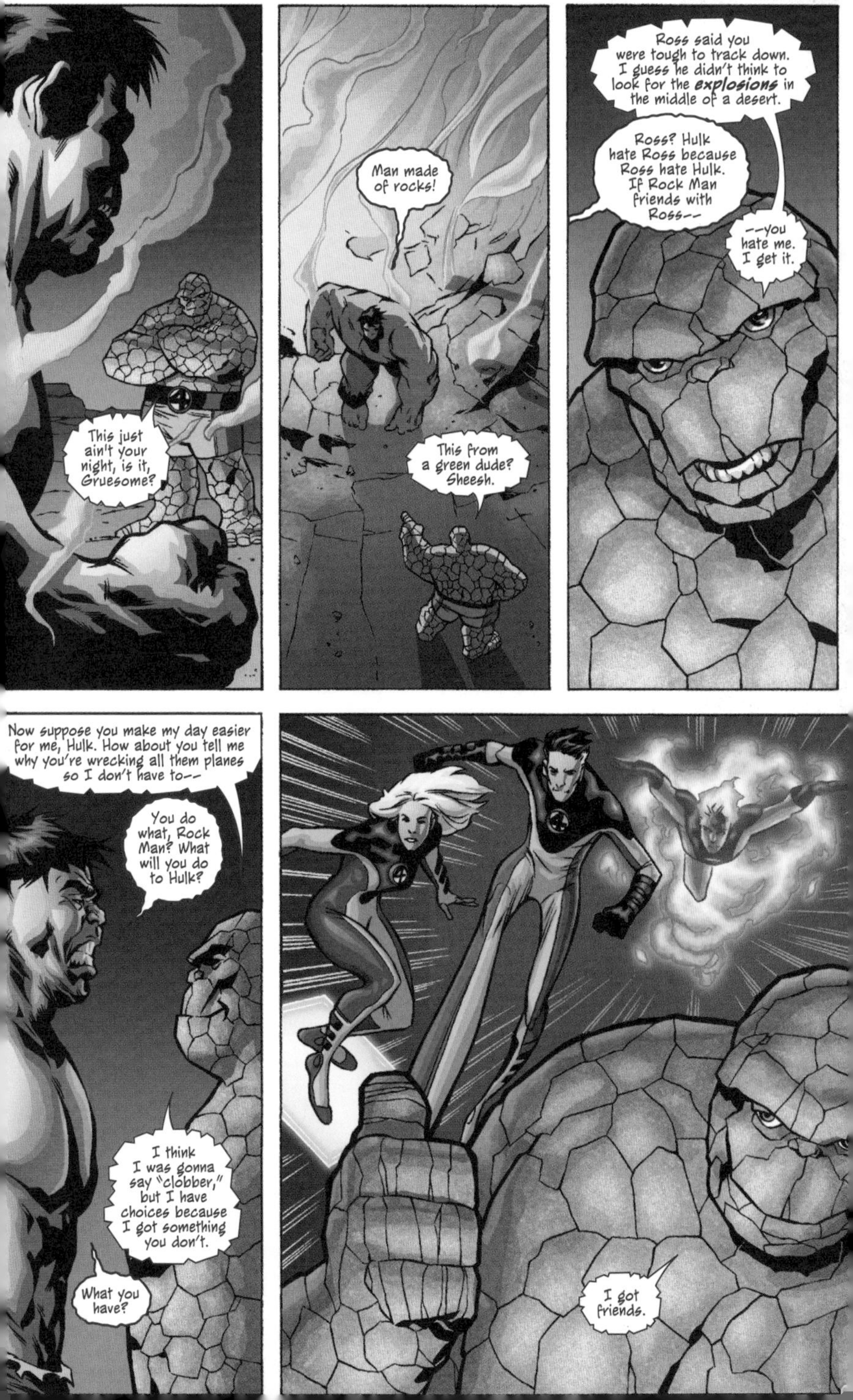
This just ain't your night, is it, Gruesome?
Man made of rocks!
This from a green dude? Sheesh.
Ross said you were tough to track down. I guess he didn't think to look for the *explosions* in the middle of a desert.
Ross? Hulk hate Ross because Ross hate Hulk. If Rock Man friends with Ross--
--you hate me. I get it.
Now suppose you make my day easier for me, Hulk. How about you tell me why you're wrecking all them planes so I don't have to--
You do what, Rock Man? What will you do to Hulk?
I think I was gonna say "clobber," but I have choices because I got something you don't.
What you have?
I got friends.

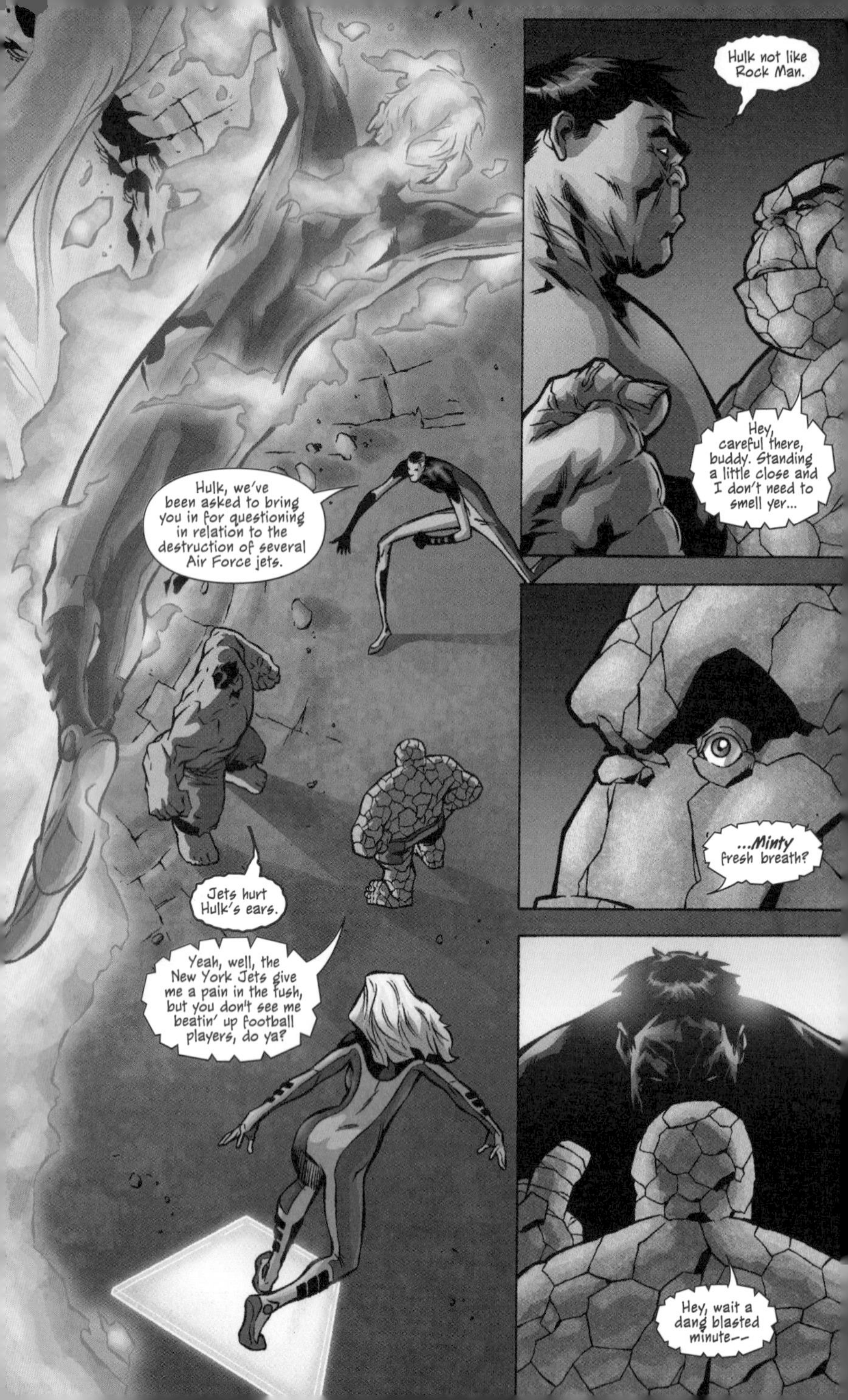
Hulk, we've been asked to bring you in for questioning in relation to the destruction of several Air Force jets.
Jets hurt Hulk's ears.
Yeah, well, the New York Jets give me a pain in the tush, but you don't see me beatin' up football players, do ya?
Hulk not like Rock Man.
Hey, careful there, buddy. Standing a little close and I don't need to smell yer...
...Minty fresh breath?
Hey, wait a dang blasted minute--

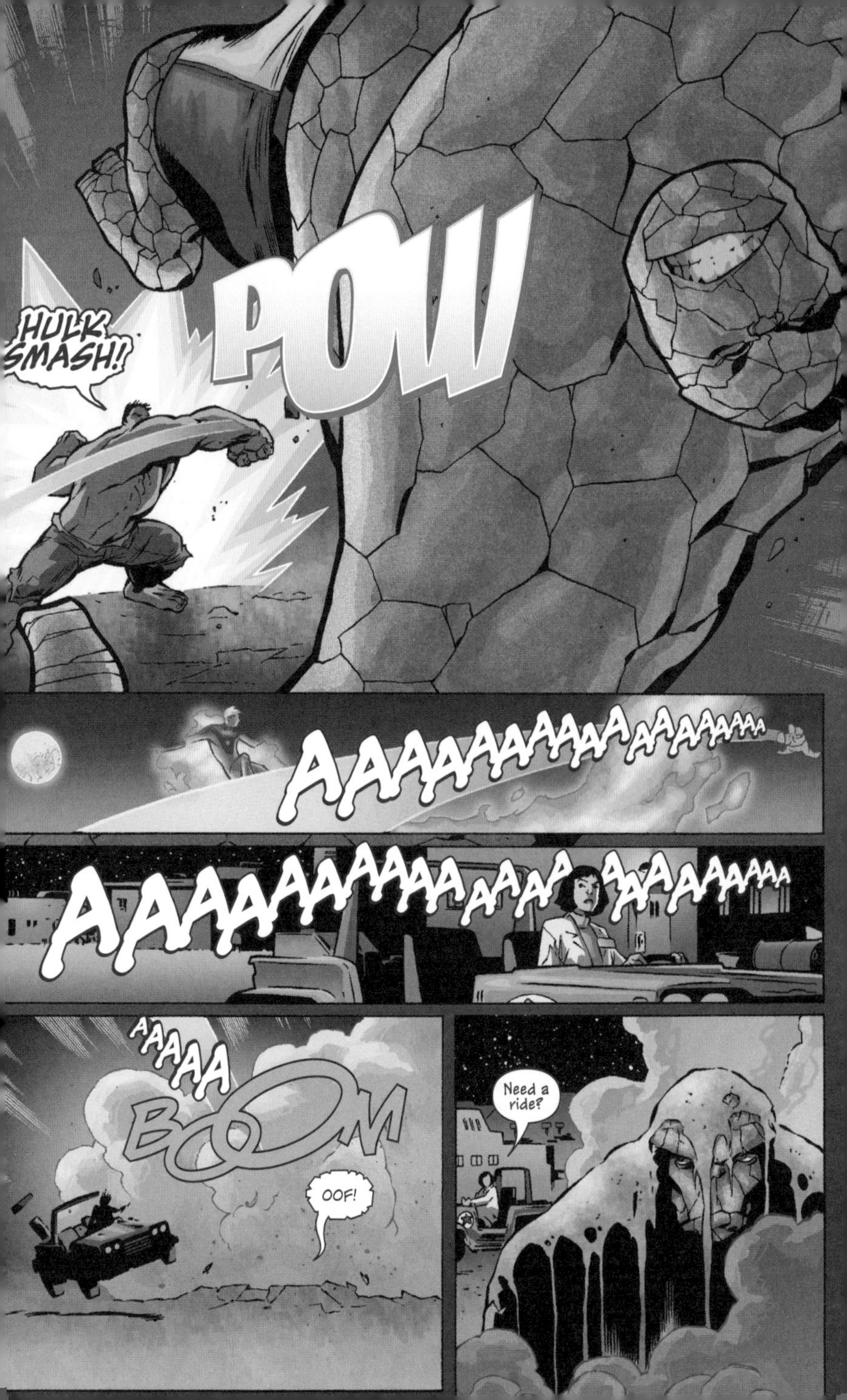
HULK SMASH!
POW
AAAAAAAAAAAAAAAAAAA
AAAAAAAAAAAAAAAAAAAAAAA
AAAAA
BOOM
OOF!
Need a ride?

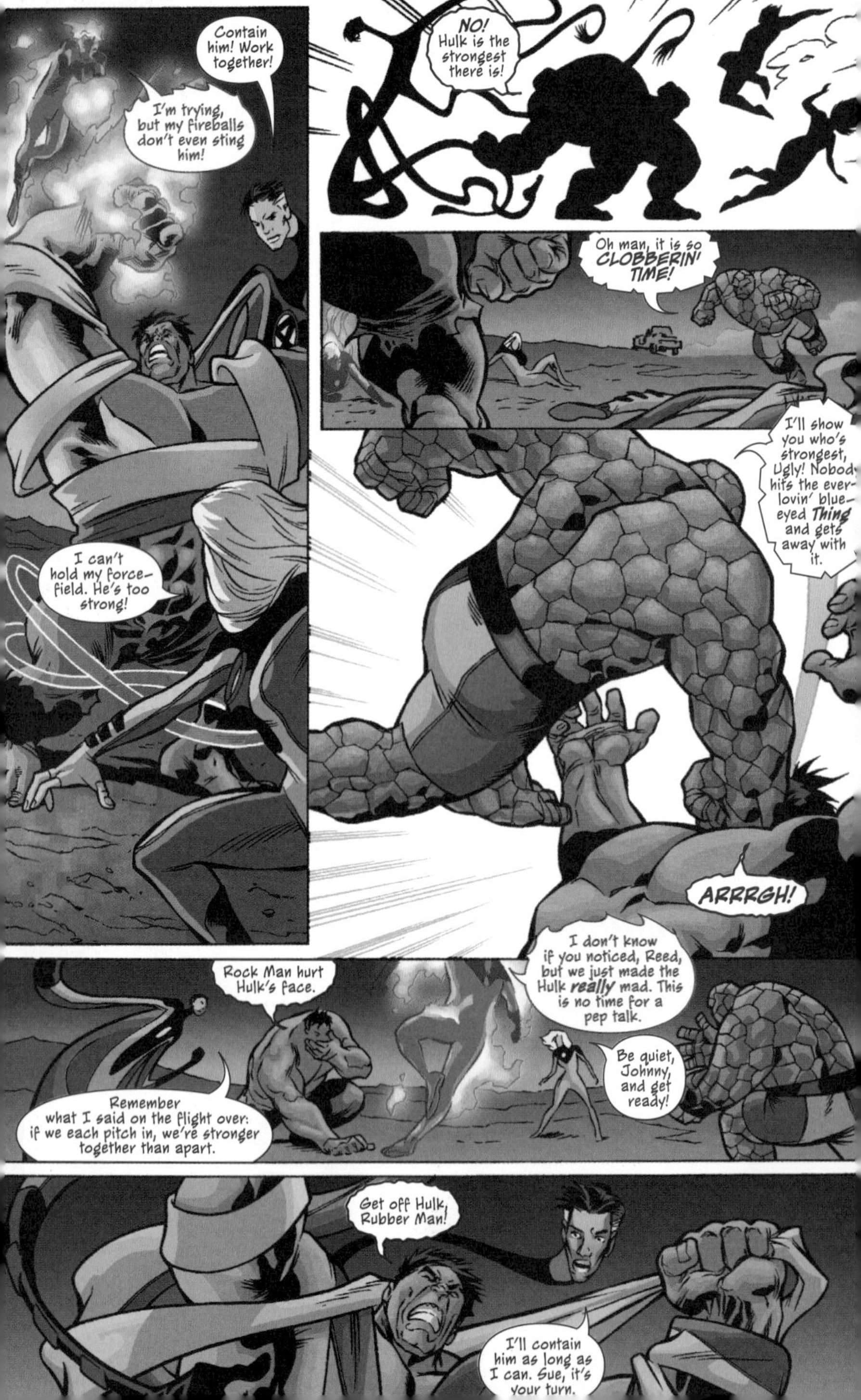
Contain him! Work together!
I'm trying, but my fireballs don't even sting him!
NO! Hulk is the strongest there is!
I can't hold my force-field. He's too strong!
Oh man, it is so CLOBBERIN' TIME!
I'll show you who's strongest, Ugly! Nobod hits the ever-lovin' blue-eyed Thing and gets away with it.
ARRRGH!
Rock Man hurt Hulk's face.
I don't know if you noticed, Reed, but we just made the Hulk really mad. This is no time for a pep talk.
Remember what I said on the flight over: if we each pitch in, we're stronger together than apart.
Be quiet, Johnny, and get ready!
Get off Hulk, Rubber Man!
I'll contain him as long as I can. Sue, it's your turn.

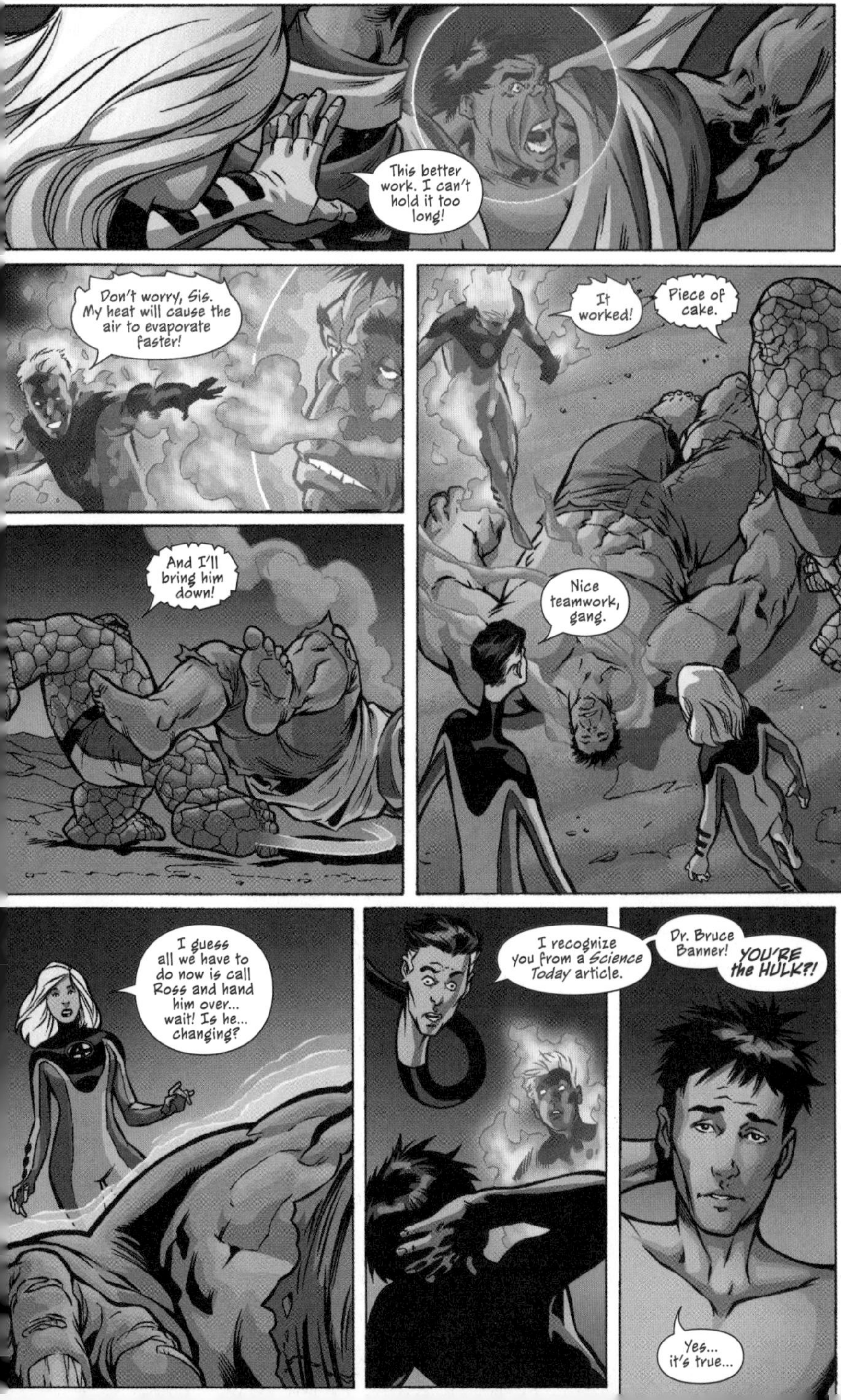
This better work. I can't hold it too long!
Don't worry, Sis. My heat will cause the air to evaporate faster!
And I'll bring him down!
It worked!
Piece of cake.
Nice teamwork, gang.
I guess all we have to do now is call Ross and hand him over... wait! Is he... changing?
I recognize you from a *Science Today* article.
Dr. Bruce Banner! YOU'RE the HULK?!
Yes... it's true...

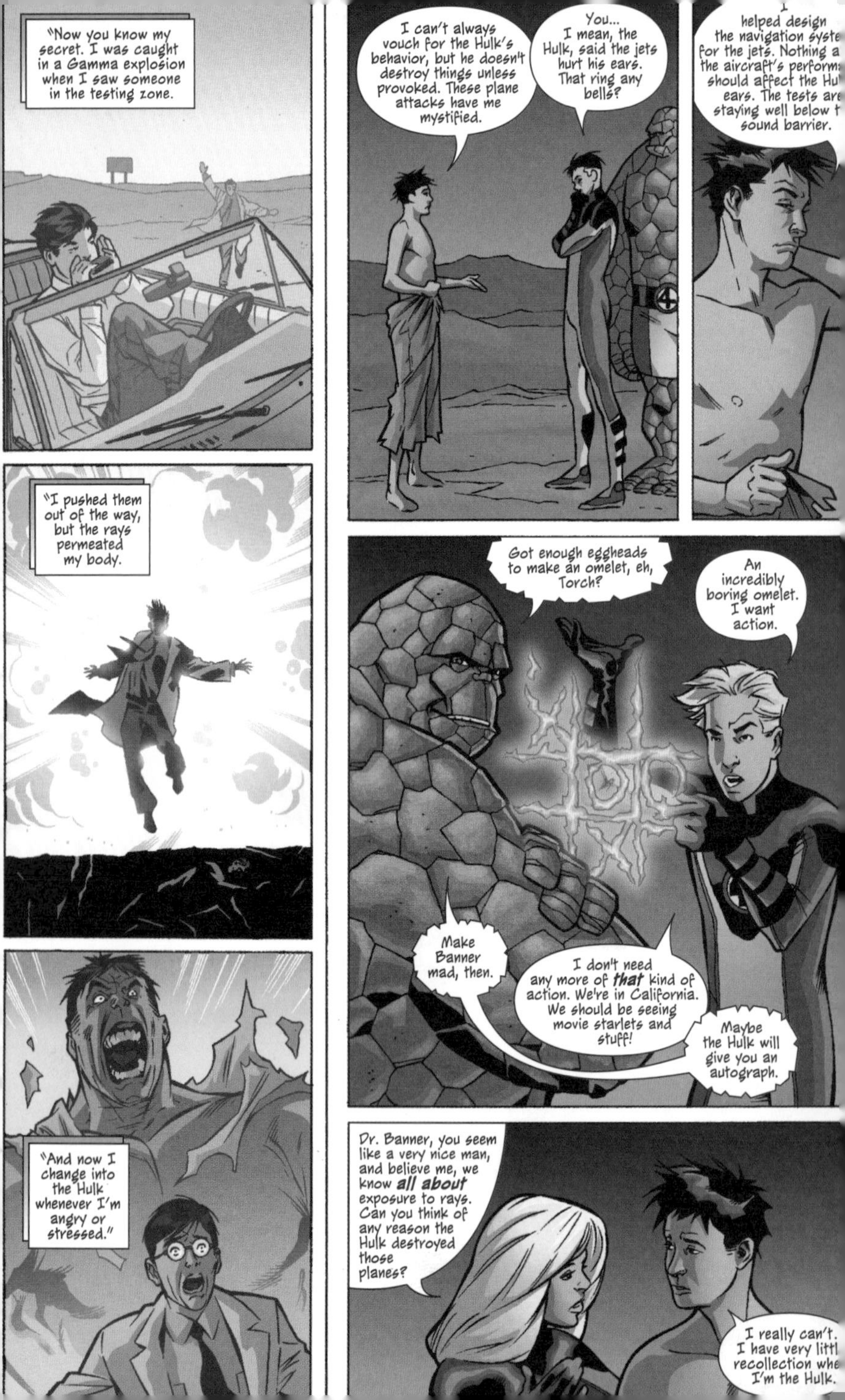

"Now you know my secret. I was caught in a Gamma explosion when I saw someone in the testing zone.
"I pushed them out of the way, but the rays permeated my body.
"And now I change into the Hulk whenever I'm angry or stressed."
I can't always vouch for the Hulk's behavior, but he doesn't destroy things unless provoked. These plane attacks have me mystified.
You... I mean, the Hulk, said the jets hurt his ears. That ring any bells?
I helped design the navigation syste for the jets. Nothing a the aircraft's perform should affect the Hu ears. The tests are staying well below t sound barrier.
Got enough eggheads to make an omelet, eh, Torch?
An incredibly boring omelet. I want action.
Make Banner mad, then.
I don't need any more of that kind of action. We're in California. We should be seeing movie starlets and stuff!
Maybe the Hulk will give you an autograph.
Dr. Banner, you seem like a very nice man, and believe me, we know all about exposure to rays. Can you think of any reason the Hulk destroyed those planes?
I really can't. I have very littl recollection whe I'm the Hulk.

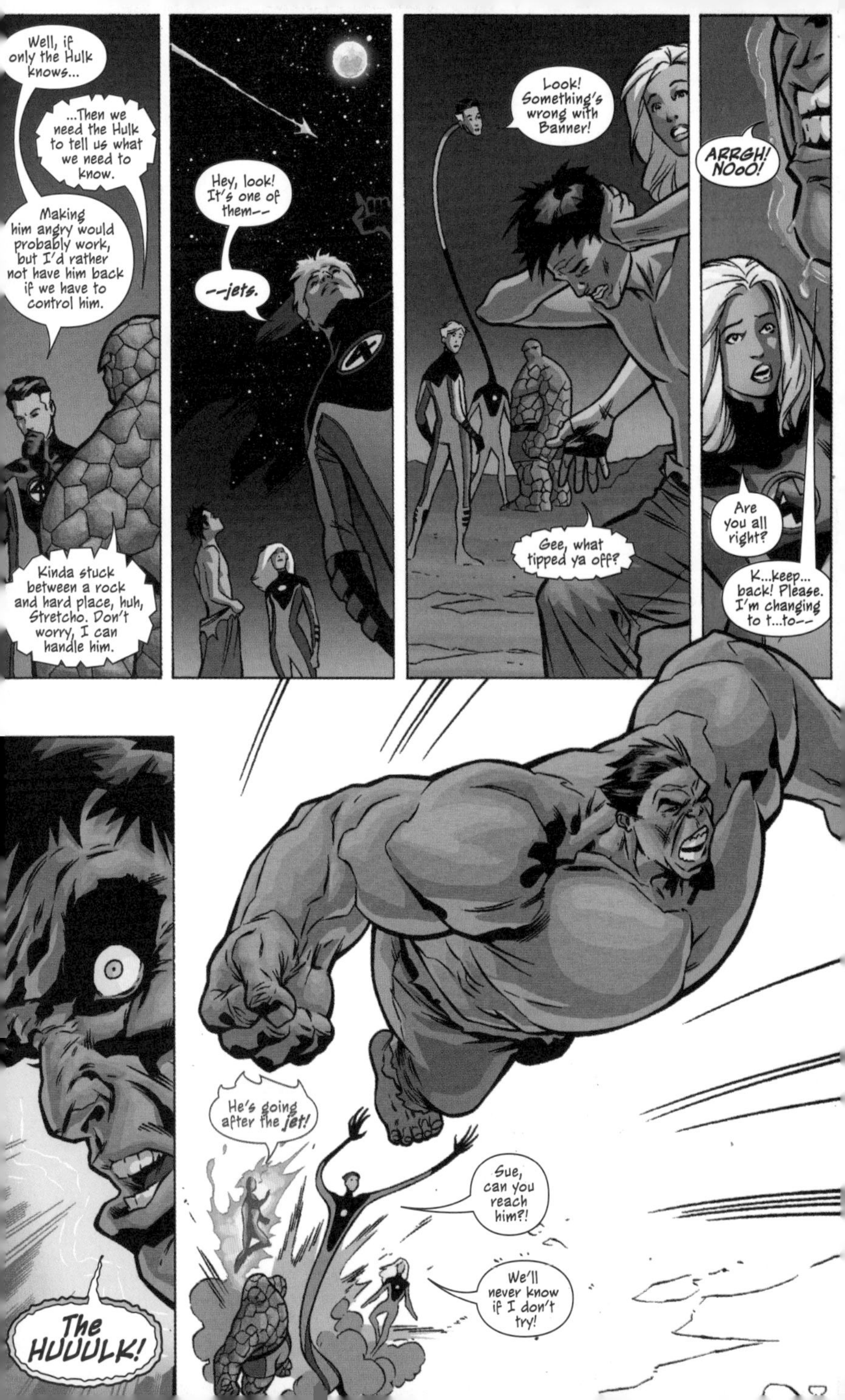
Well, if only the Hulk knows...
...Then we need the Hulk to tell us what we need to know.
Making him angry would probably work, but I'd rather not have him back if we have to control him.
Kinda stuck between a rock and hard place, huh, Stretcho. Don't worry, I can handle him.
Hey, look! It's one of them--
--jets.
Look! Something's wrong with Banner!
Gee, what tipped ya off?
ARRGH! NOoO!
Are you all right?
K...keep... back! Please. I'm changing to t...to--
The HUUULK!
He's going after the jet!
Sue, can you reach him?!
We'll never know if I don't try!

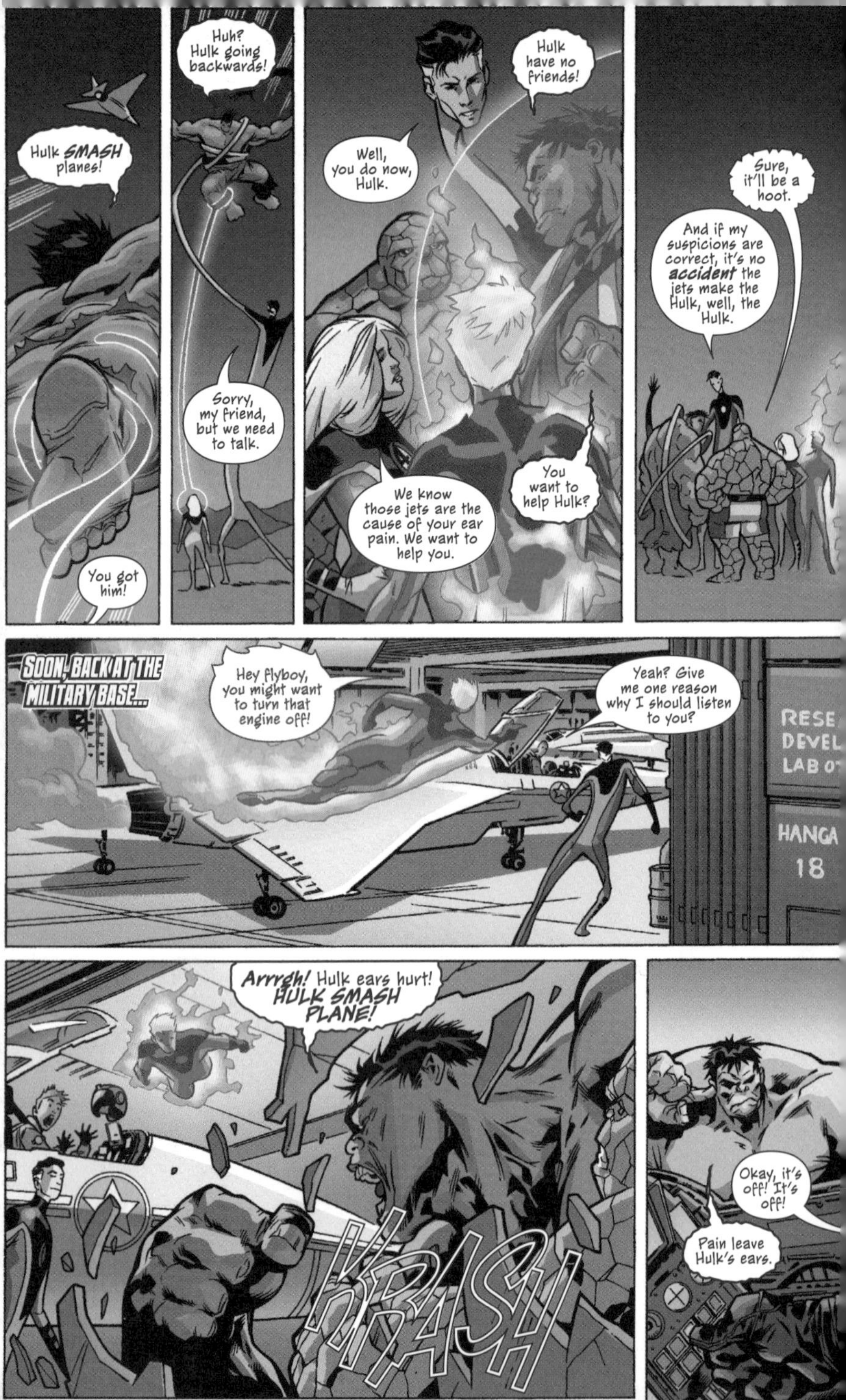

Hulk SMASH planes!
You got him!
Huh? Hulk going backwards!
Sorry, my friend, but we need to talk.
Hulk have no friends!
Well, you do now, Hulk.
We know those jets are the cause of your ear pain. We want to help you.
You want to help Hulk?
Sure, it'll be a hoot.
And if my suspicions are correct, it's no accident the jets make the Hulk, well, the Hulk.
SOON, BACK AT THE MILITARY BASE...
Hey flyboy, you might want to turn that engine off!
Yeah? Give me one reason why I should listen to you?
RESE
DEVEL
LAB O
HANGA
18
Arrrgh! Hulk ears hurt! HULK SMASH PLANE!
KRASH
Okay, it's off! It's off!
Pain leave Hulk's ears.

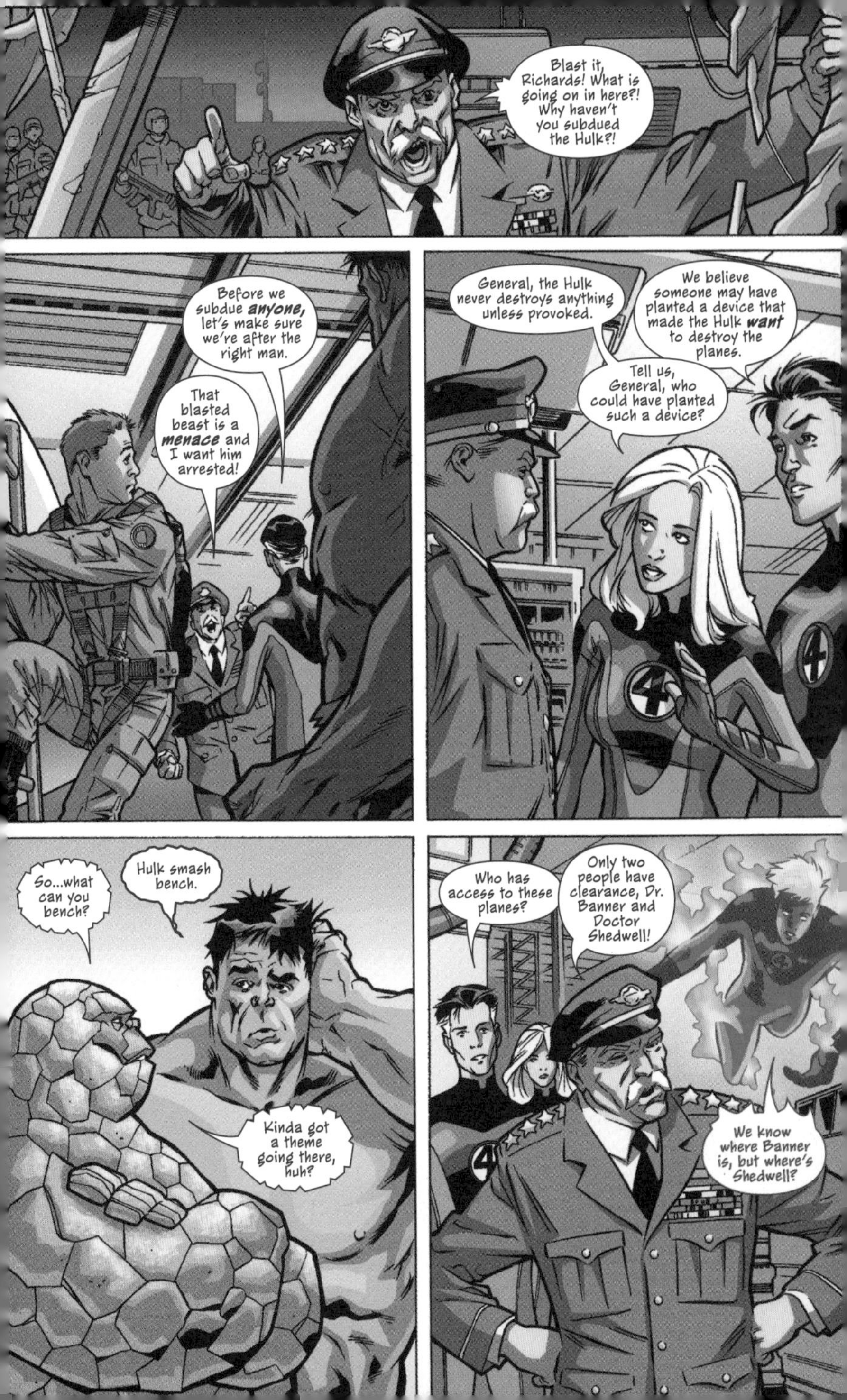
Blast it, Richards! What is going on in here?! Why haven't you subdued the Hulk?!
Before we subdue ***anyone,*** let's make sure we're after the right man.
That blasted beast is a ***menace*** and I want him arrested!
General, the Hulk never destroys anything unless provoked.
We believe someone may have planted a device that made the Hulk ***want*** to destroy the planes.
Tell us, General, who could have planted such a device?
So...what can you bench?
Hulk smash bench.
Kinda got a theme going there, huh?
Who has access to these planes?
Only two people have clearance, Dr. Banner and Doctor Shedwell!
We know where Banner is, but where's Shedwell?

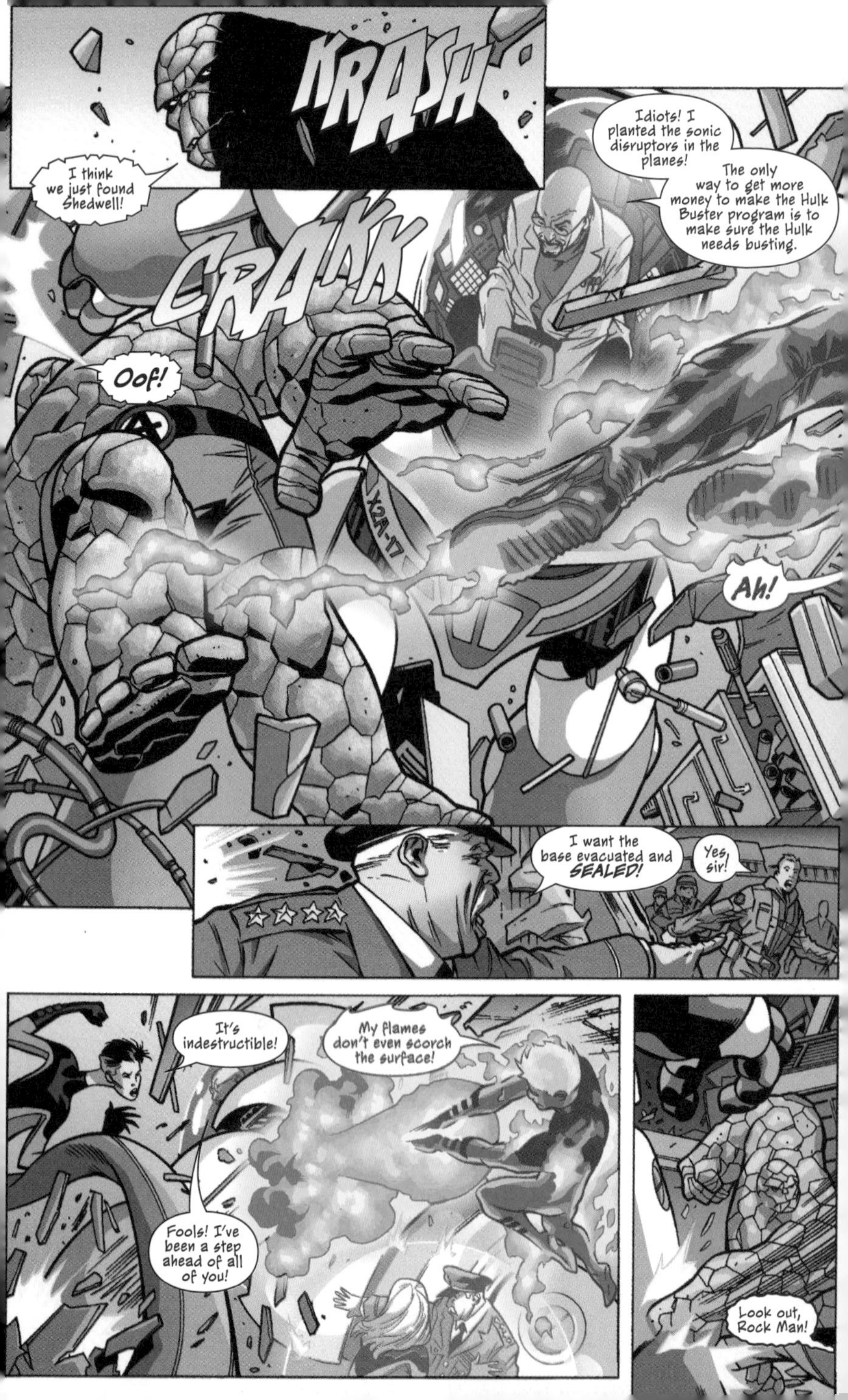
KRASH
I think we just found Shedwell!
Idiots! I planted the sonic disruptors in the planes!
The only way to get more money to make the Hulk Buster program is to make sure the Hulk needs busting.
CRAKK
Oof!
X2A-17
Ah!
I want the base evacuated and SEALED!
Yes, sir!
It's indestructible!
My flames don't even scorch the surface!
Fools! I've been a step ahead of all of you!
Look out, Rock Man!

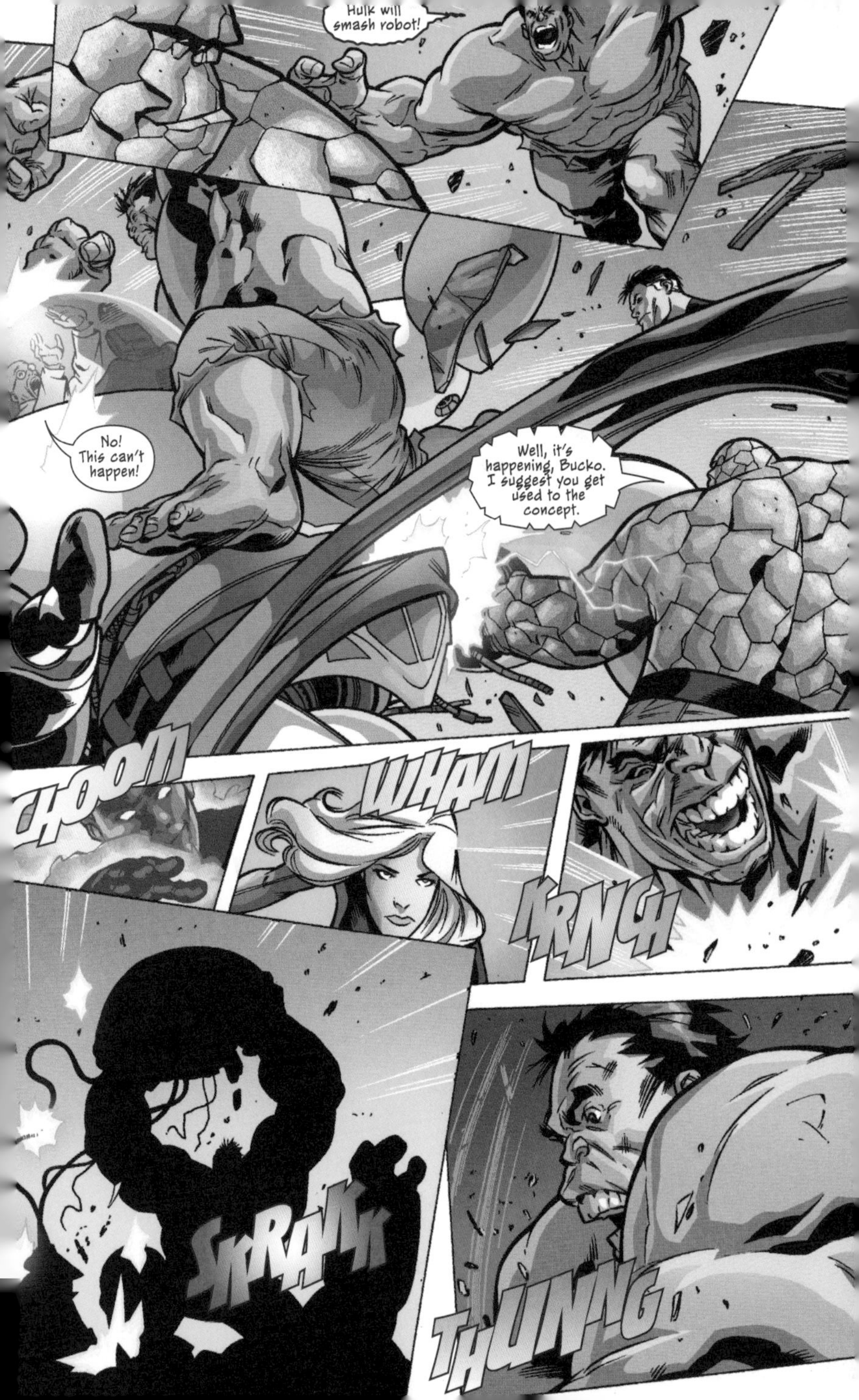

Hulk will smash robot!
No! This can't happen!
Well, it's happening, Bucko. I suggest you get used to the concept.
CHOOM
WHAM
KRNCH
SKRANK
THUNNG

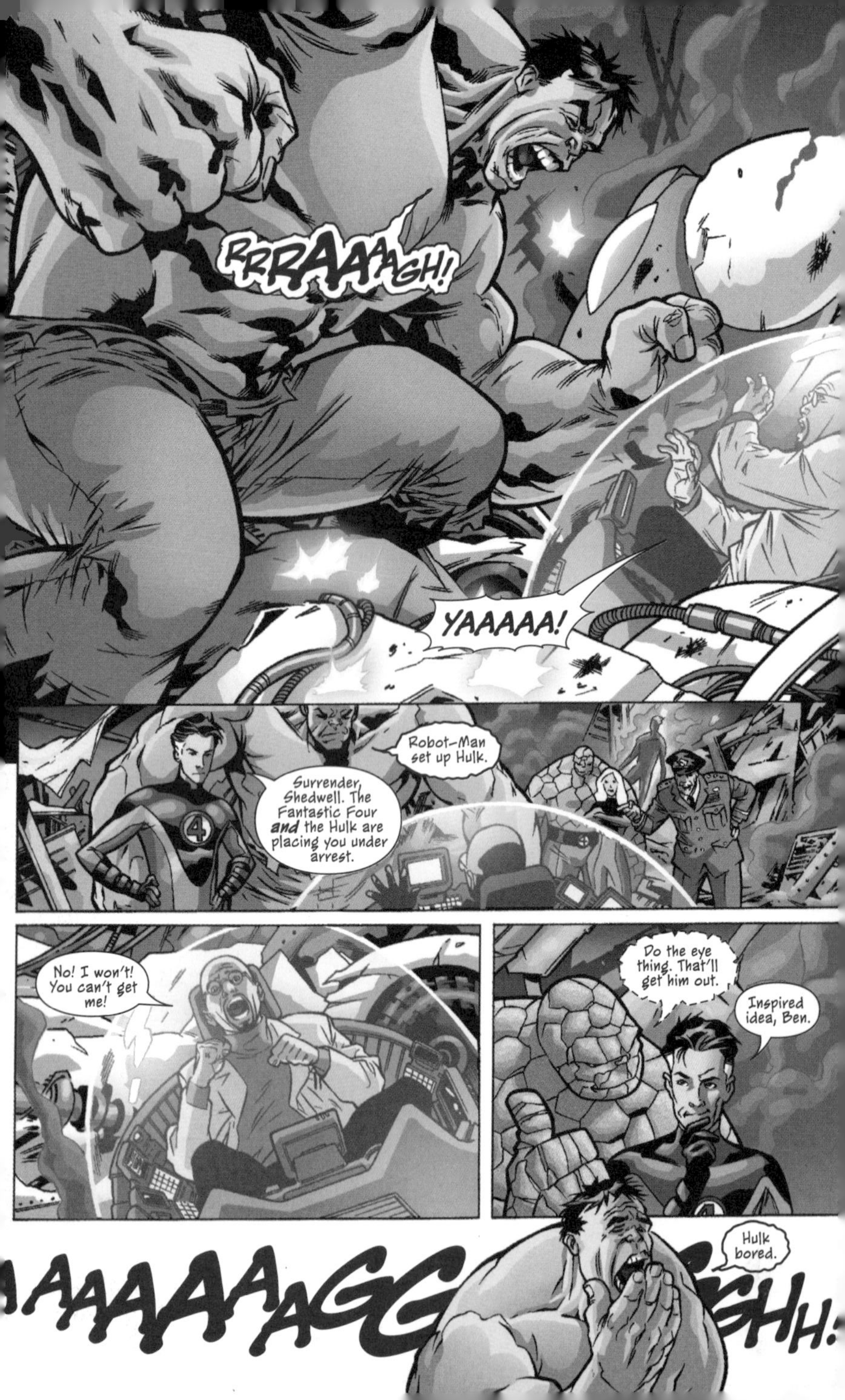
RRRAAAAGH!
YAAAAA!
Robot-Man set up Hulk.
Surrender, Shedwell. The Fantastic Four **and** the Hulk are placing you under arrest.
No! I won't! You can't get me!
Do the eye thing. That'll get him out.
Inspired idea, Ben.
Hulk bored.

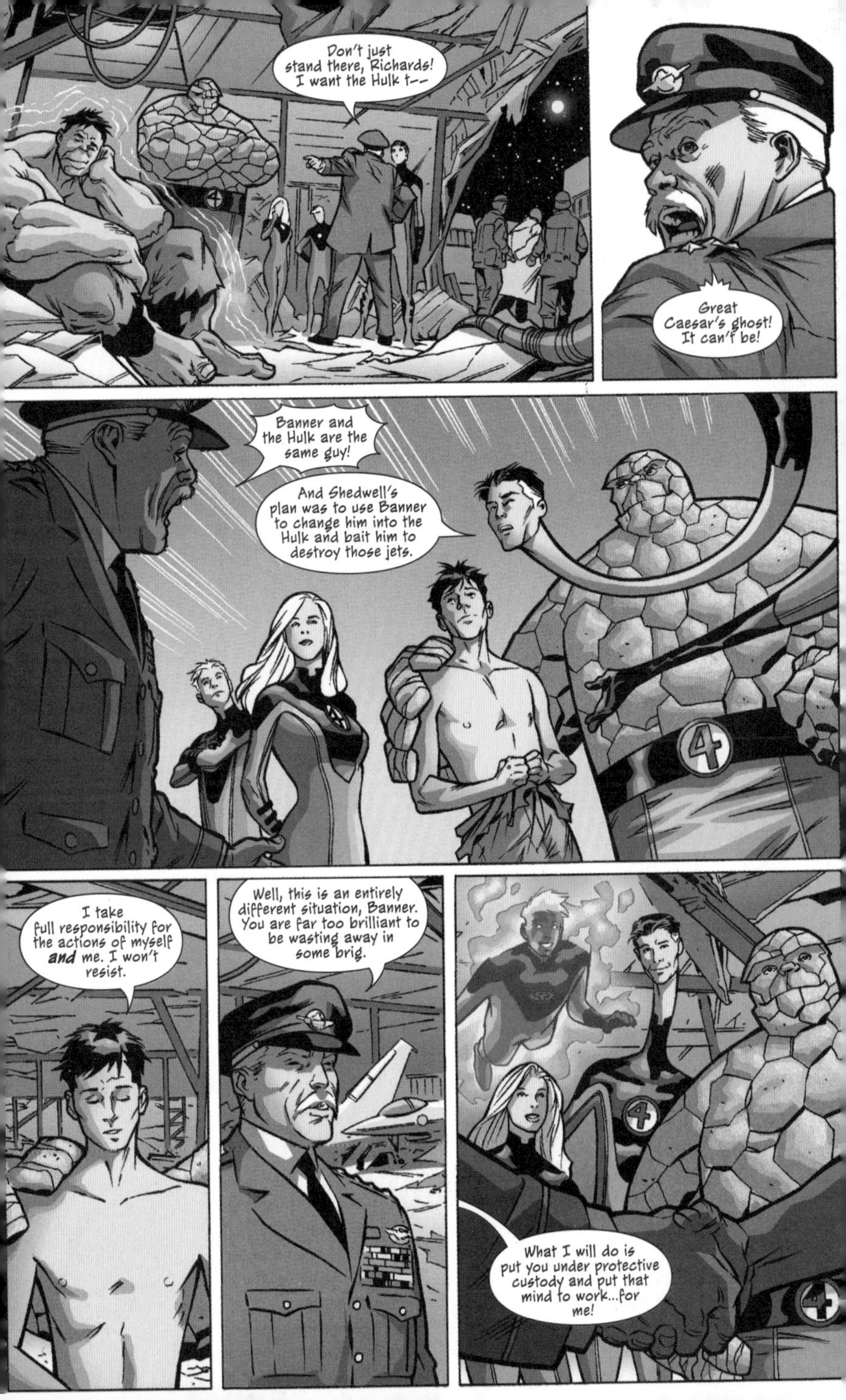
Don't just stand there, Richards! I want the Hulk t--
Great Caesar's ghost! It can't be!
Banner and the Hulk are the same guy!
And Shedwell's plan was to use Banner to change him into the Hulk and bait him to destroy those jets.
I take full responsibility for the actions of myself and me. I won't resist.
Well, this is an entirely different situation, Banner. You are far too brilliant to be wasting away in some brig.
What I will do is put you under protective custody and put that mind to work...for me!

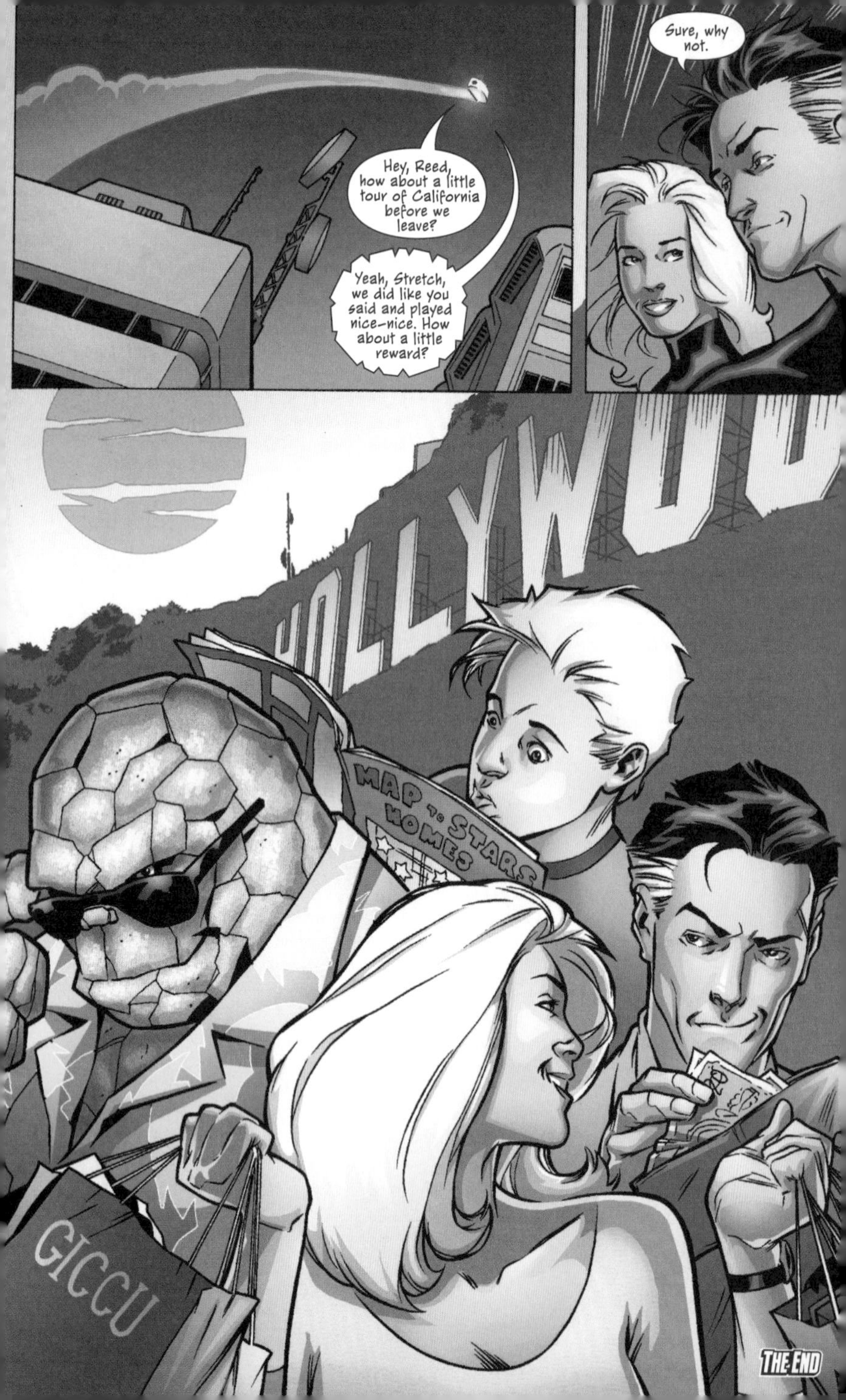
Hey, Reed, how about a little tour of California before we leave?
Yeah, Stretch, we did like you said and played nice-nice. How about a little reward?
Sure, why not.
HOLLYWOOD
MAP TO STARS HOMES
GICCU
THE END

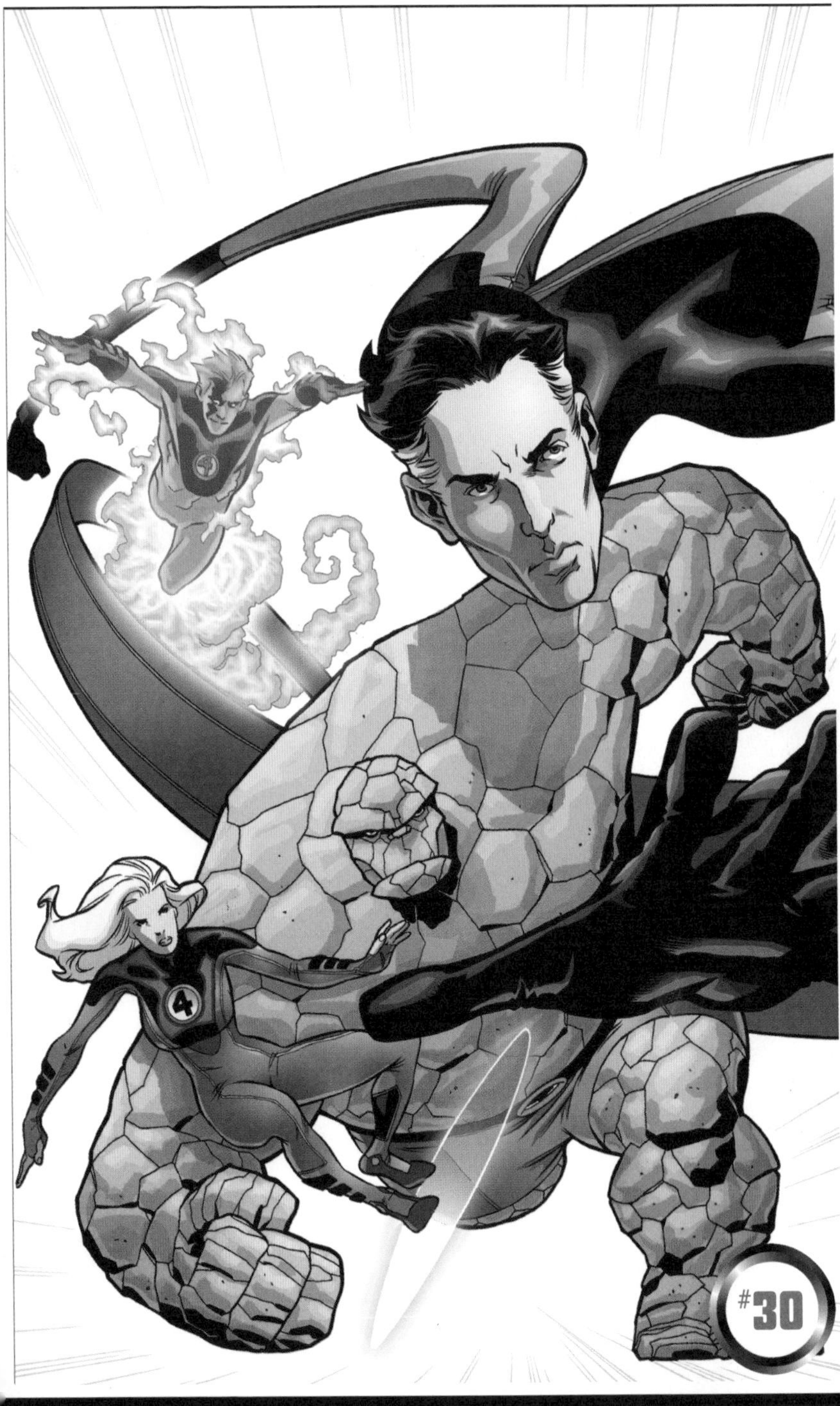
#30

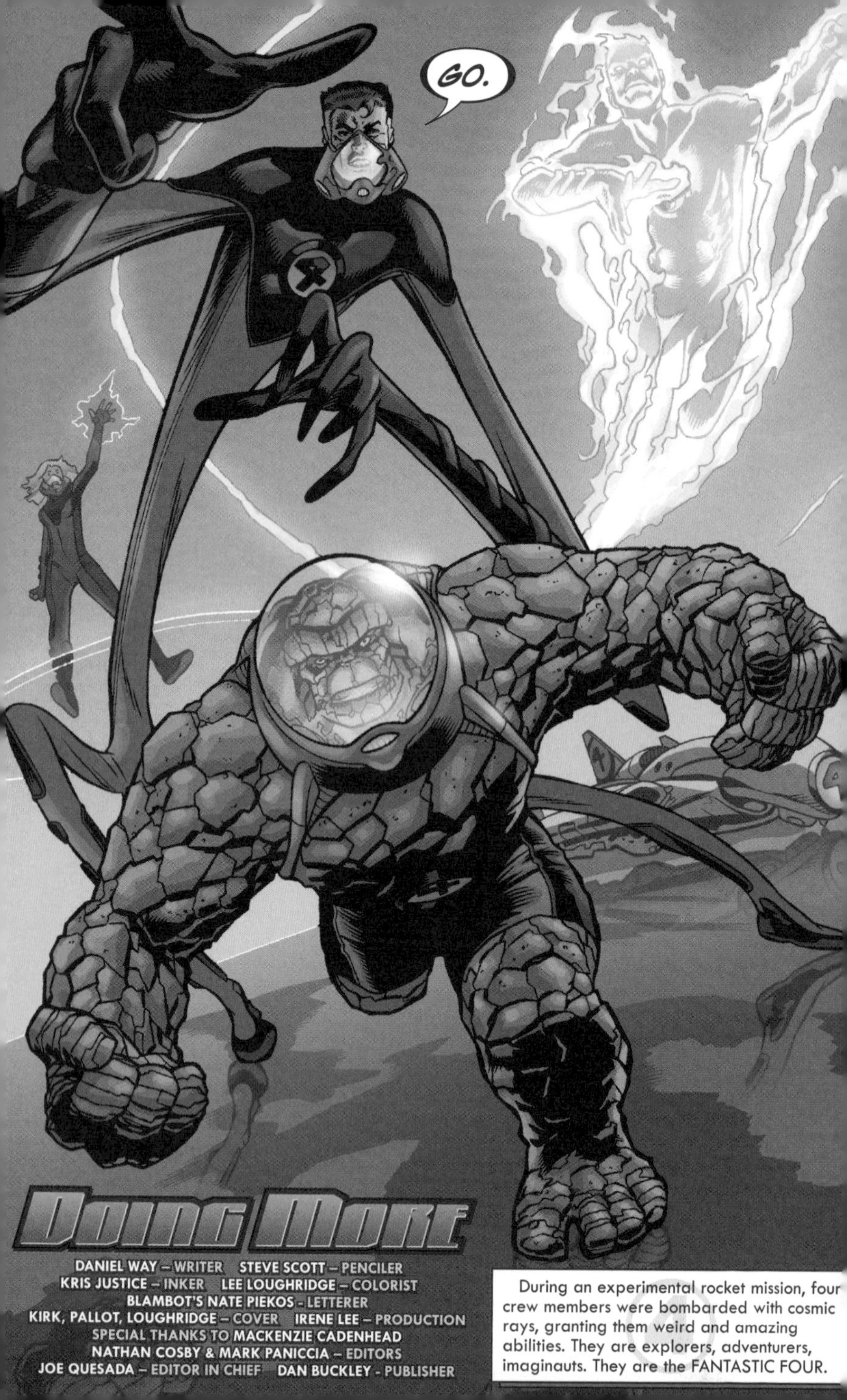
GO.
DOING MORE
DANIEL WAY – WRITER STEVE SCOTT – PENCILER
KRIS JUSTICE – INKER LEE LOUGHRIDGE – COLORIST
BLAMBOT'S NATE PIEKOS - LETTERER
KIRK, PALLOT, LOUGHRIDGE – COVER IRENE LEE – PRODUCTION
SPECIAL THANKS TO MACKENZIE CADENHEAD
NATHAN COSBY & MARK PANICCIA – EDITORS
JOE QUESADA – EDITOR IN CHIEF DAN BUCKLEY - PUBLISHER
During an experimental rocket mission, four crew members were bombarded with cosmic rays, granting them weird and amazing abilities. They are explorers, adventurers, imaginauts. They are the FANTASTIC FOUR.

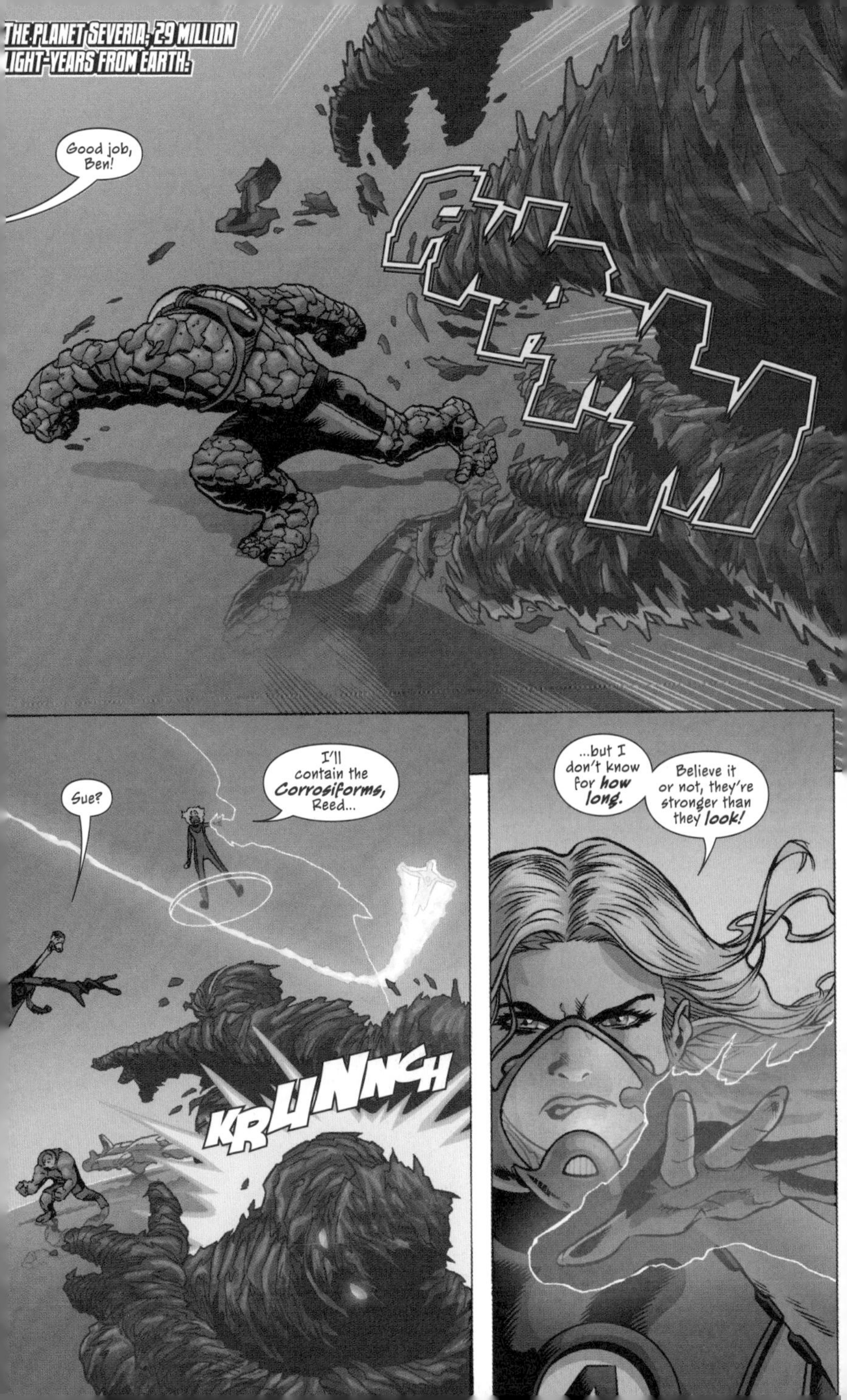
THE PLANET SEVERIA, 29 MILLION LIGHT-YEARS FROM EARTH:
Good job, Ben!
Sue?
I'll contain the Corrosiforms, Reed...
KRUNNCH
...but I don't know for how long.
Believe it or not, they're stronger than they look!

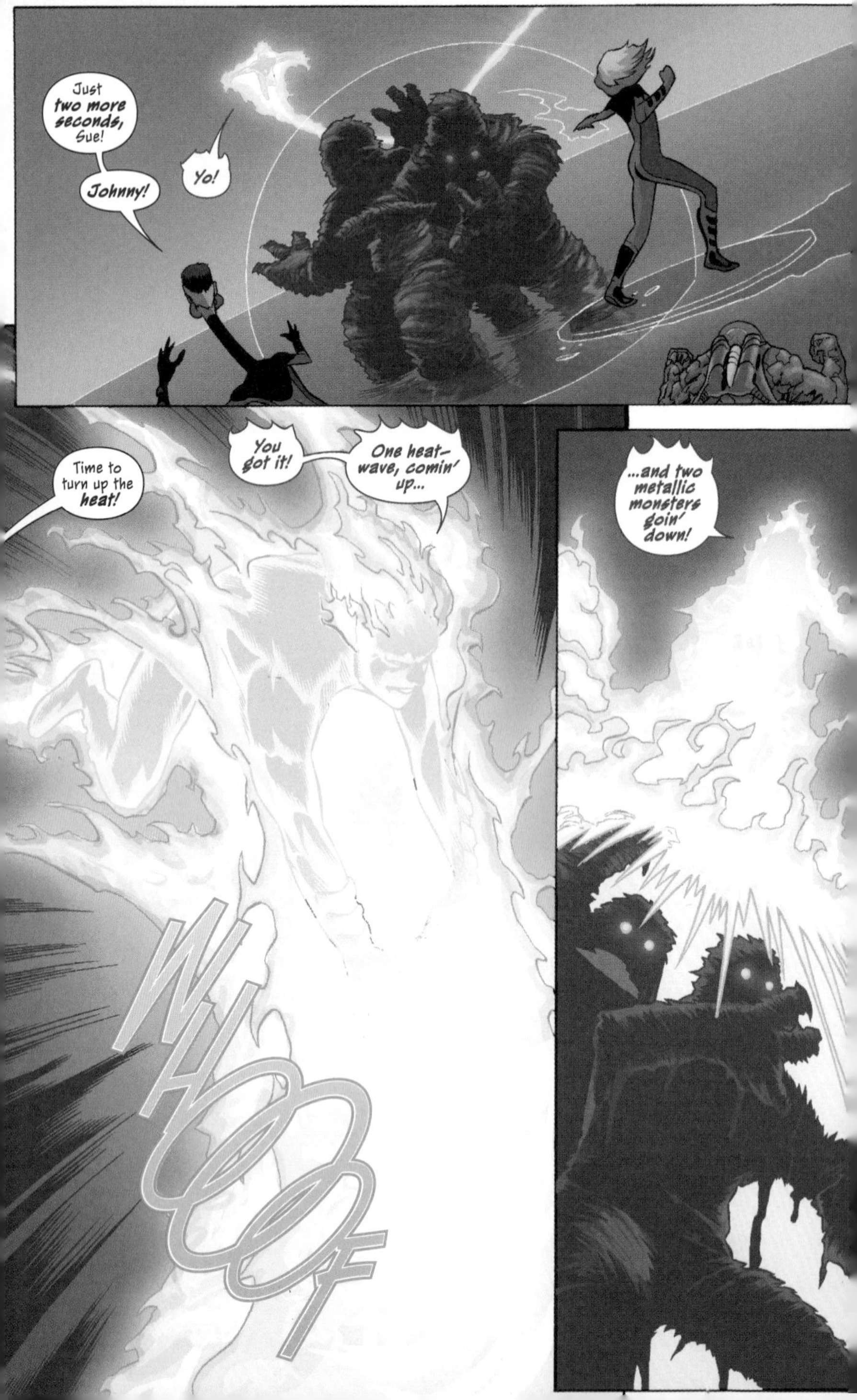

Just two more seconds, Sue!
Johnny!
Yo!
Time to turn up the heat!
You got it!
One heat-wave, comin' up...
...and two metallic monsters goin' down!

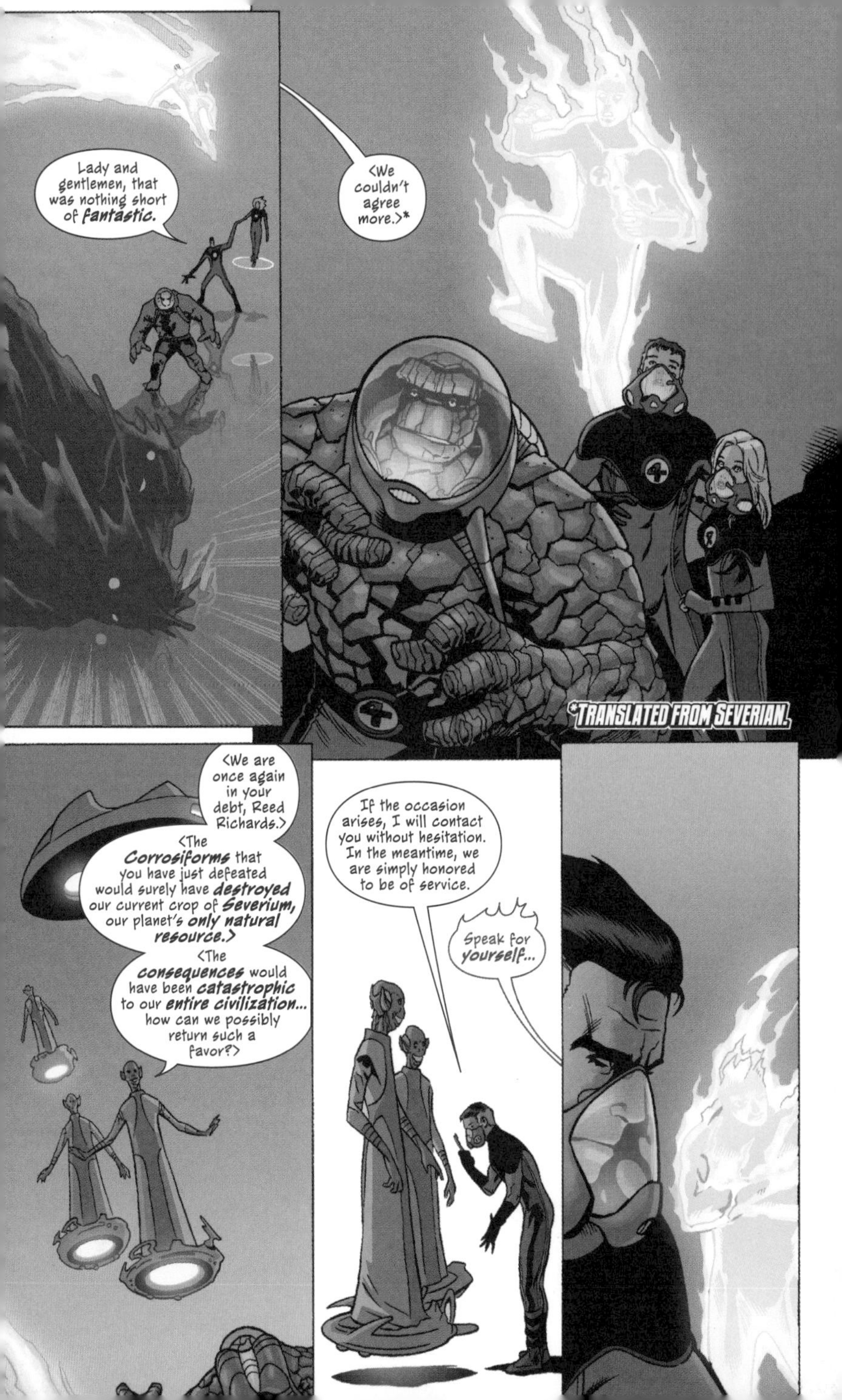

Lady and gentlemen, that was nothing short of *fantastic.*
<We couldn't agree more.>*
*TRANSLATED FROM SEVERIAN.
<We are once again in your debt, Reed Richards.>
<The **Corrosiforms** that you have just defeated would surely have **destroyed** our current crop of **Severium,** our planet's **only natural resource.**>
<The **consequences** would have been **catastrophic** to our **entire civilization...** how can we possibly return such a favor?>
If the occasion arises, I will contact you without hesitation. In the meantime, we are simply honored to be of service.
Speak for *yourself...*

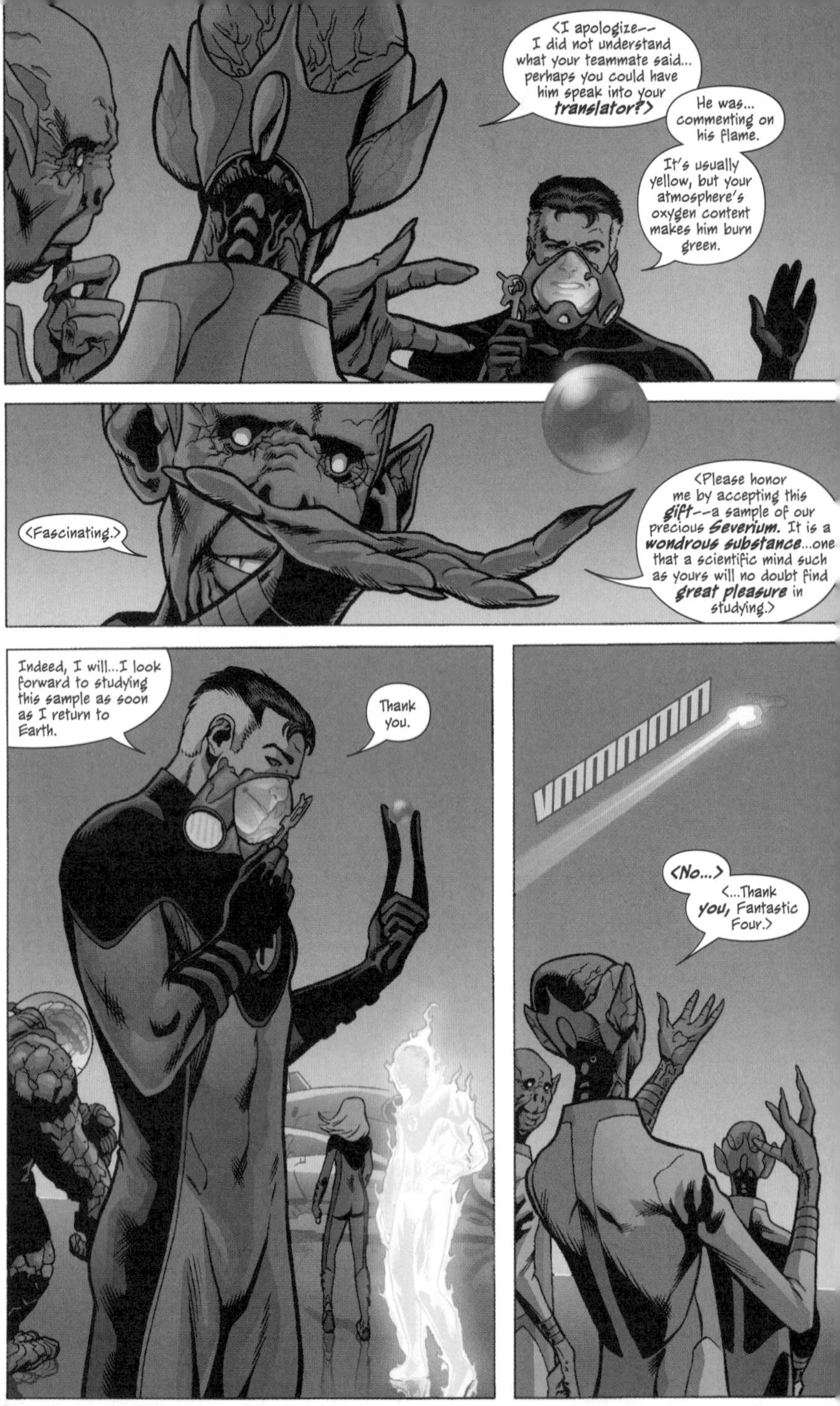

<I apologize-- I did not understand what your teammate said... perhaps you could have him speak into your translator?>
He was... commenting on his flame.
It's usually yellow, but your atmosphere's oxygen content makes him burn green.
<Fascinating.>
<Please honor me by accepting this gift--a sample of our precious Severium. It is a wondrous substance...one that a scientific mind such as yours will no doubt find great pleasure in studying.>
Indeed, I will...I look forward to studying this sample as soon as I return to Earth.
Thank you.
VMMMMMM
<No...>
<...Thank you, Fantastic Four.>

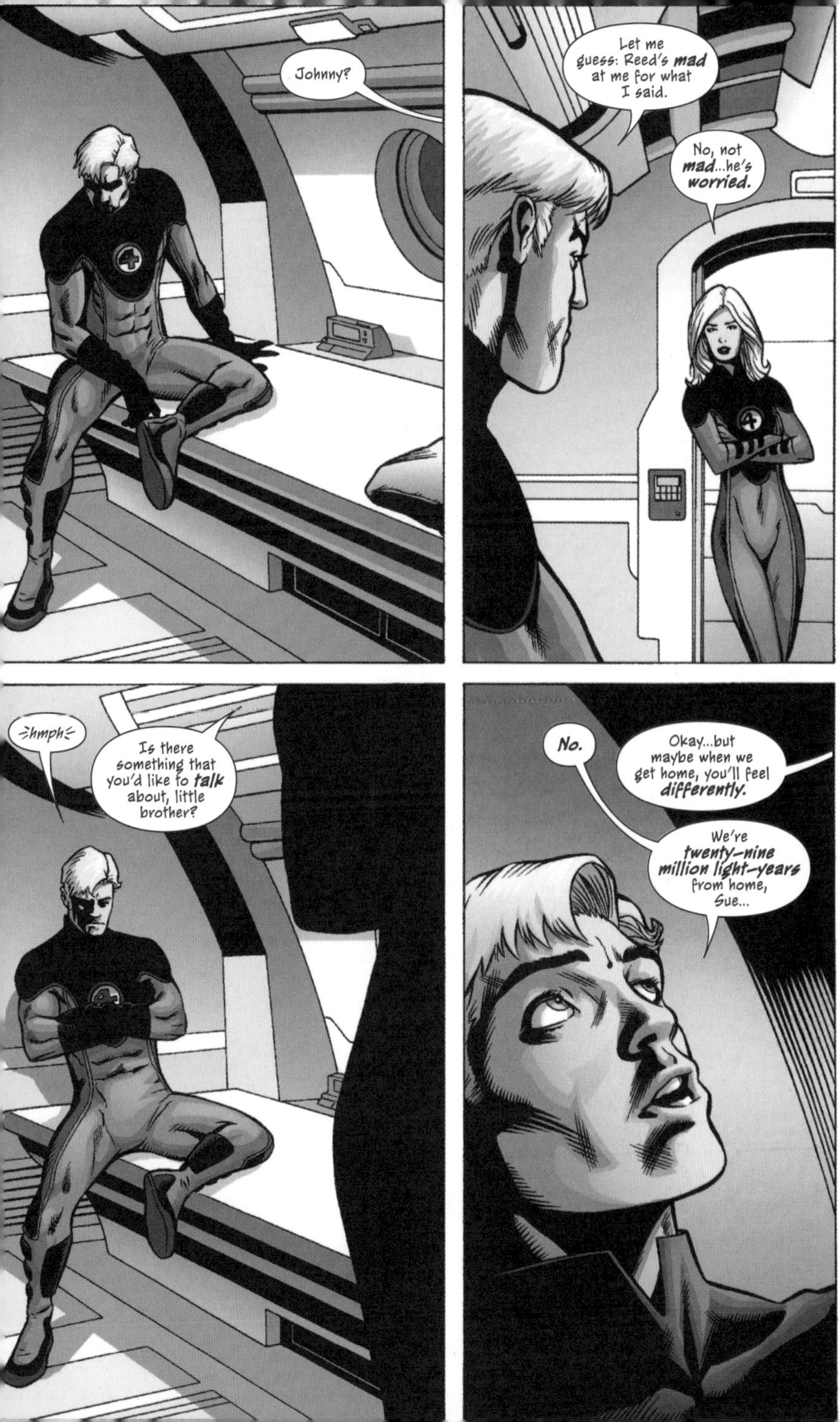
Johnny?
Let me guess: Reed's mad at me for what I said.
No, not mad...he's worried.
=hmph=
Is there something that you'd like to talk about, little brother?
No.
Okay...but maybe when we get home, you'll feel differently.
We're twenty-nine million light-years from home, Sue...

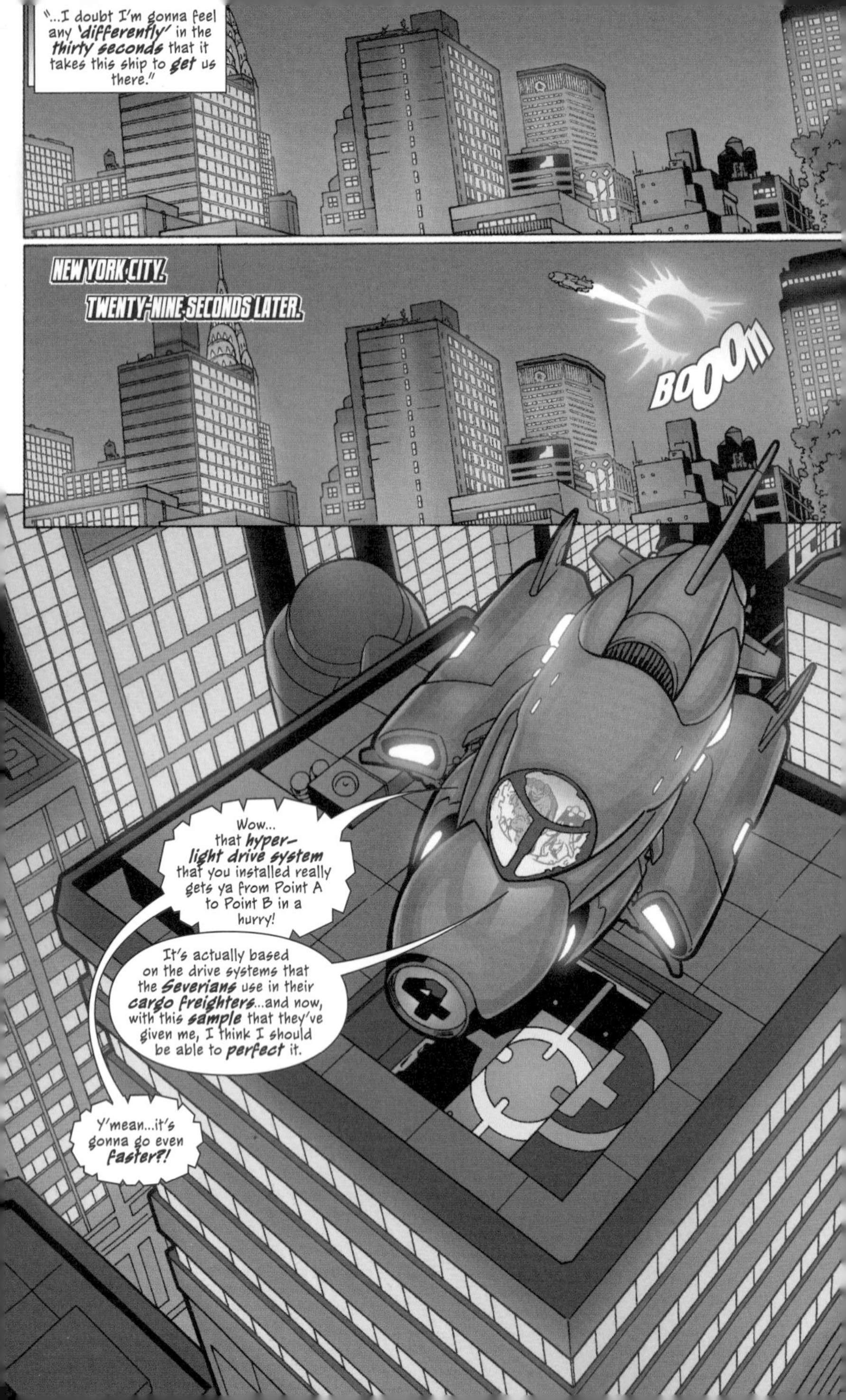
"...I doubt I'm gonna feel any 'differenfly' in the thirty seconds that it takes this ship to get us there."
NEW YORK CITY.
TWENTY-NINE SECONDS LATER.
BOOOM
Wow... that hyper-light drive system that you installed really gets ya from Point A to Point B in a hurry!
It's actually based on the drive systems that the Severians use in their cargo freighters...and now, with this sample that they've given me, I think I should be able to perfect it.
Y'mean...it's gonna go even faster?!

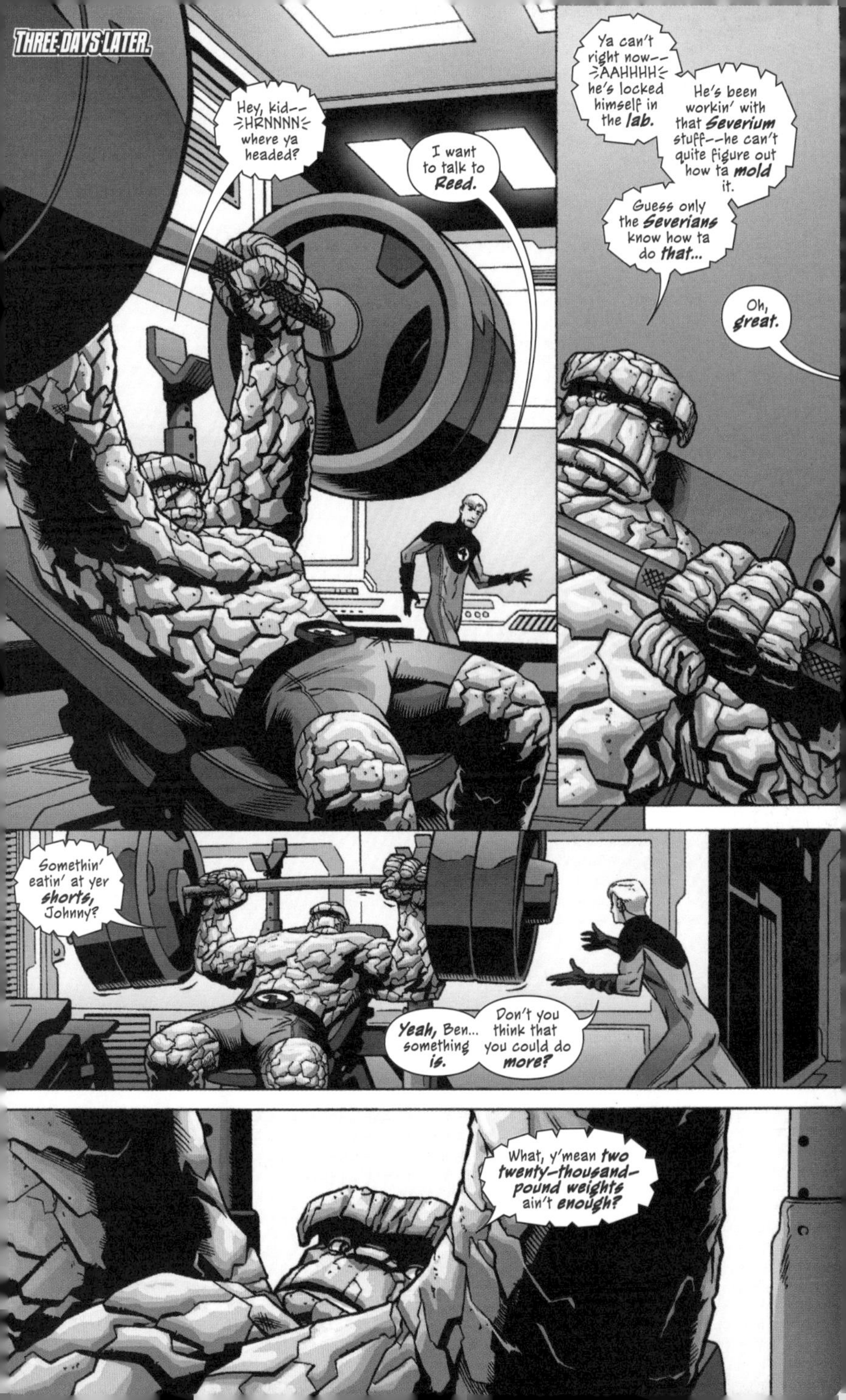
THREE DAYS LATER.
Hey, kid-- HRNNNN where ya headed?
I want to talk to Reed.
Ya can't right now-- AAHHHH he's locked himself in the lab.
He's been workin' with that Severium stuff--he can't quite figure out how ta mold it.
Guess only the Severians know how ta do that...
Oh, great.
Somethin' eatin' at yer shorts, Johnny?
Yeah, Ben... something is.
Don't you think that you could do more?
What, y'mean two twenty-thousand-pound weights ain't enough?

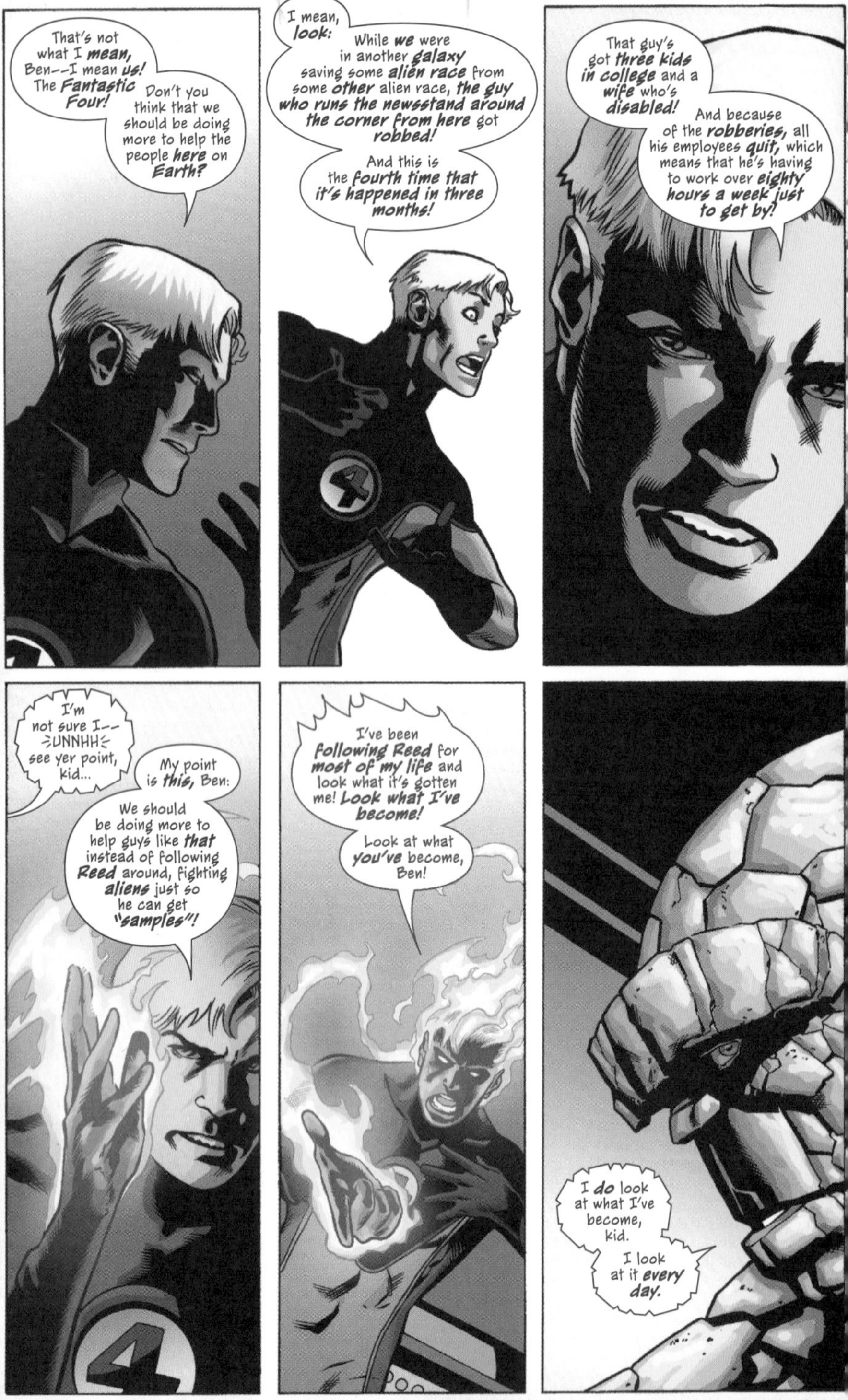
That's not what I mean, Ben--I mean us! The Fantastic Four!
Don't you think that we should be doing more to help the people here on Earth?
I mean, look:
While we were in another galaxy saving some alien race from some other alien race, the guy who runs the newsstand around the corner from here got robbed!
And this is the fourth time that it's happened in three months!
That guy's got three kids in college and a wife who's disabled!
And because of the robberies, all his employees quit, which means that he's having to work over eighty hours a week just to get by!
I'm not sure I-- UNNHH see yer point, kid...
My point is this, Ben:
We should be doing more to help guys like that instead of following Reed around, fighting aliens just so he can get "samples"!
I've been following Reed for most of my life and look what it's gotten me! Look what I've become!
Look at what you've become, Ben!
I do look at what I've become, kid.
I look at it every day.

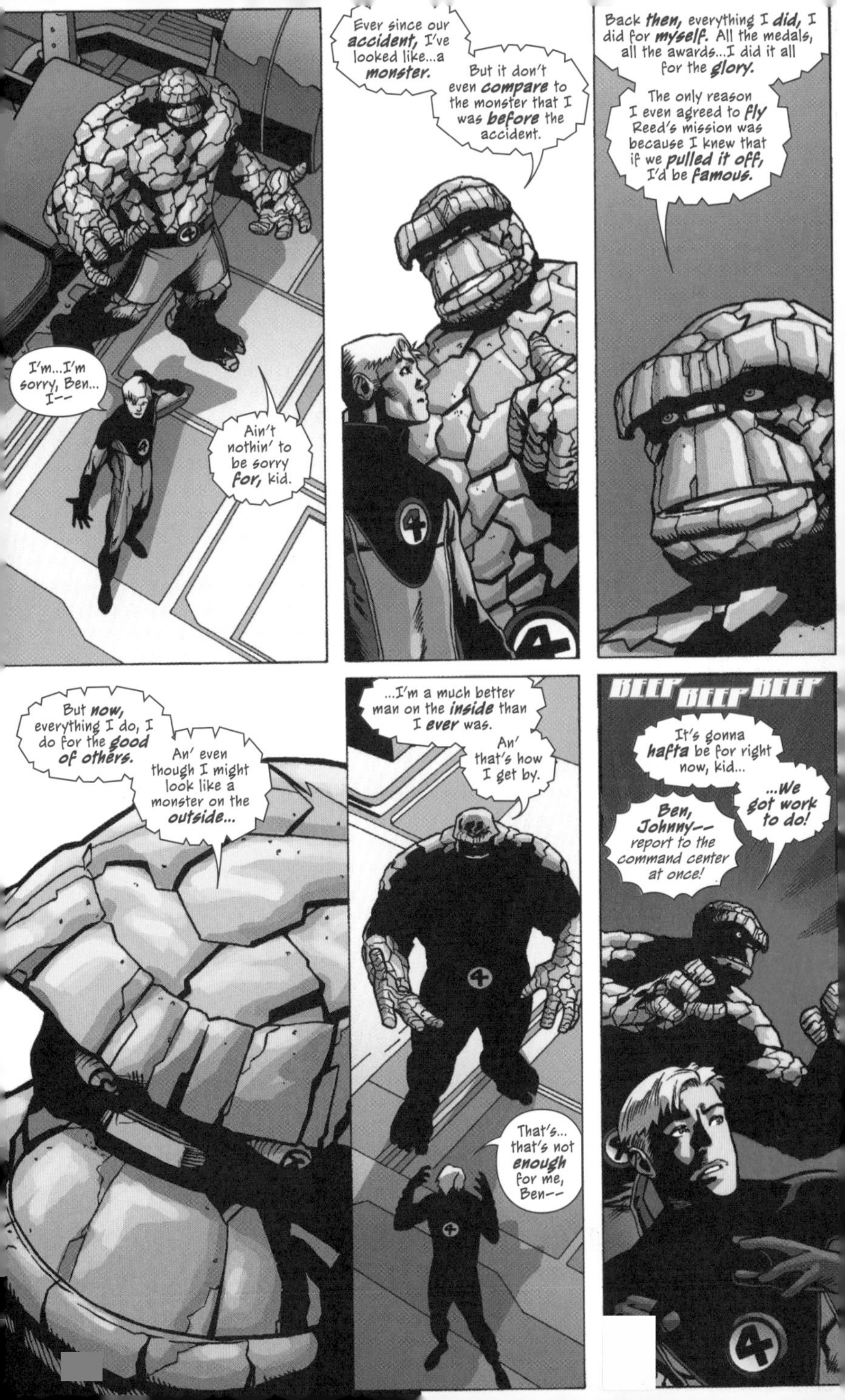

I'm...I'm sorry, Ben... I--
Ain't nothin' to be sorry for, kid.
Ever since our accident, I've looked like...a monster.
But it don't even compare to the monster that I was before the accident.
Back then, everything I did, I did for myself. All the medals, all the awards...I did it all for the glory.
The only reason I even agreed to fly Reed's mission was because I knew that if we pulled it off, I'd be famous.
But now, everything I do, I do for the good of others.
An' even though I might look like a monster on the outside...
...I'm a much better man on the inside than I ever was.
An' that's how I get by.
That's... that's not enough for me, Ben--
BEEP BEEP BEEP
It's gonna hafta be for right now, kid...
Ben, Johnny-- report to the command center at once!
...We got work to do!

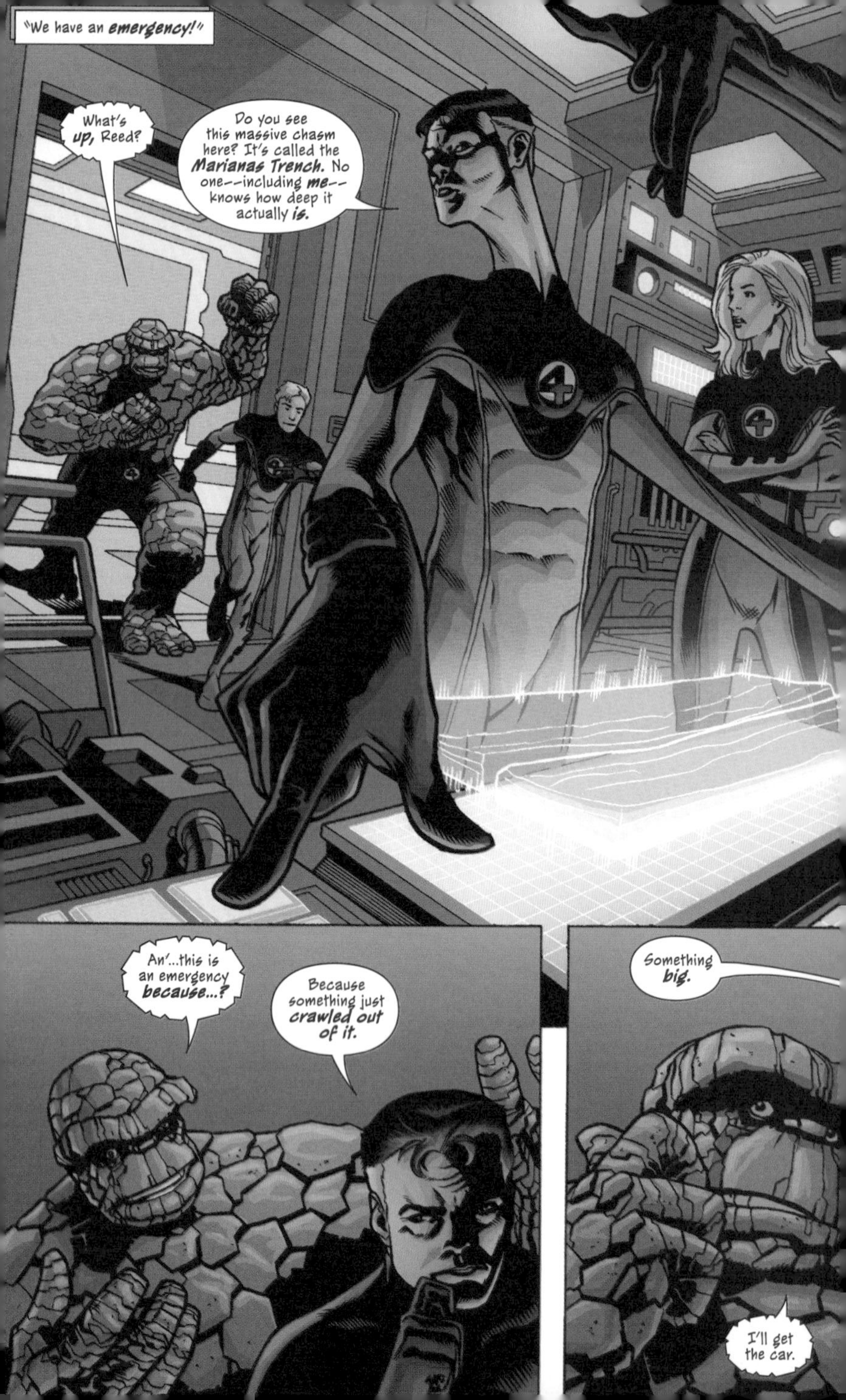
"We have an emergency!"
What's up, Reed?
Do you see this massive chasm here? It's called the Marianas Trench. No one--including me--knows how deep it actually is.
An'...this is an emergency because...?
Because something just crawled out of it.
Something big.
I'll get the car.

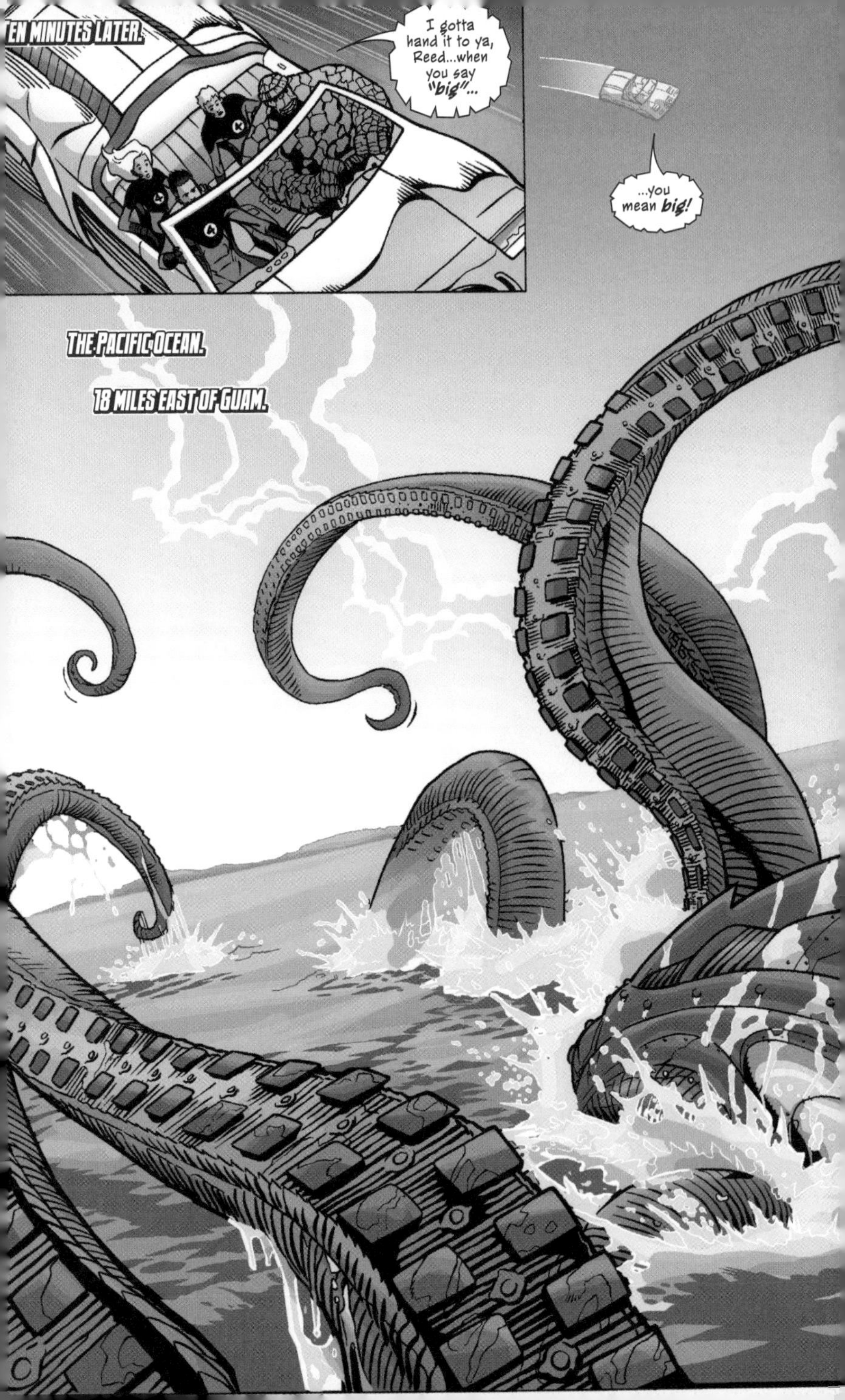
TEN MINUTES LATER.
I gotta hand it to ya, Reed...when you say "big"...
...you mean big!
THE PACIFIC OCEAN.
18 MILES EAST OF GUAM.

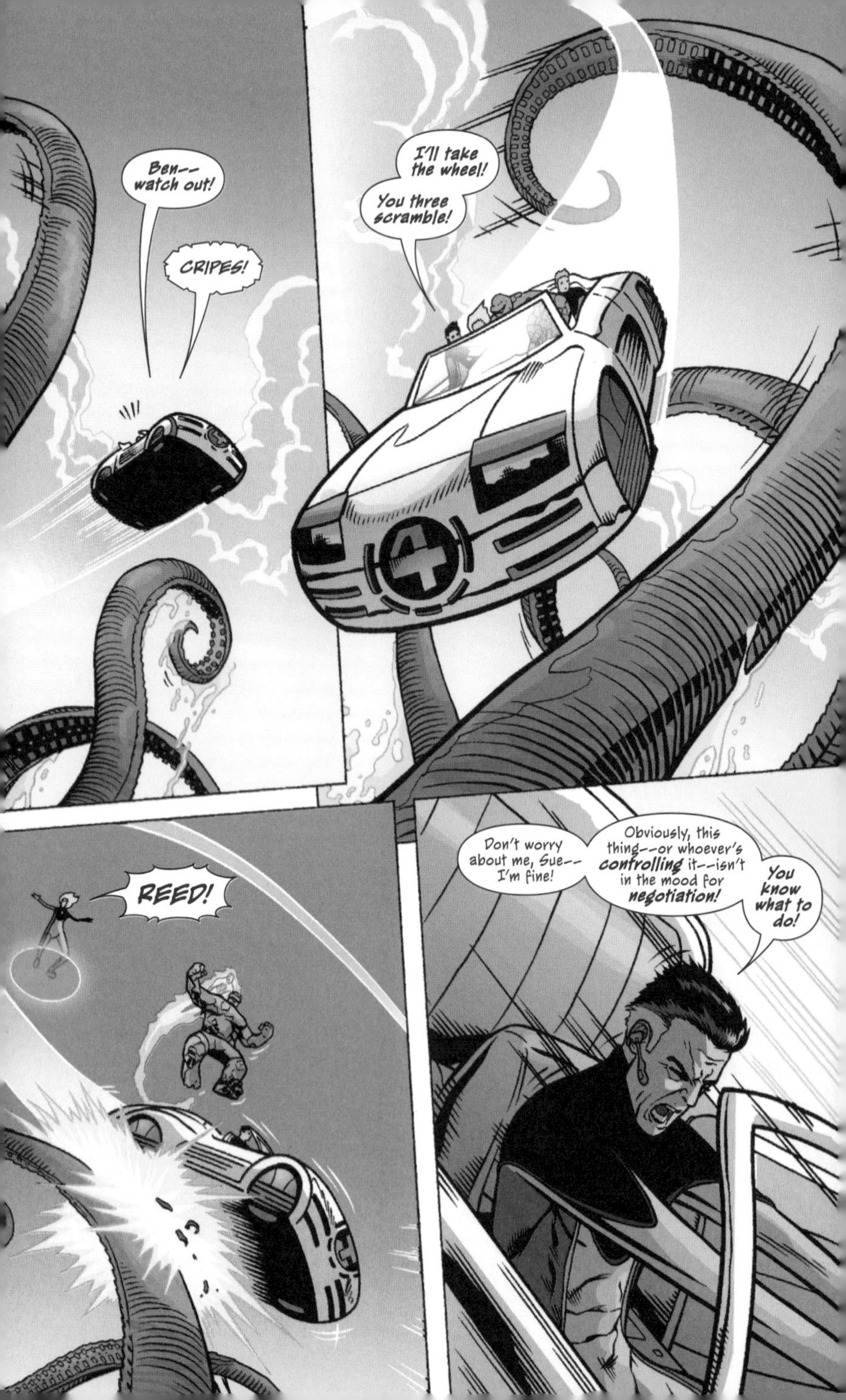
Ben--
watch out!
CRIPES!
I'll take the wheel!
You three scramble!
REED!
Don't worry about me, Sue-- I'm fine!
Obviously, this thing--or whoever's controlling it--isn't in the mood for negotiation!
You know what to do!

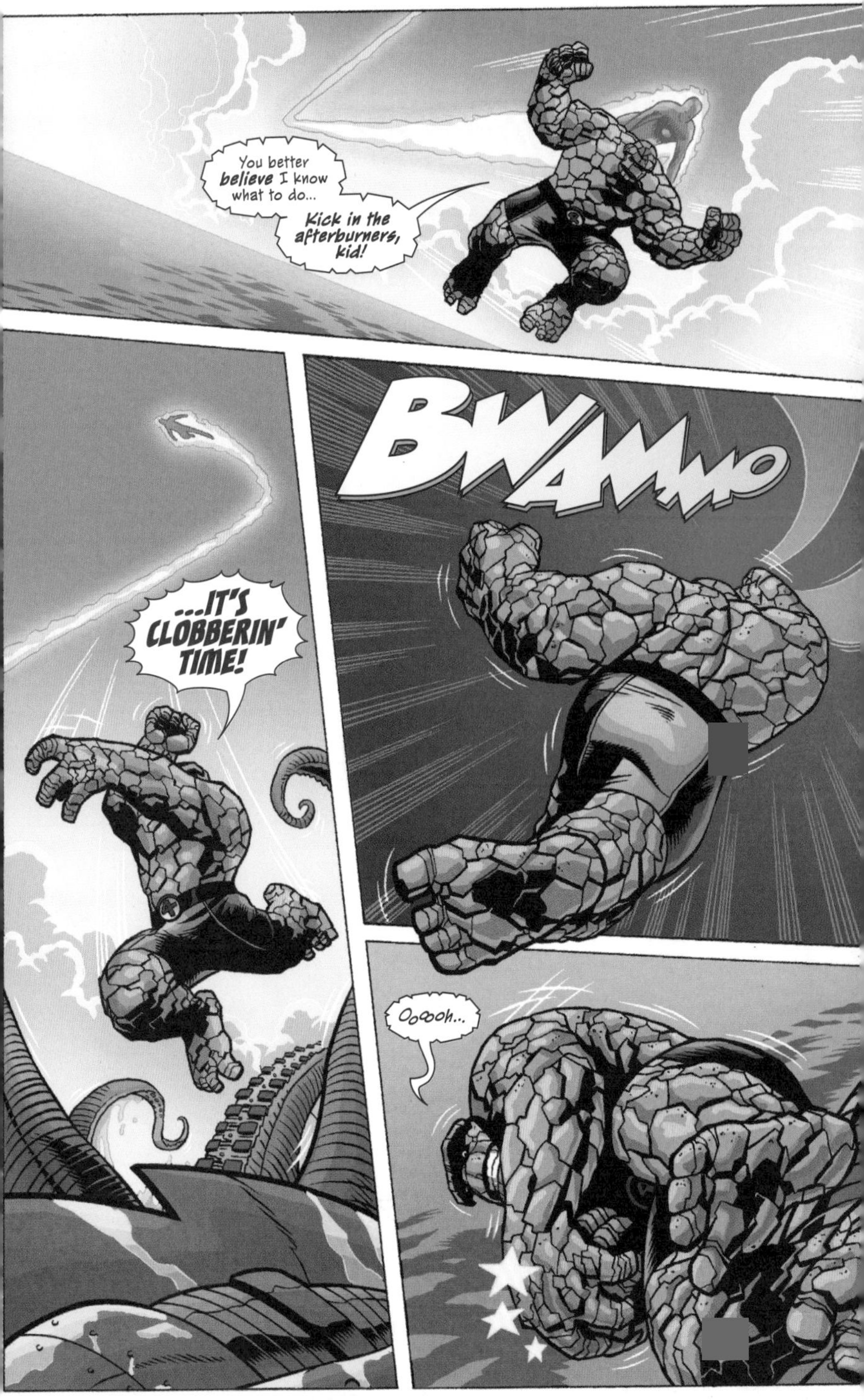

You better believe I know what to do...
Kick in the afterburners, kid!
...IT'S CLOBBERIN' TIME!
BWAMMO
Ooooh...

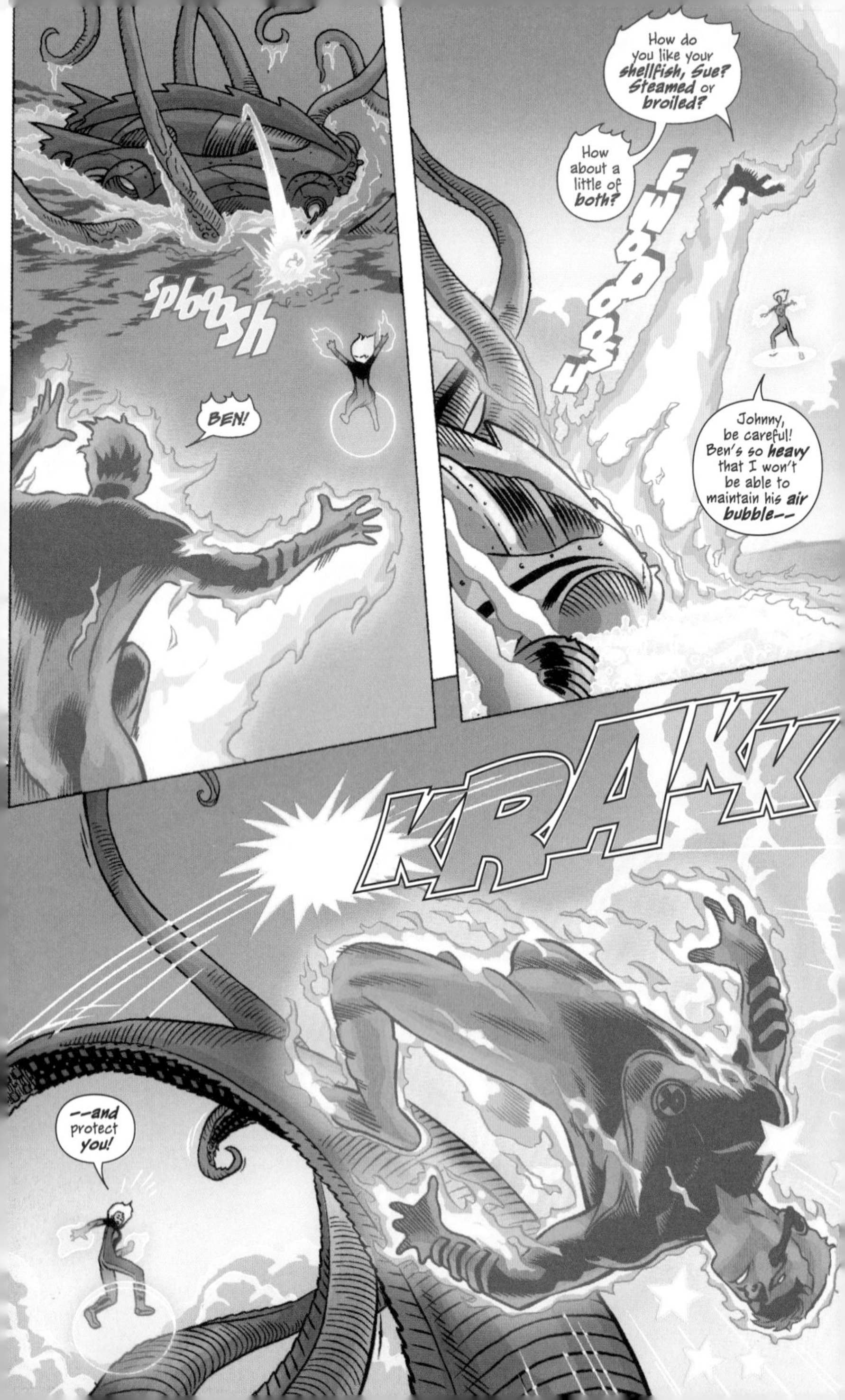

sploosh
BEN!
How do you like your shellfish, Sue? Steamed or broiled?
How about a little of both?
FWOOOOOSH
Johnny, be careful! Ben's so heavy that I won't be able to maintain his air bubble--
KRAKK
--and protect you!

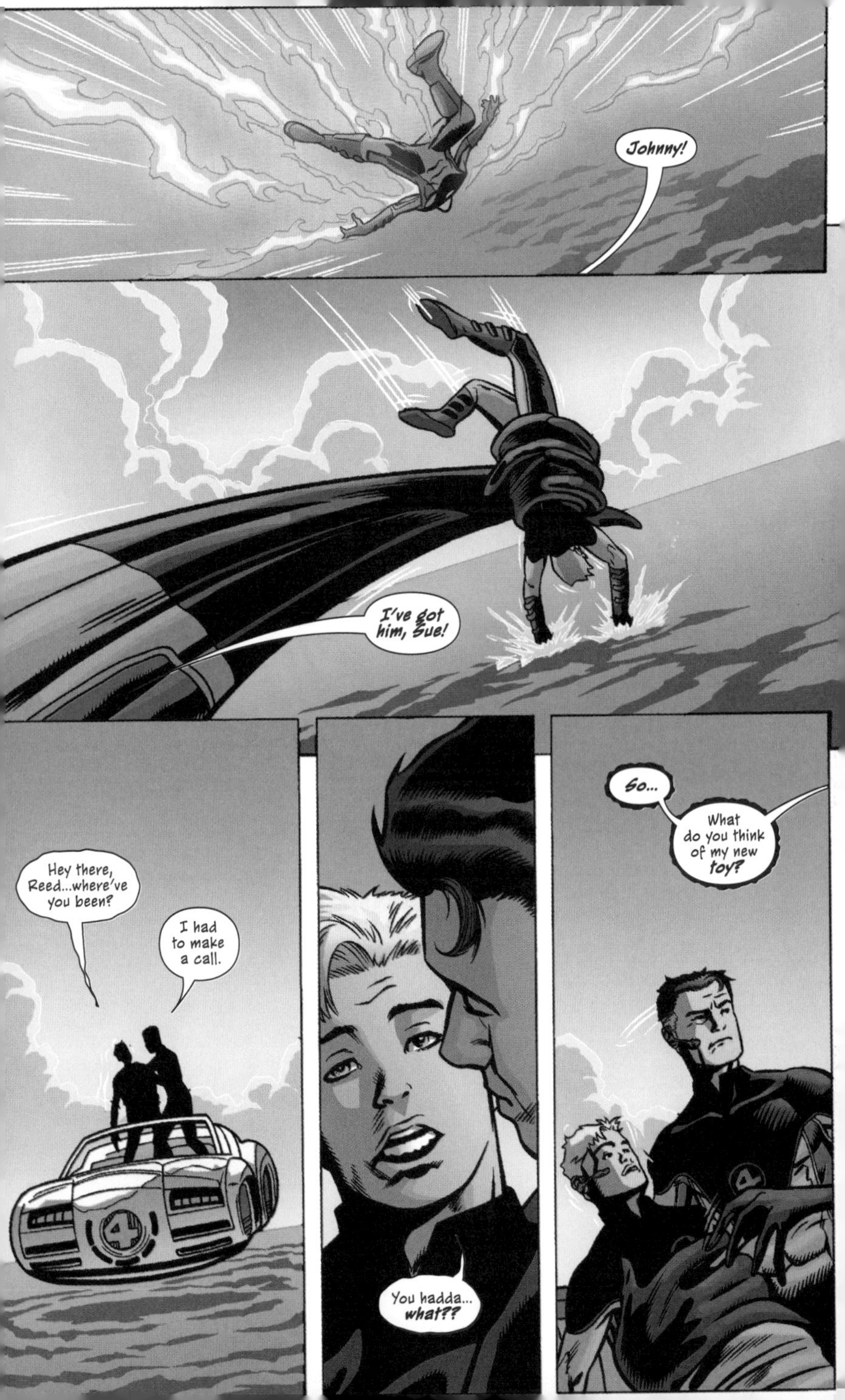
Johnny!
I've got him, Sue!
Hey there, Reed...where've you been?
I had to make a call.
You hadda... what??
So...
What do you think of my new toy?

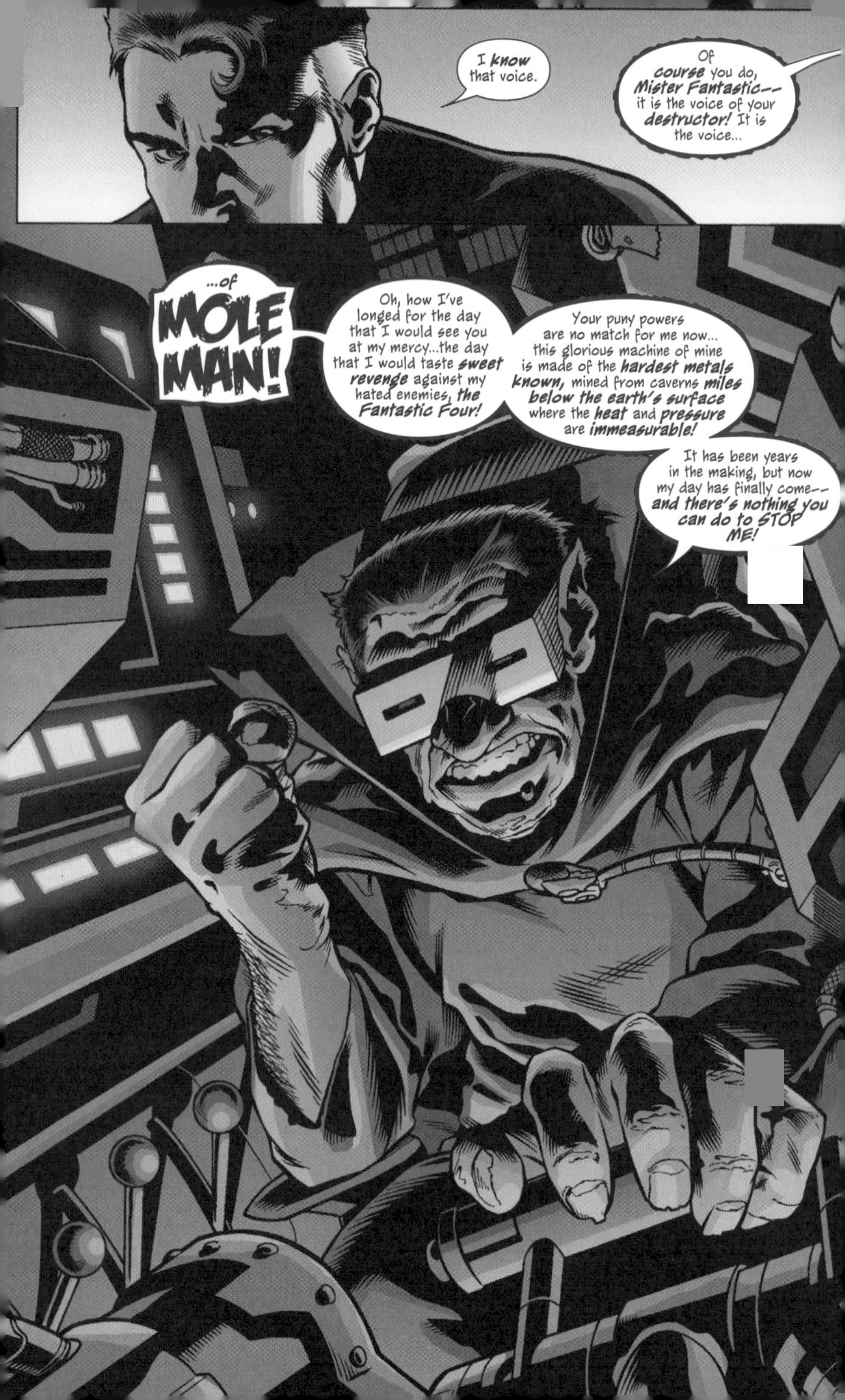
I **know** that voice.
Of **course** you do, **Mister Fantastic--** it is the voice of your **destructor!** It is the voice...
...of MOLE MAN!
Oh, how I've longed for the day that I would see you at my mercy...the day that I would taste **sweet revenge** against my hated enemies, **the Fantastic Four!**
Your puny powers are no match for me now... this glorious machine of mine is made of the **hardest metals known,** mined from caverns **miles below the earth's surface** where the **heat** and **pressure** are **immeasurable!**
It has been years in the making, but now my day has finally come-- **and there's nothing you can do to STOP ME!**

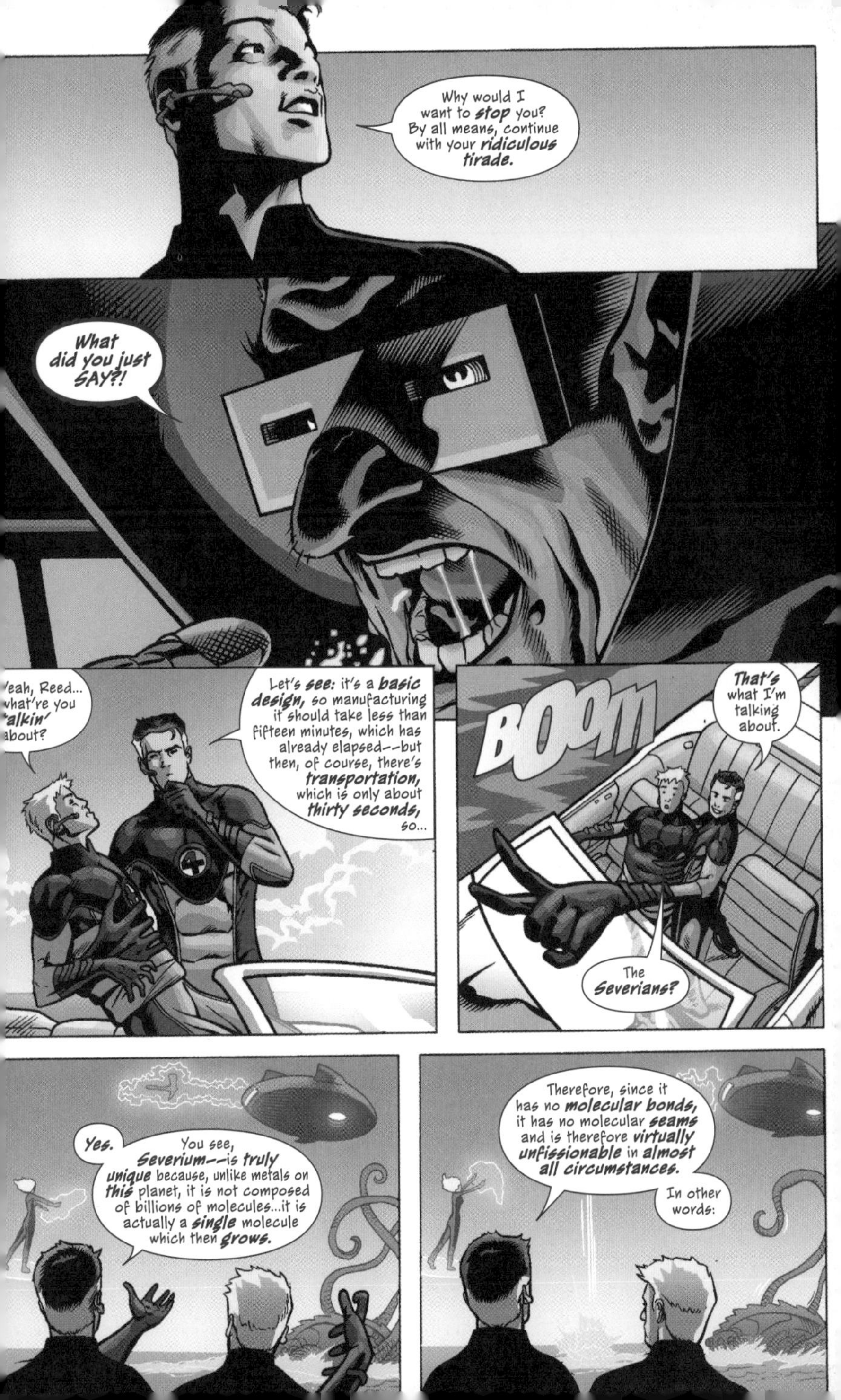
Why would I want to stop you? By all means, continue with your ridiculous tirade.
What did you just SAY?!
Yeah, Reed... what're you talkin' about?
Let's see: it's a basic design, so manufacturing it should take less than fifteen minutes, which has already elapsed--but then, of course, there's transportation, which is only about thirty seconds, so...
BOOM
That's what I'm talking about.
The Severians?
Yes.
You see, Severium--is truly unique because, unlike metals on this planet, it is not composed of billions of molecules...it is actually a single molecule which then grows.
Therefore, since it has no molecular bonds, it has no molecular seams and is therefore virtually unfissionable in almost all circumstances.
In other words:

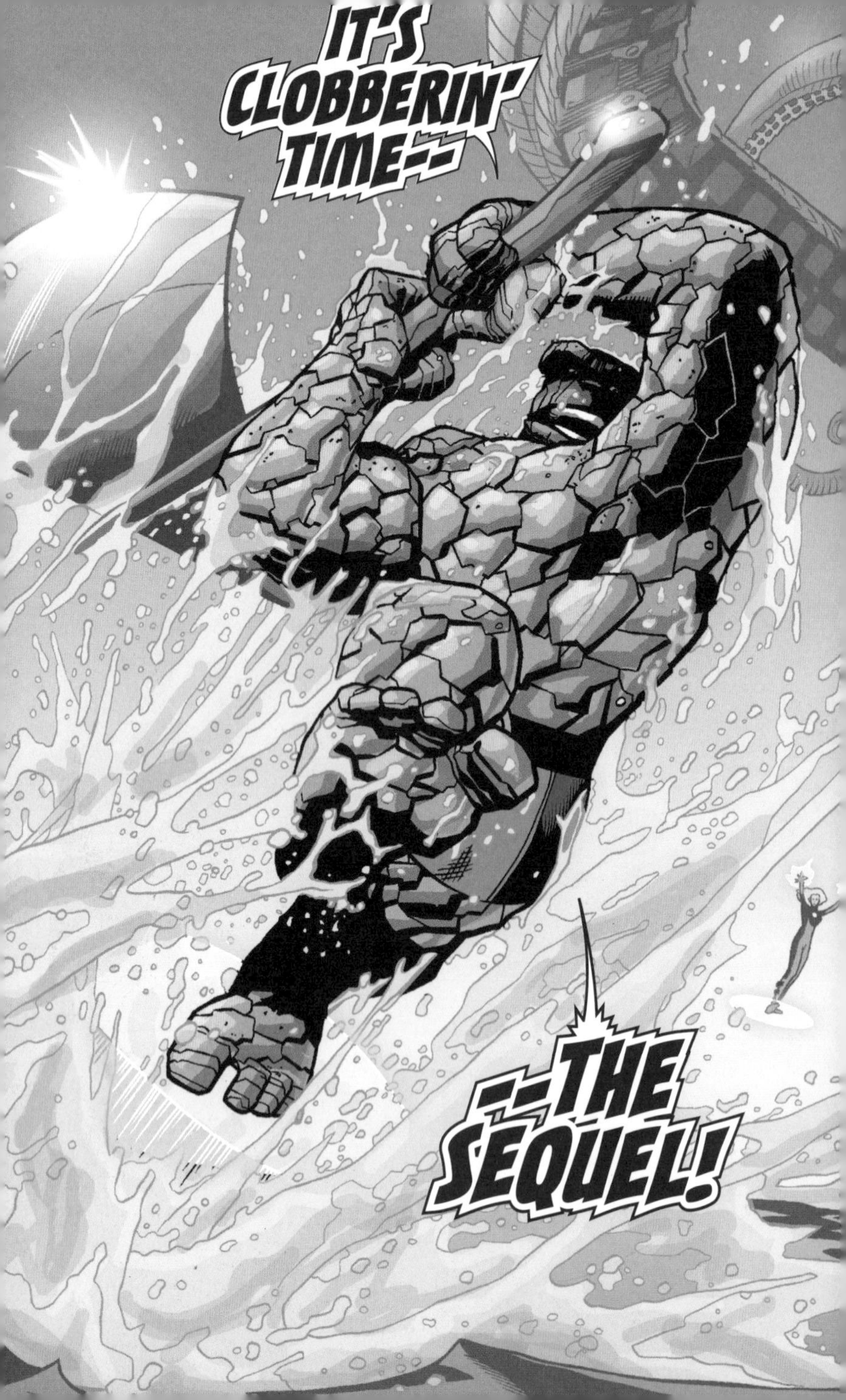
IT'S CLOBBERIN' TIME--
--THE SEQUEL!

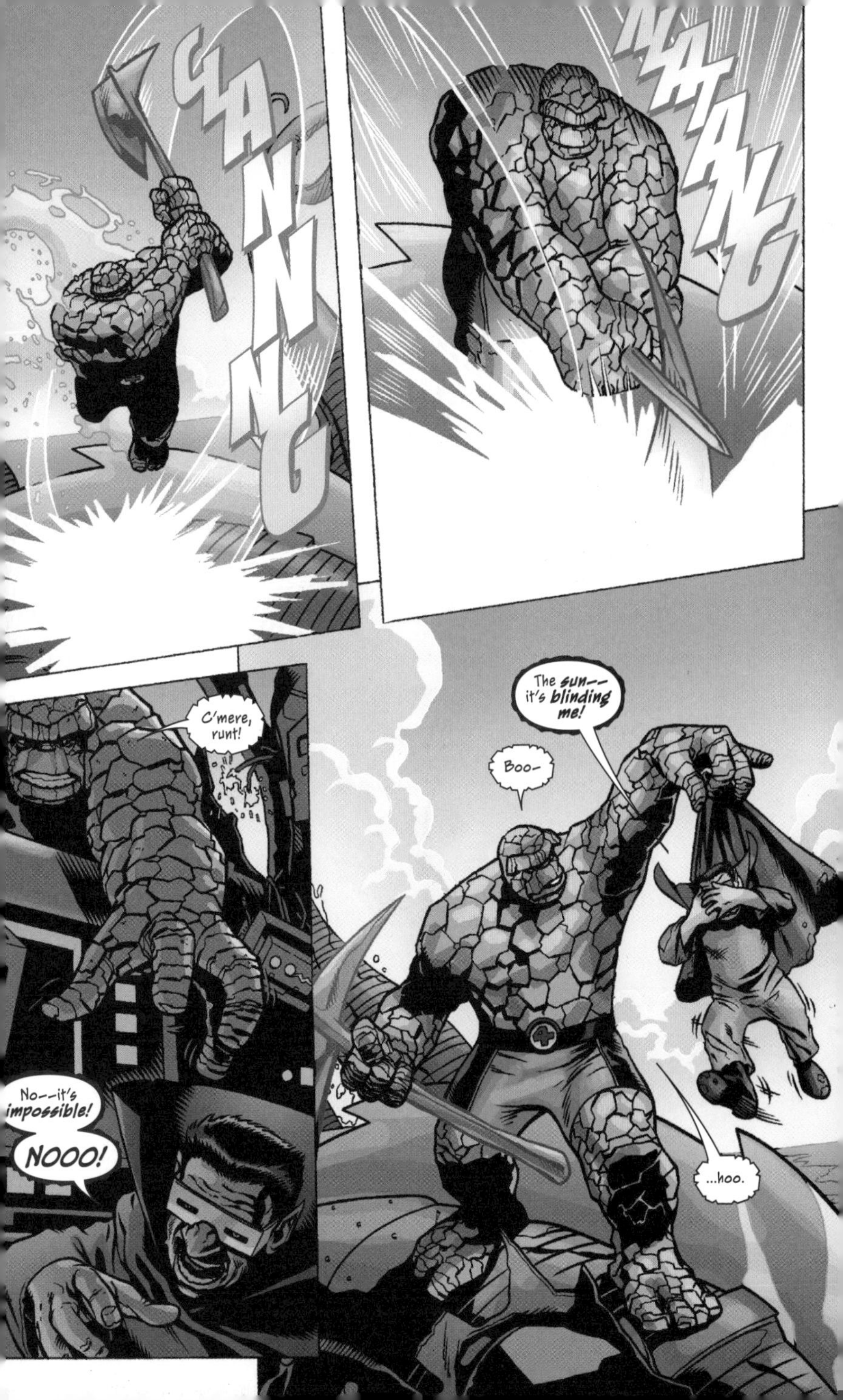
CLANNNNG
NNTANG
C'mere, runt!
No--it's impossible!
NOOO!
The sun-- it's blinding me!
Boo-
...hoo.

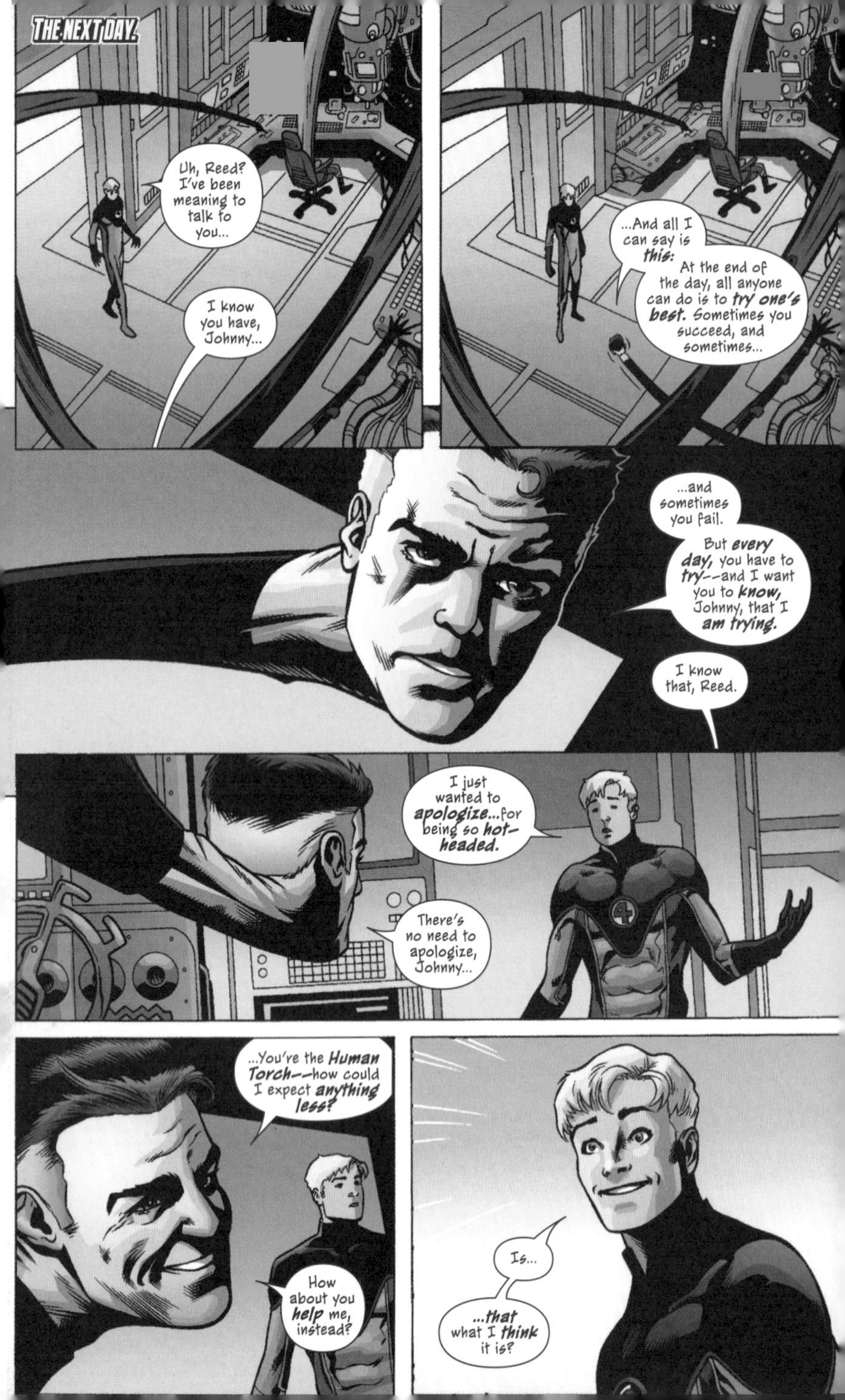

THE NEXT DAY.
Uh, Reed? I've been meaning to talk to you...
I know you have, Johnny...
...And all I can say is this:
At the end of the day, all anyone can do is to try one's best. Sometimes you succeed, and sometimes...
...and sometimes you fail.
But every day, you have to try--and I want you to know, Johnny, that I am trying.
I know that, Reed.
I just wanted to apologize...for being so hot-headed.
There's no need to apologize, Johnny...
...You're the Human Torch--how could I expect anything less?
How about you help me, instead?
Is...
...that what I think it is?

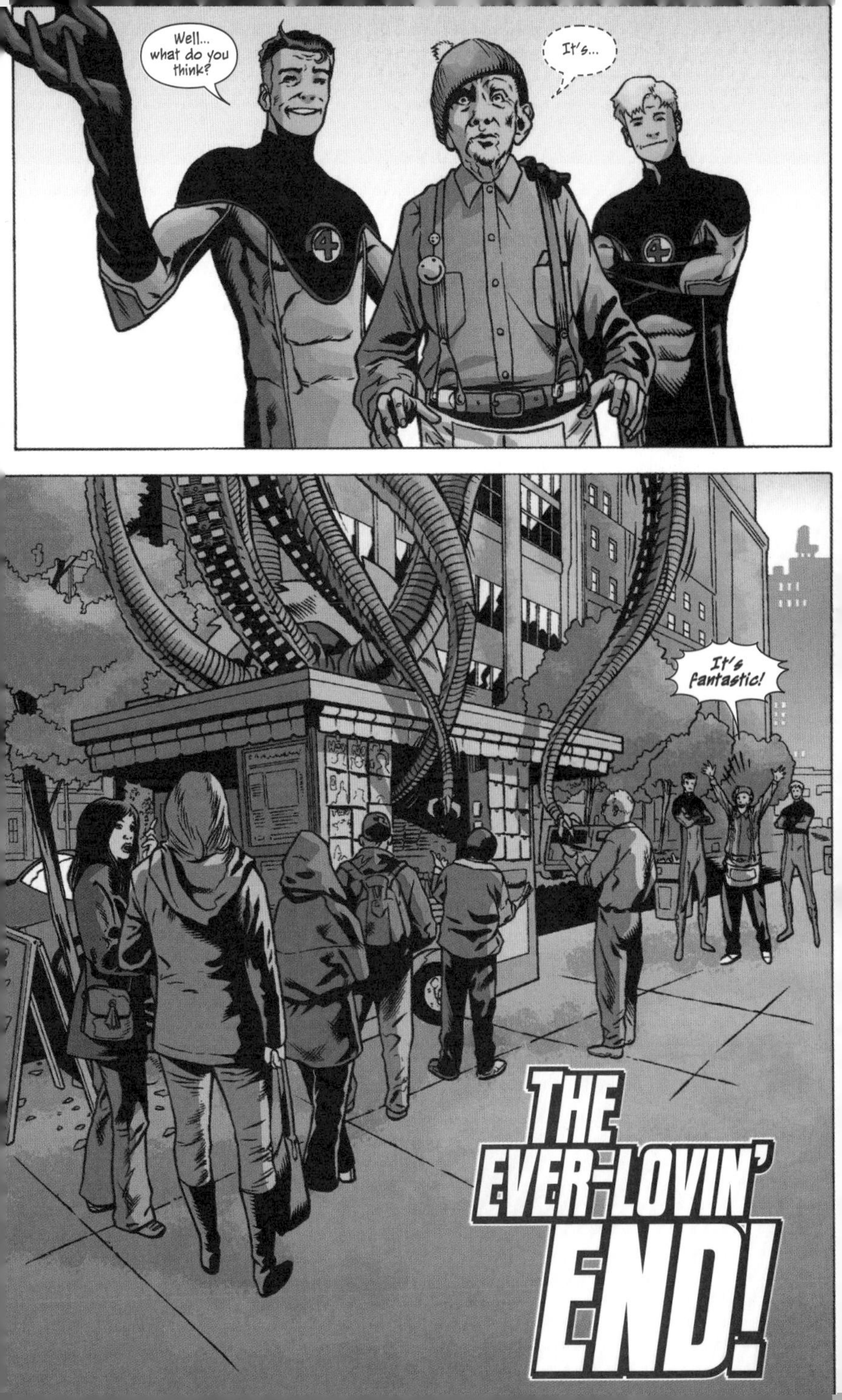
Well... what do you think?
It's...
It's fantastic!
THE EVER-LOVIN' END!

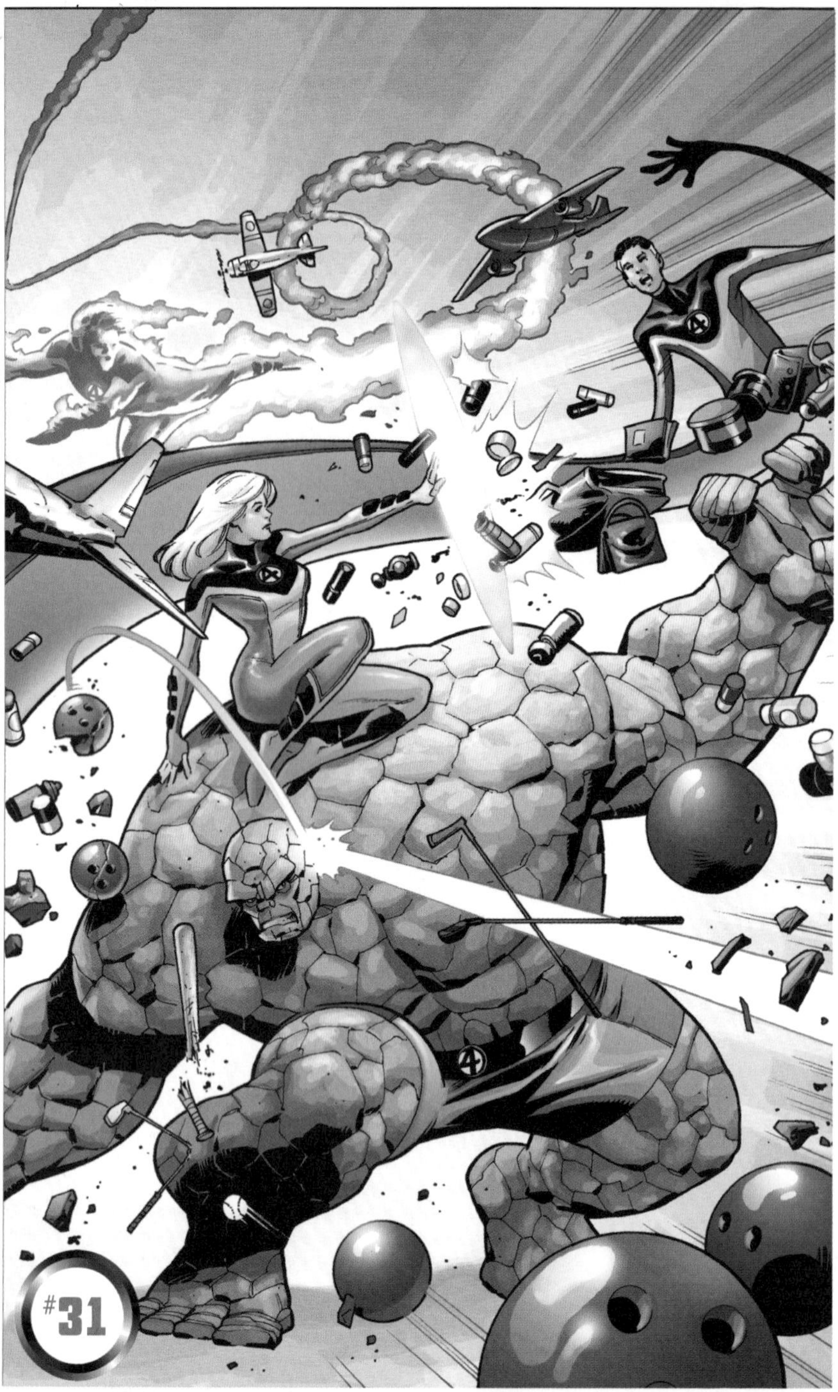
#31

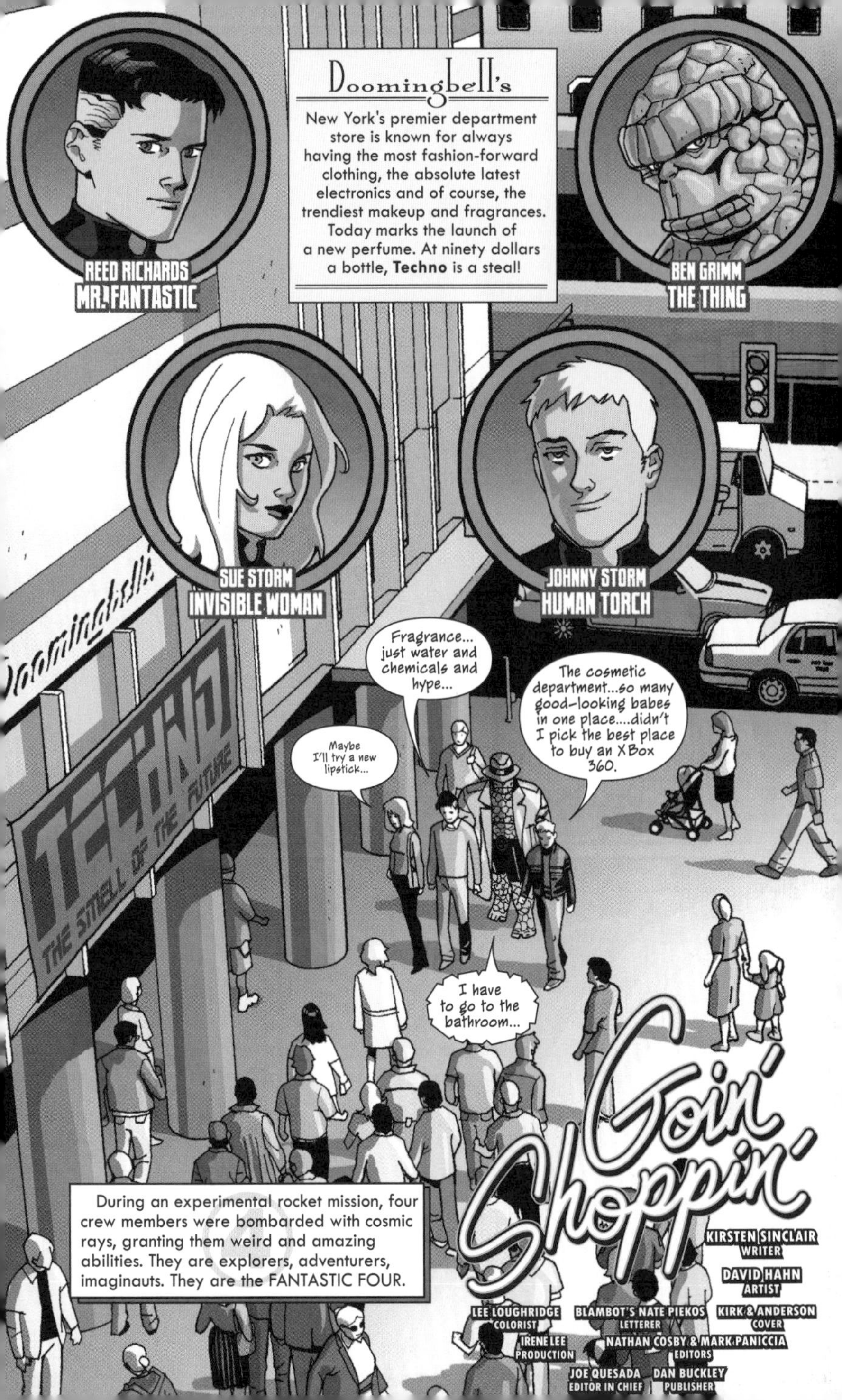

Doomingbell's
New York's premier department store is known for always having the most fashion-forward clothing, the absolute latest electronics and of course, the trendiest makeup and fragrances. Today marks the launch of a new perfume. At ninety dollars a bottle, **Techno** is a steal!
REED RICHARDS
MR. FANTASTIC
BEN GRIMM
THE THING
SUE STORM
INVISIBLE WOMAN
JOHNNY STORM
HUMAN TORCH
TECHNO
THE SMELL OF THE FUTURE
Fragrance... just water and chemicals and hype...
Maybe I'll try a new lipstick...
The cosmetic department...so many good-looking babes in one place....didn't I pick the best place to buy an XBox 360.
I have to go to the bathroom...
During an experimental rocket mission, four crew members were bombarded with cosmic rays, granting them weird and amazing abilities. They are explorers, adventurers, imaginauts. They are the FANTASTIC FOUR.
Goin' Shoppin'
KIRSTEN SINCLAIR WRITER
DAVID HAHN ARTIST
LEE LOUGHRIDGE COLORIST
BLAMBOT'S NATE PIEKOS LETTERER
KIRK & ANDERSON COVER
IRENE LEE PRODUCTION
NATHAN COSBY & MARK PANICCIA EDITORS
JOE QUESADA EDITOR IN CHIEF
DAN BUCKLEY PUBLISHER

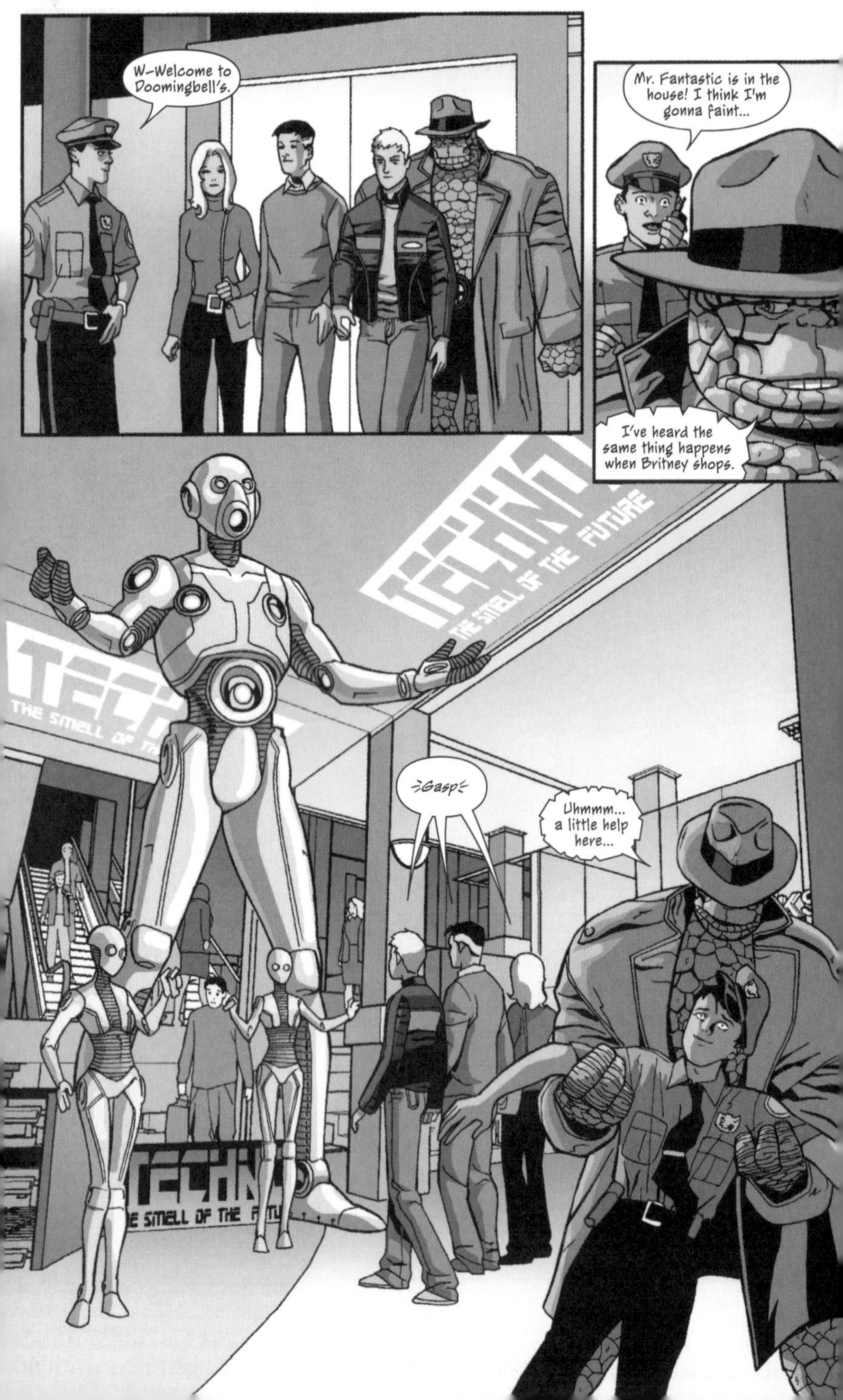
W-Welcome to Doomingbell's.
Mr. Fantastic is in the house! I think I'm gonna faint...
I've heard the same thing happens when Britney shops.
THE SMELL OF THE FUTURE
THE SMELL OF THE FUTURE
⋾Gasp⋸
Uhmmm... a little help here...

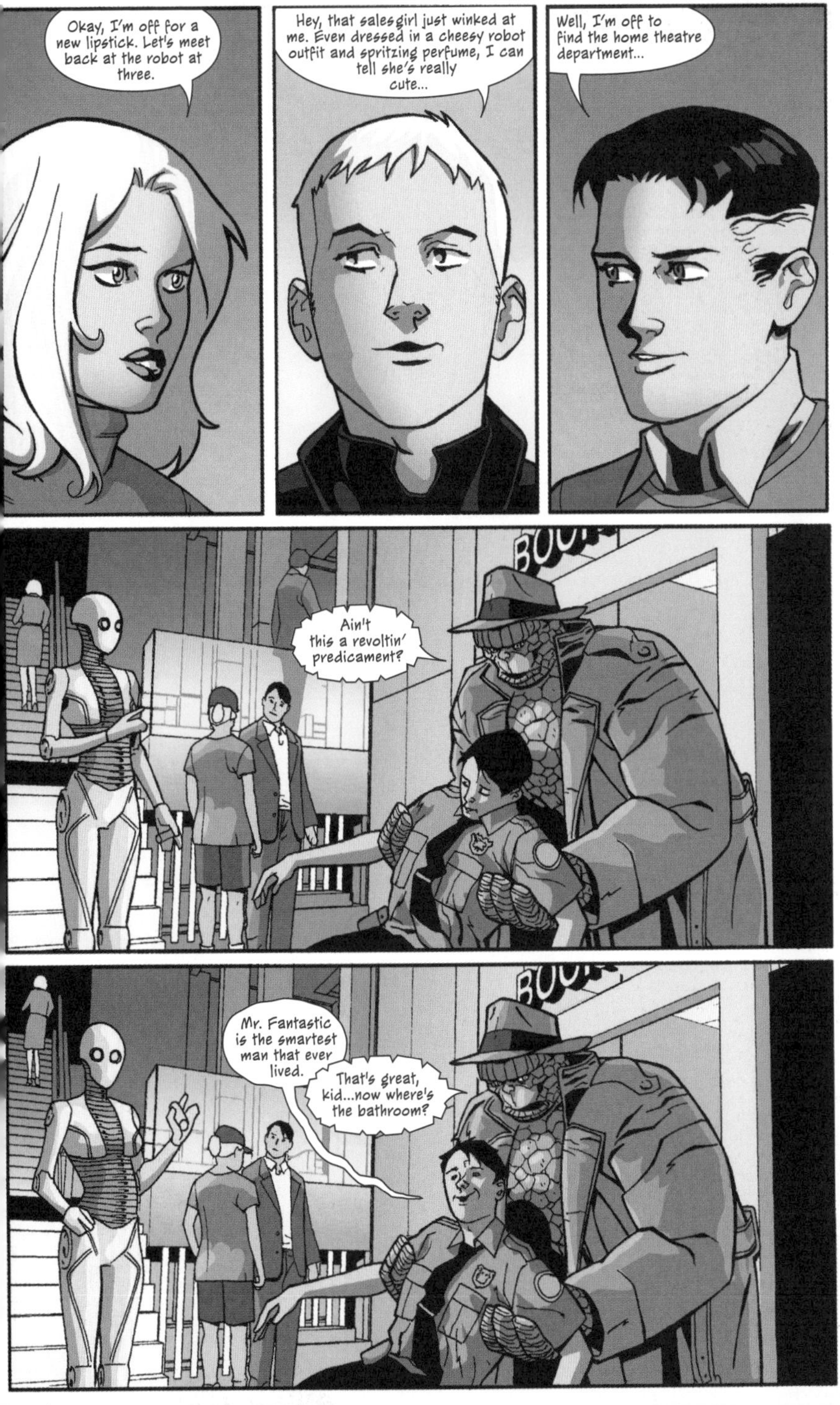
Okay, I'm off for a new lipstick. Let's meet back at the robot at three.
Hey, that salesgirl just winked at me. Even dressed in a cheesy robot outfit and spritzing perfume, I can tell she's really cute...
Well, I'm off to find the home theatre department...
Ain't this a revoltin' predicament?
Mr. Fantastic is the smartest man that ever lived.
That's great, kid...now where's the bathroom?

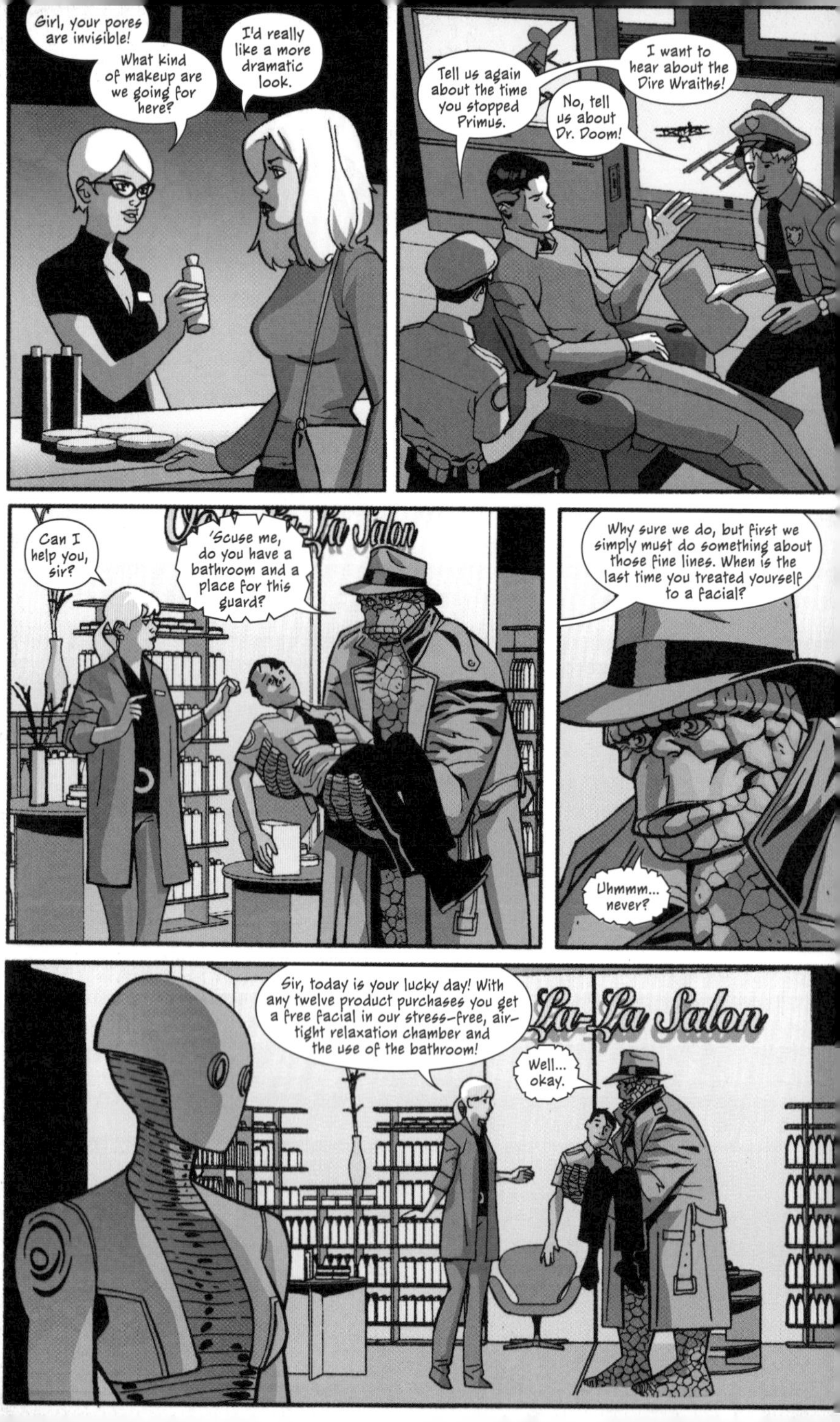

Girl, your pores are invisible!
What kind of makeup are we going for here?
I'd really like a more dramatic look.
Tell us again about the time you stopped Primus.
I want to hear about the Dire Wraiths!
No, tell us about Dr. Doom!
Can I help you, sir?
'Scuse me, do you have a bathroom and a place for this guard?
Why sure we do, but first we simply must do something about those fine lines. When is the last time you treated yourself to a facial?
Uhmmm... never?
Sir, today is your lucky day! With any twelve product purchases you get a free facial in our stress-free, air-tight relaxation chamber and the use of the bathroom!
La-La Salon
Well... okay.

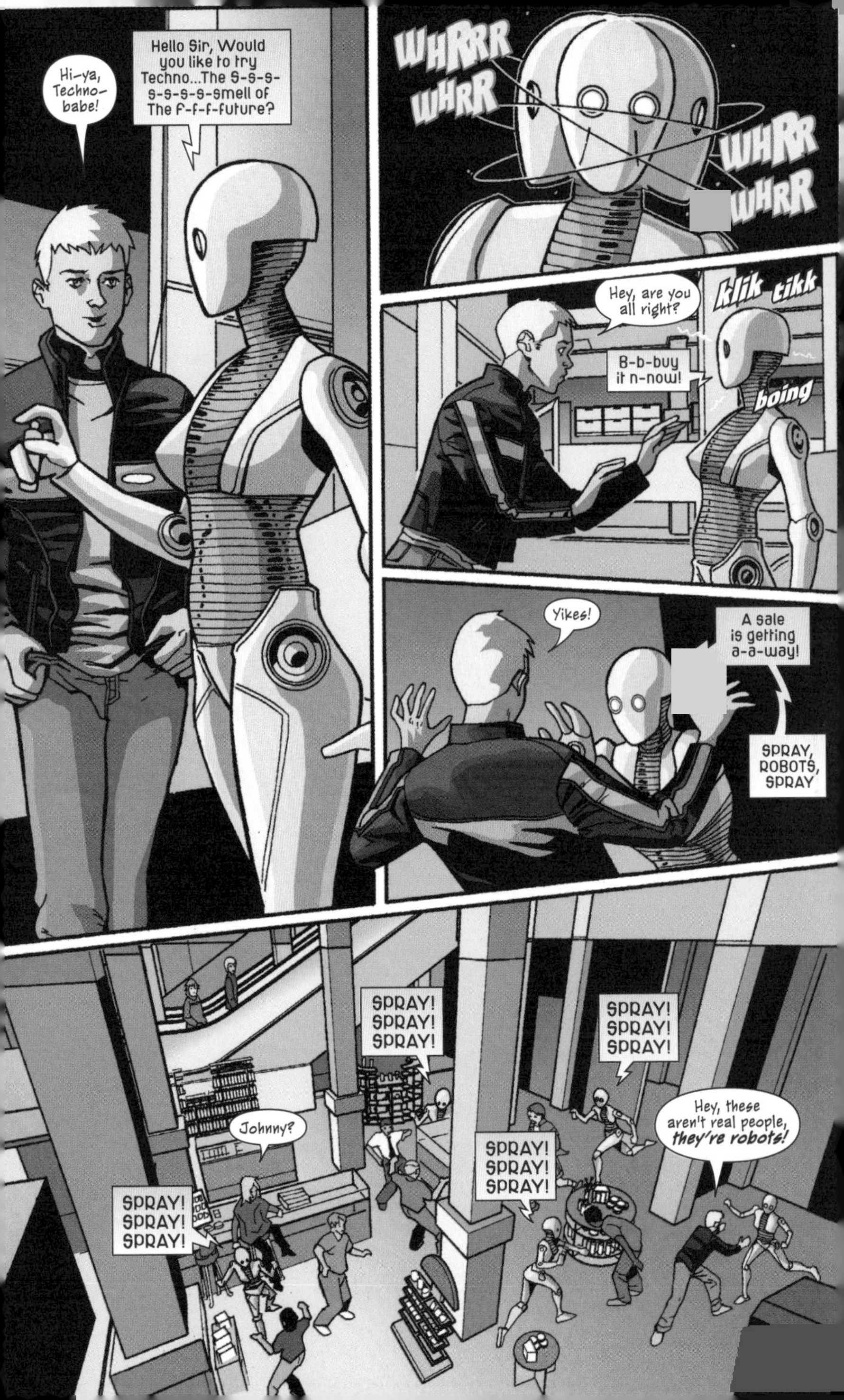
Hi-ya, Techno-babe!
Hello Sir, Would you like to try Techno...The S-s-s-s-s-s-s-smell of The f-f-f-future?
WHRRR
WHRR
WHRR
WHRR
Hey, are you all right?
klik tikk
B-b-buy it n-now!
boing
Yikes!
A sale is getting a-a-way!
SPRAY, ROBOTS, SPRAY
SPRAY! SPRAY! SPRAY!
SPRAY! SPRAY! SPRAY!
Johnny?
Hey, these aren't real people, they're robots!
SPRAY! SPRAY! SPRAY!
SPRAY! SPRAY! SPRAY!

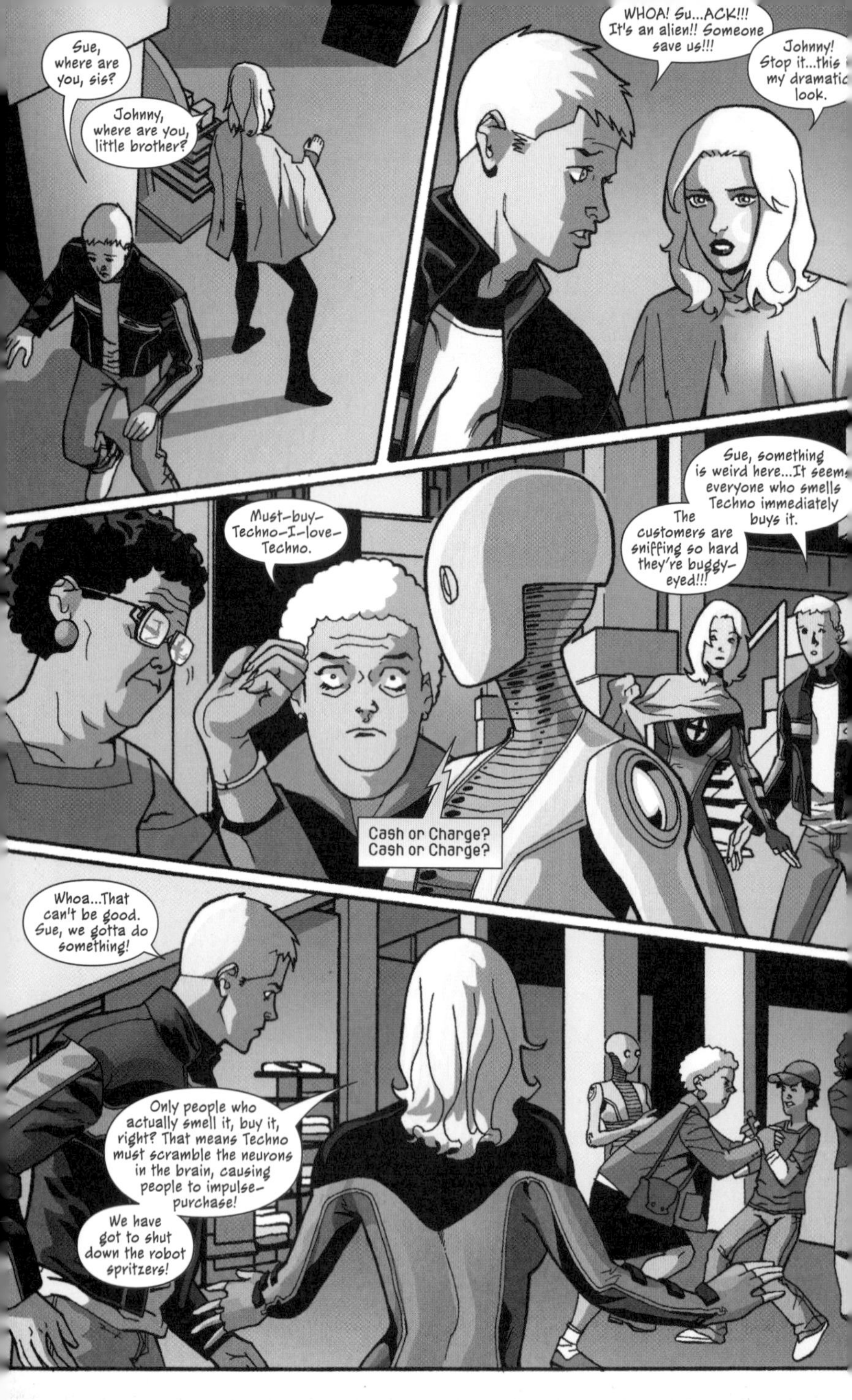
Sue, where are you, sis?
Johnny, where are you, little brother?
WHOA! Su...ACK!!! It's an alien!! Someone save us!!!
Johnny! Stop it...this is my dramatic look.
Must-buy-Techno-I-love-Techno.
Sue, something is weird here...It seems everyone who smells Techno immediately buys it.
The customers are sniffing so hard they're buggy-eyed!!!
Cash or Charge? Cash or Charge?
Whoa...That can't be good. Sue, we gotta do something!
Only people who actually smell it, buy it, right? That means Techno must scramble the neurons in the brain, causing people to impulse-purchase!
We have got to shut down the robot spritzers!

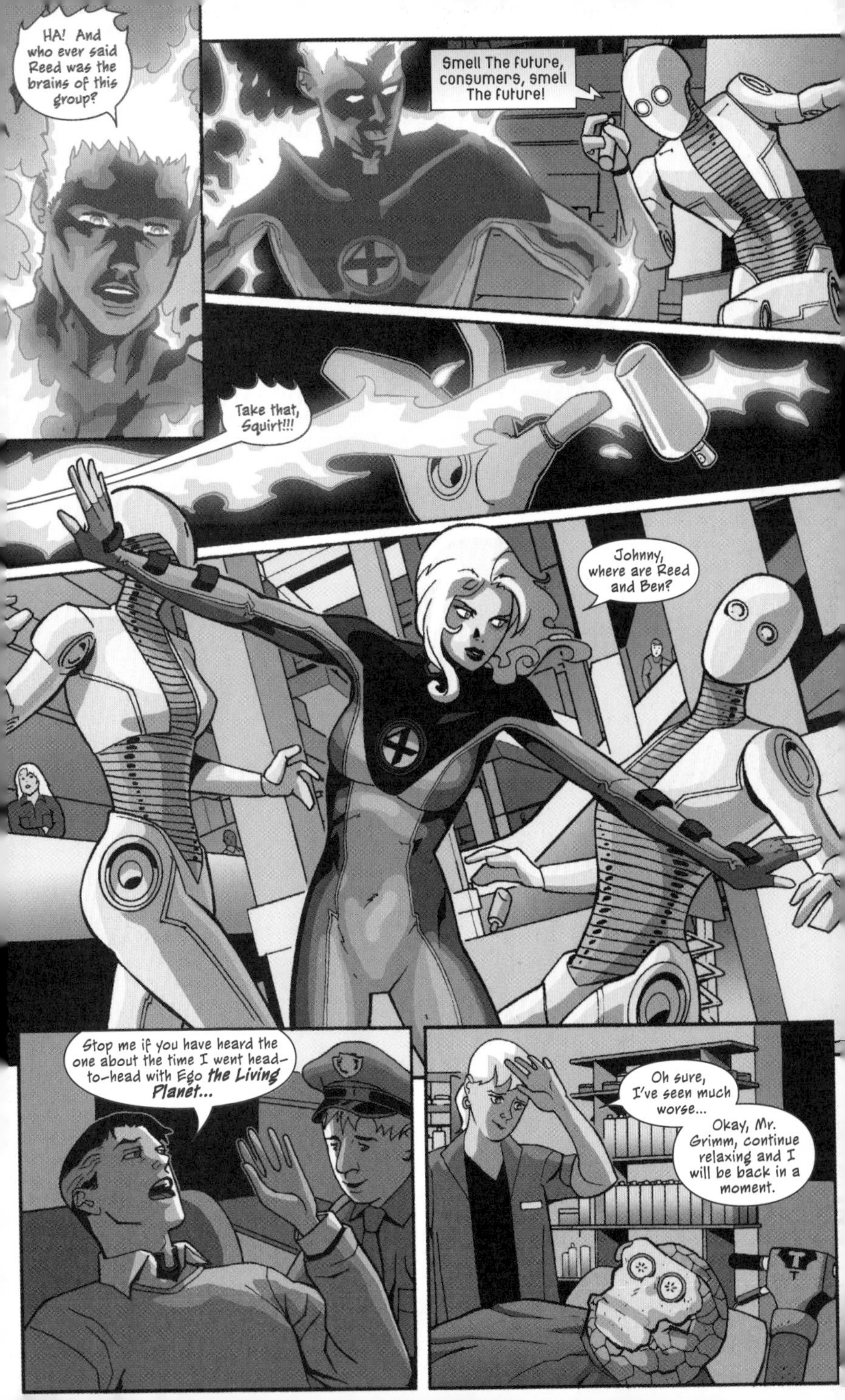
HA! And who ever said Reed was the brains of this group?
Smell The future, consumers, smell The future!
Take that, Squirt!!!
Johnny, where are Reed and Ben?
Stop me if you have heard the one about the time I went head-to-head with Ego *the Living Planet...*
Oh sure, I've seen much worse...
Okay, Mr. Grimm, continue relaxing and I will be back in a moment.

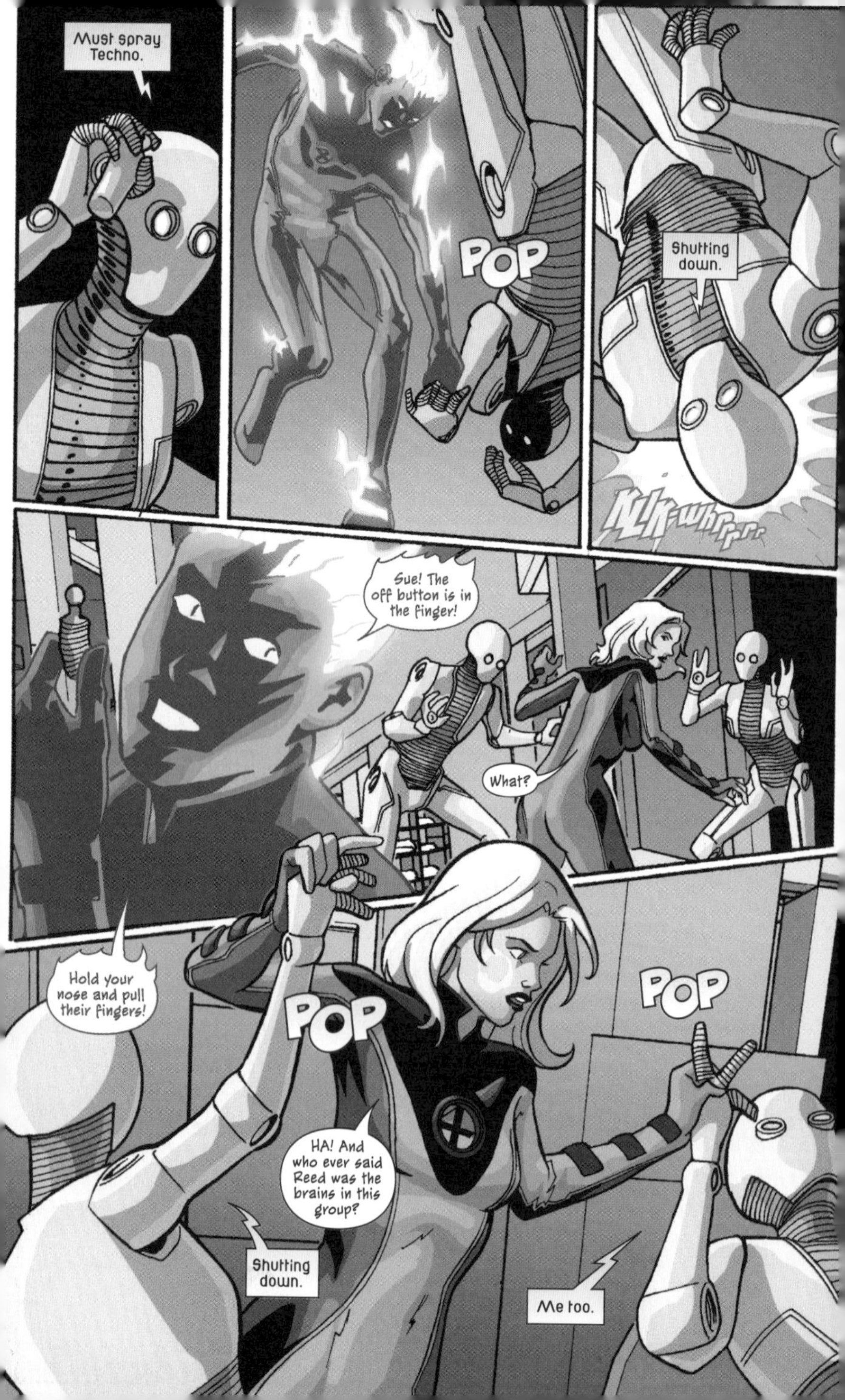
Must spray Techno.
POP
Shutting down.
KLIK-whrrr
Sue! The off button is in the finger!
What?
Hold your nose and pull their fingers!
POP
POP
HA! And who ever said Reed was the brains in this group?
Shutting down.
Me too.

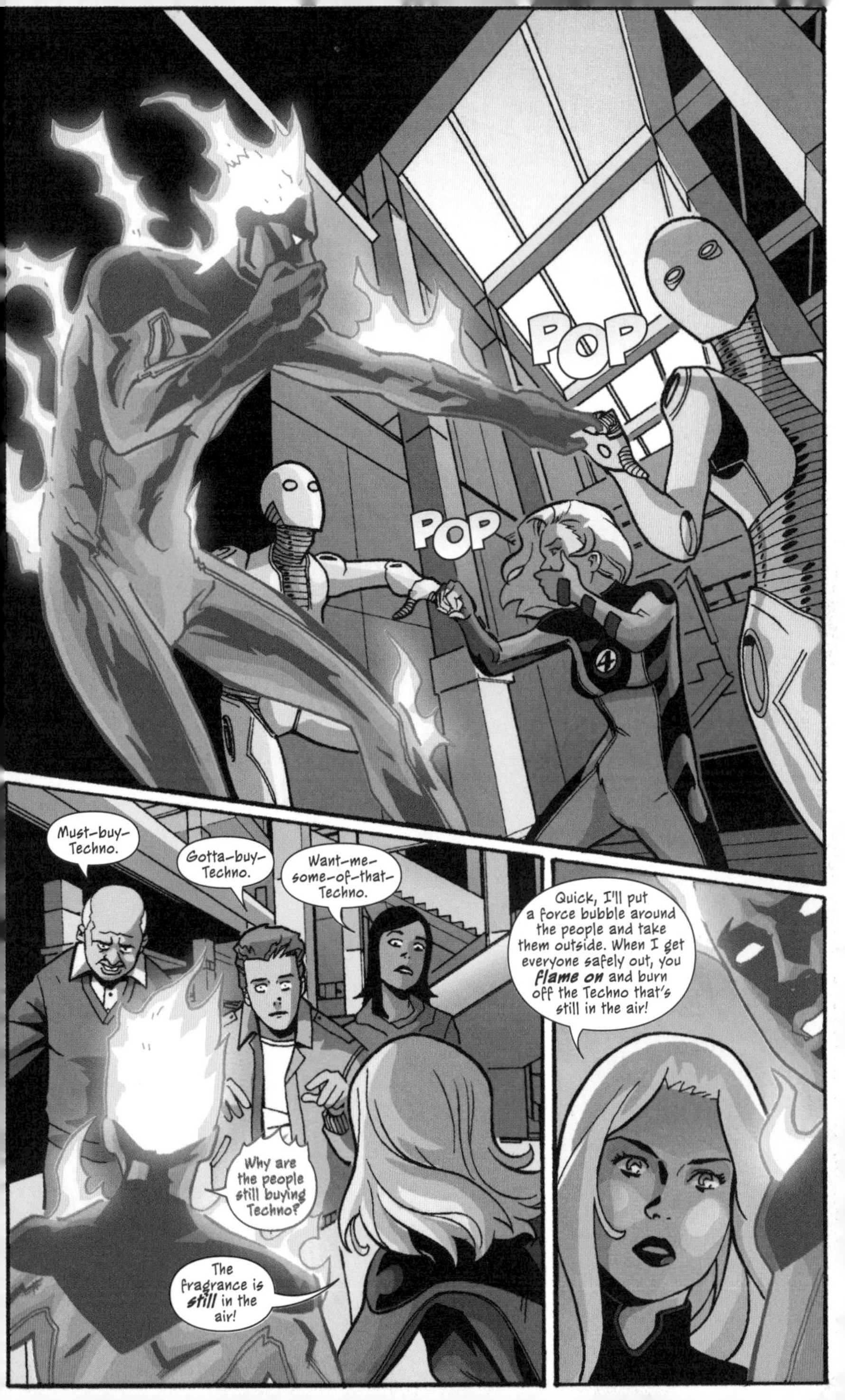
POP
POP
Must-buy-Techno.
Gotta-buy-Techno.
Want-me-some-of-that-Techno.
Why are the people still buying Techno?
The fragrance is *still* in the air!
Quick, I'll put a force bubble around the people and take them outside. When I get everyone safely out, you *flame on* and burn off the Techno that's still in the air!

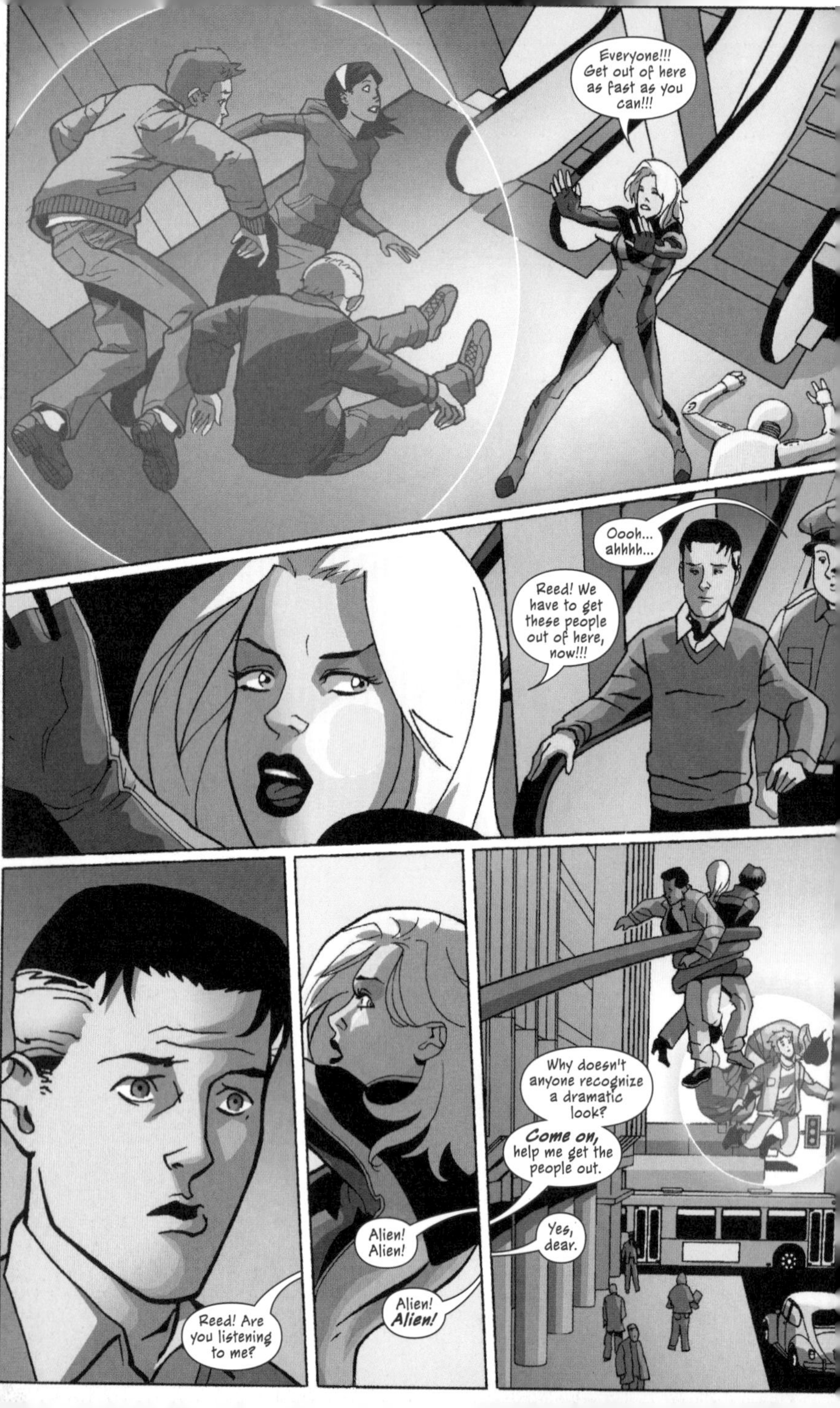
Everyone!!! Get out of here as fast as you can!!!
Oooh... ahhhh...
Reed! We have to get these people out of here, now!!!
Reed! Are you listening to me?
Alien! Alien!
Alien! **Alien!**
Why doesn't anyone recognize a dramatic look?
Come on, help me get the people out.
Yes, dear.

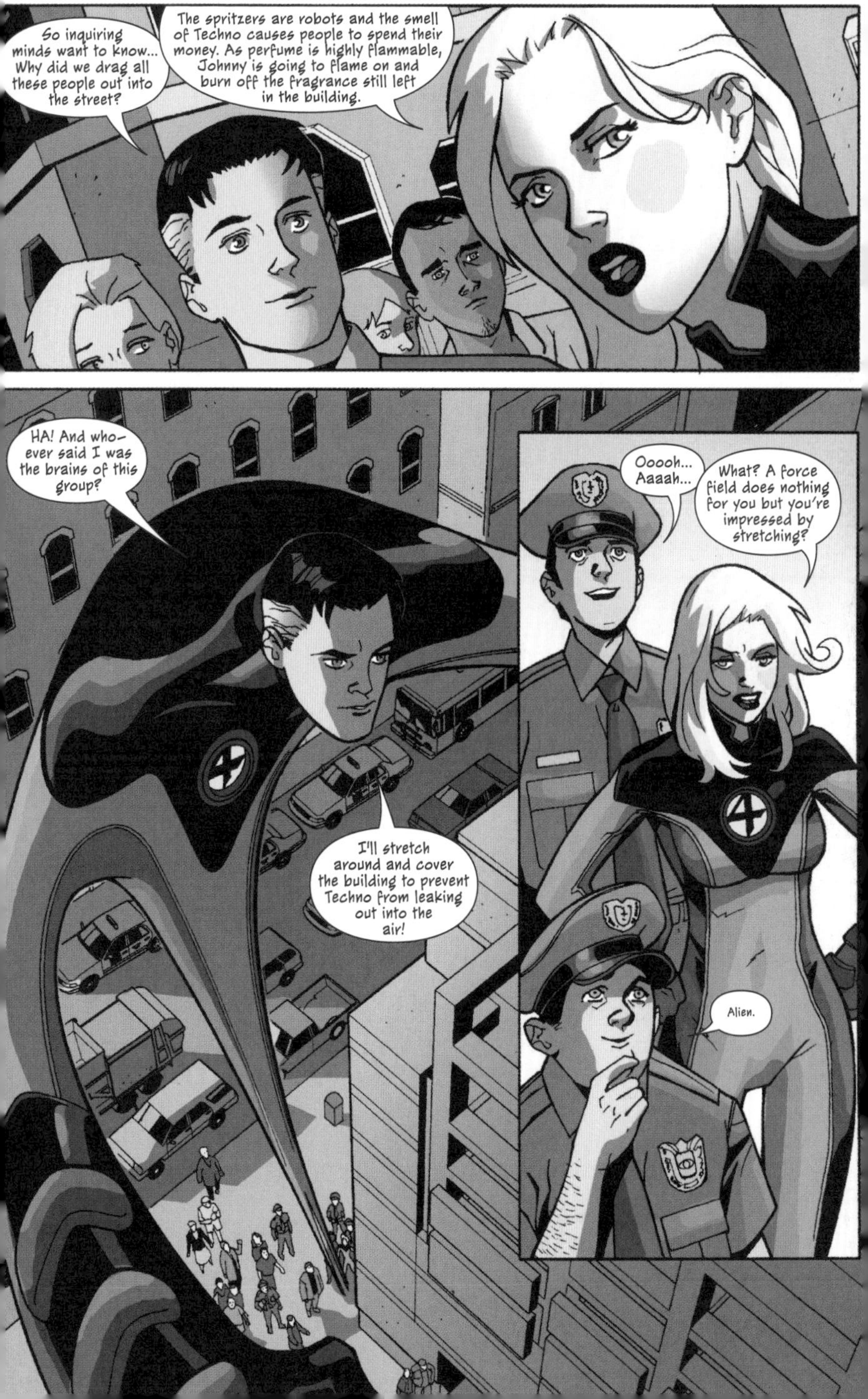
So inquiring minds want to know... Why did we drag all these people out into the street?
The spritzers are robots and the smell of Techno causes people to spend their money. As perfume is highly flammable, Johnny is going to flame on and burn off the fragrance still left in the building.
HA! And who-ever said I was the brains of this group?
I'll stretch around and cover the building to prevent Techno from leaking out into the air!
Ooooh... Aaaah...
What? A force field does nothing for you but you're impressed by stretching?
Alien.

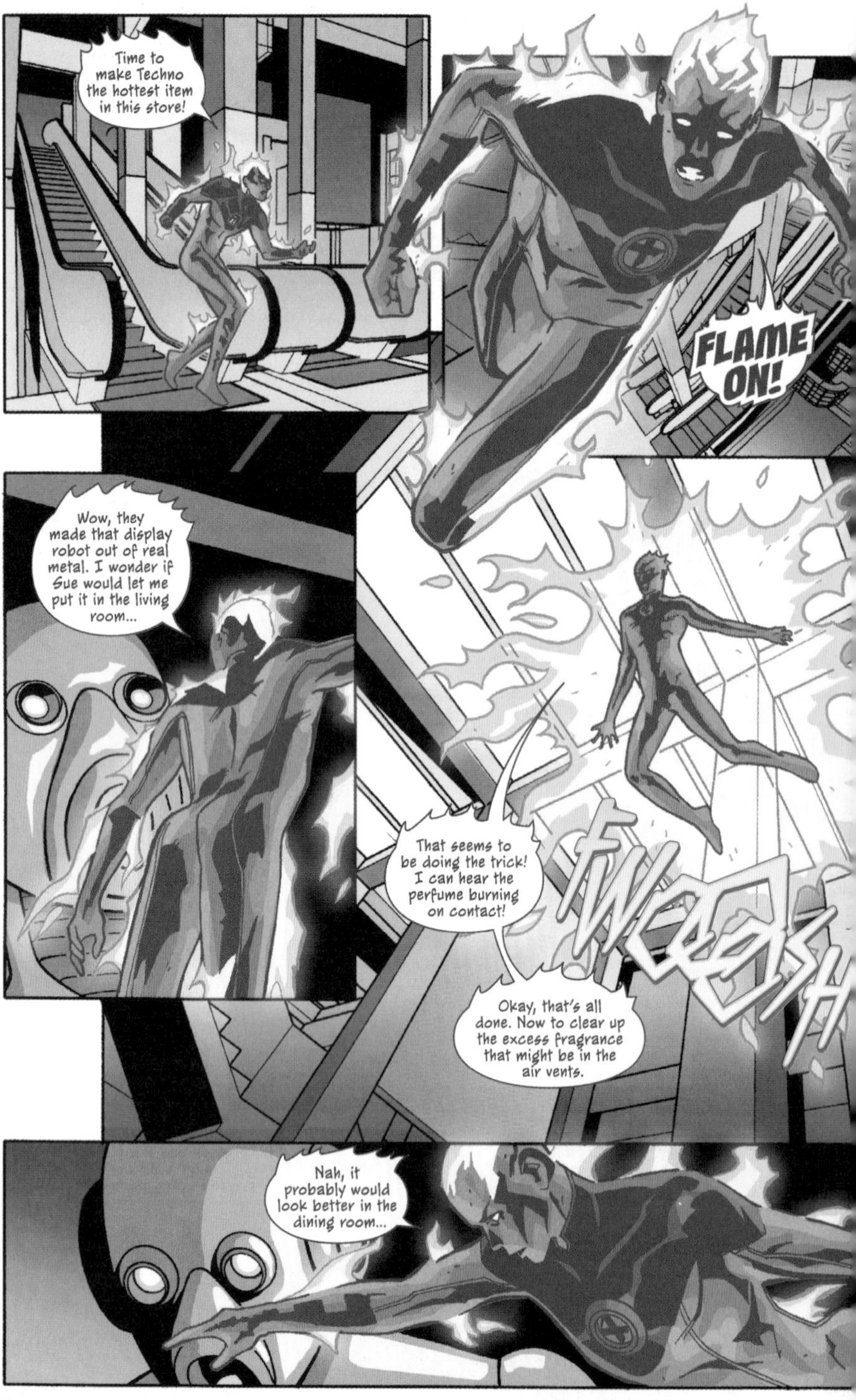
Time to make Techno the hottest item in this store!
FLAME ON!
Wow, they made that display robot out of real metal. I wonder if Sue would let me put it in the living room...
That seems to be doing the trick! I can hear the perfume burning on contact!
FWOOSH
Okay, that's all done. Now to clear up the excess fragrance that might be in the air vents.
Nah, it probably would look better in the dining room...

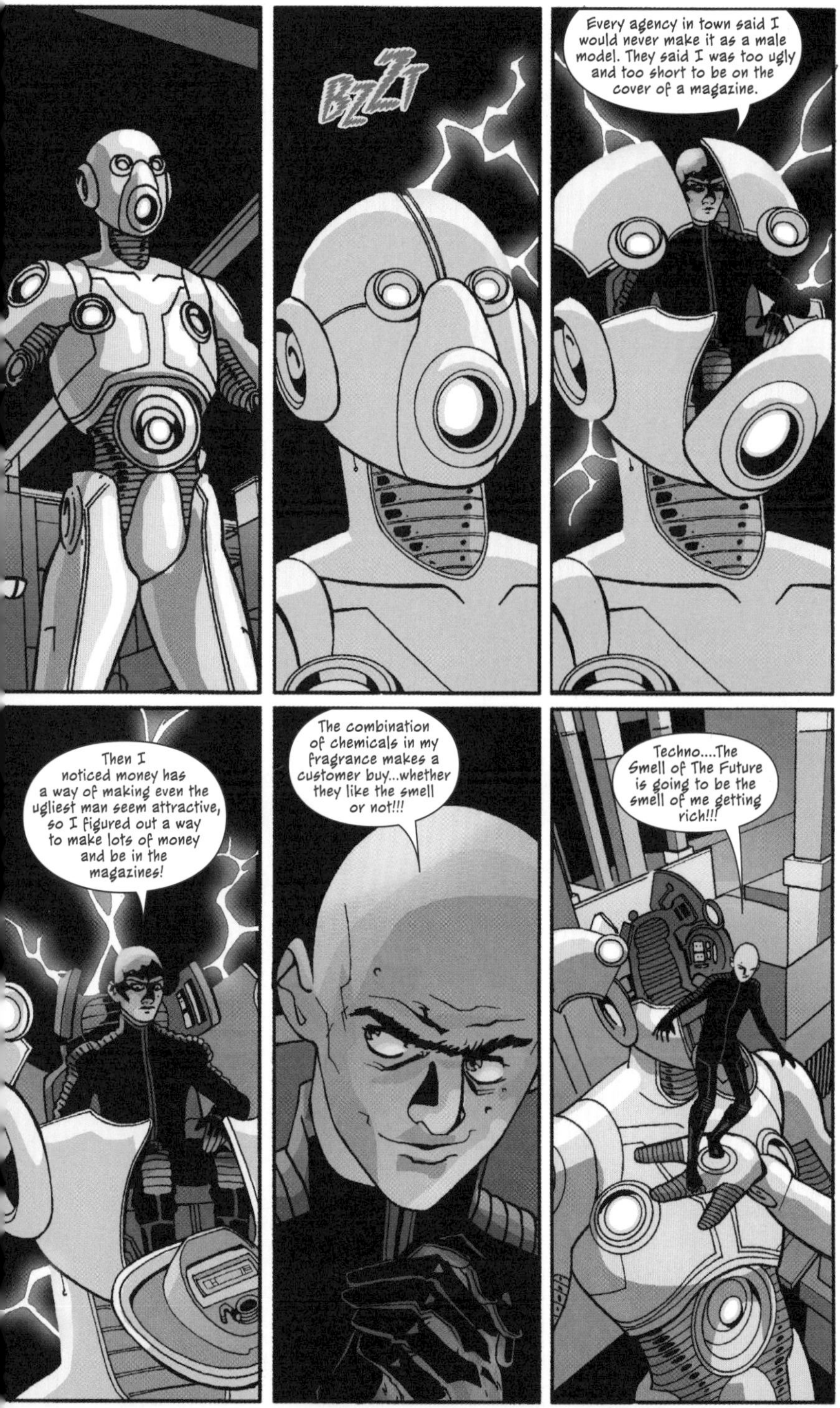
BZZZT
Every agency in town said I would never make it as a male model. They said I was too ugly and too short to be on the cover of a magazine.
Then I noticed money has a way of making even the ugliest man seem attractive, so I figured out a way to make lots of money and be in the magazines!
The combination of chemicals in my fragrance makes a customer buy...whether they like the smell or not!!!
Techno....The Smell of The Future is going to be the smell of me getting rich!!!

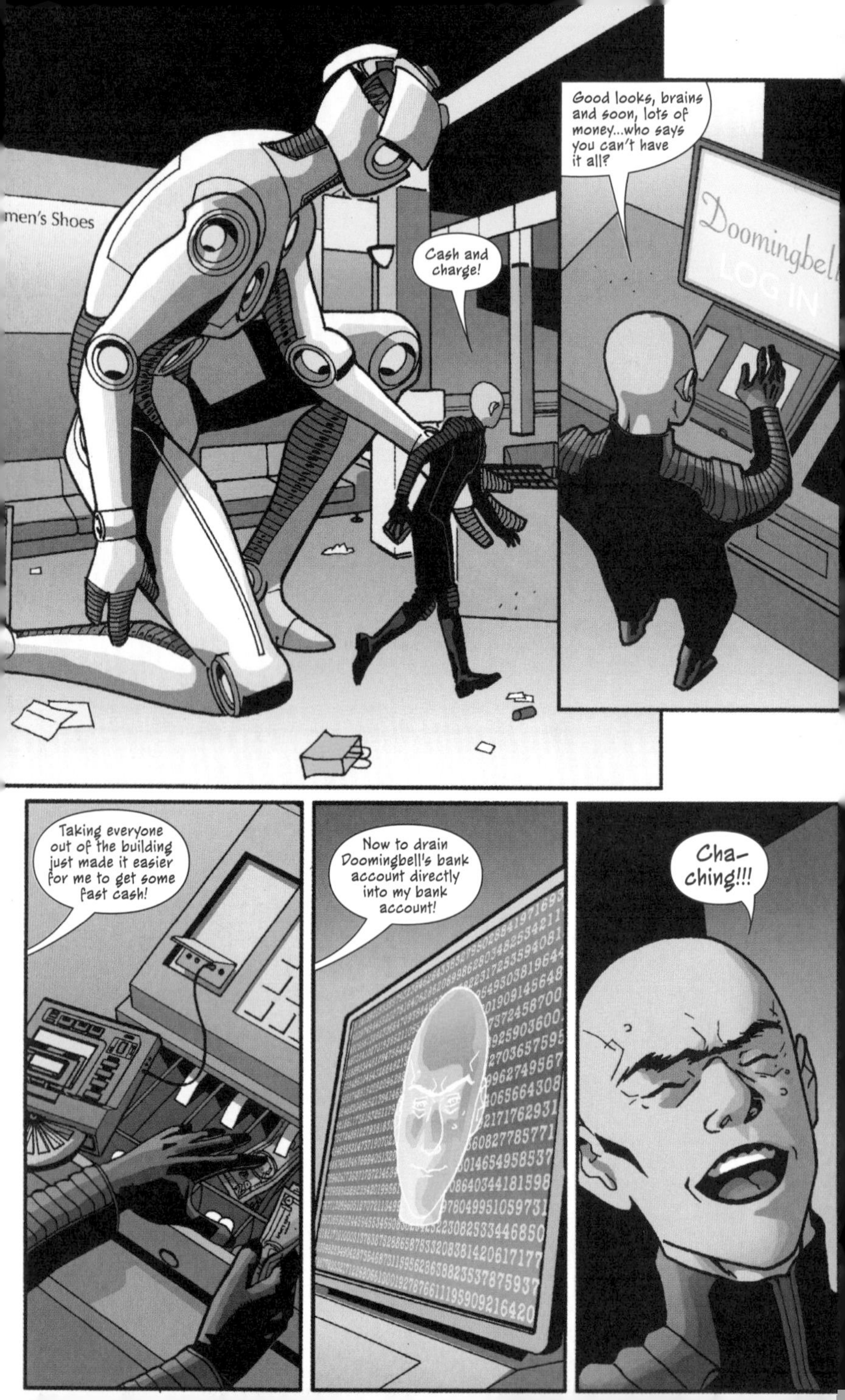
men's Shoes
Cash and charge!
Good looks, brains and soon, lots of money...who says you can't have it all?
Doomingbell
LOG IN
Taking everyone out of the building just made it easier for me to get some fast cash!
Now to drain Doomingbell's bank account directly into my bank account!
Cha-ching!!!

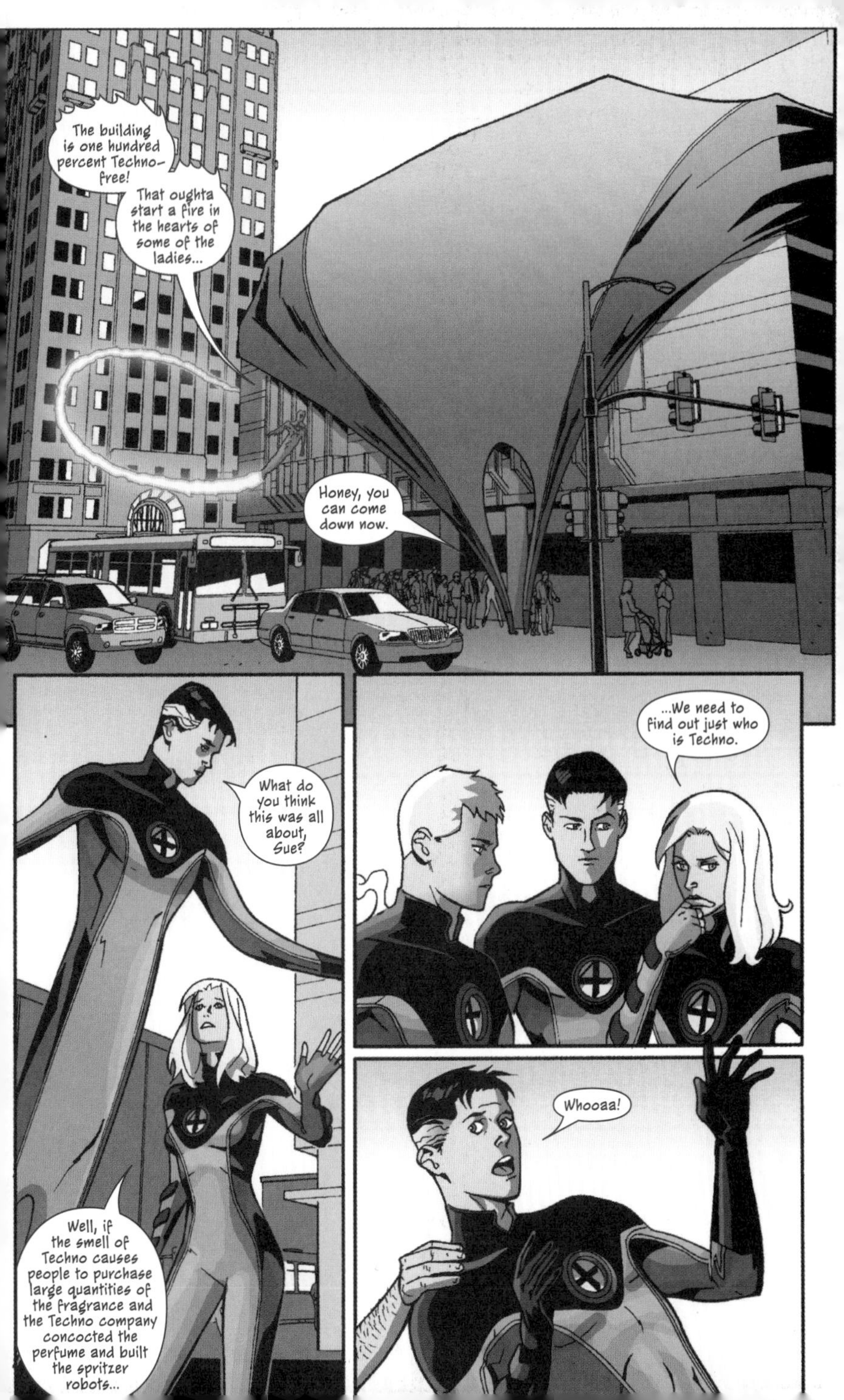

The building is one hundred percent Techno-free!
That oughta start a fire in the hearts of some of the ladies...
Honey, you can come down now.
What do you think this was all about, Sue?
Well, if the smell of Techno causes people to purchase large quantities of the fragrance and the Techno company concocted the perfume and built the spritzer robots...
...We need to find out just who is Techno.
Whooaa!

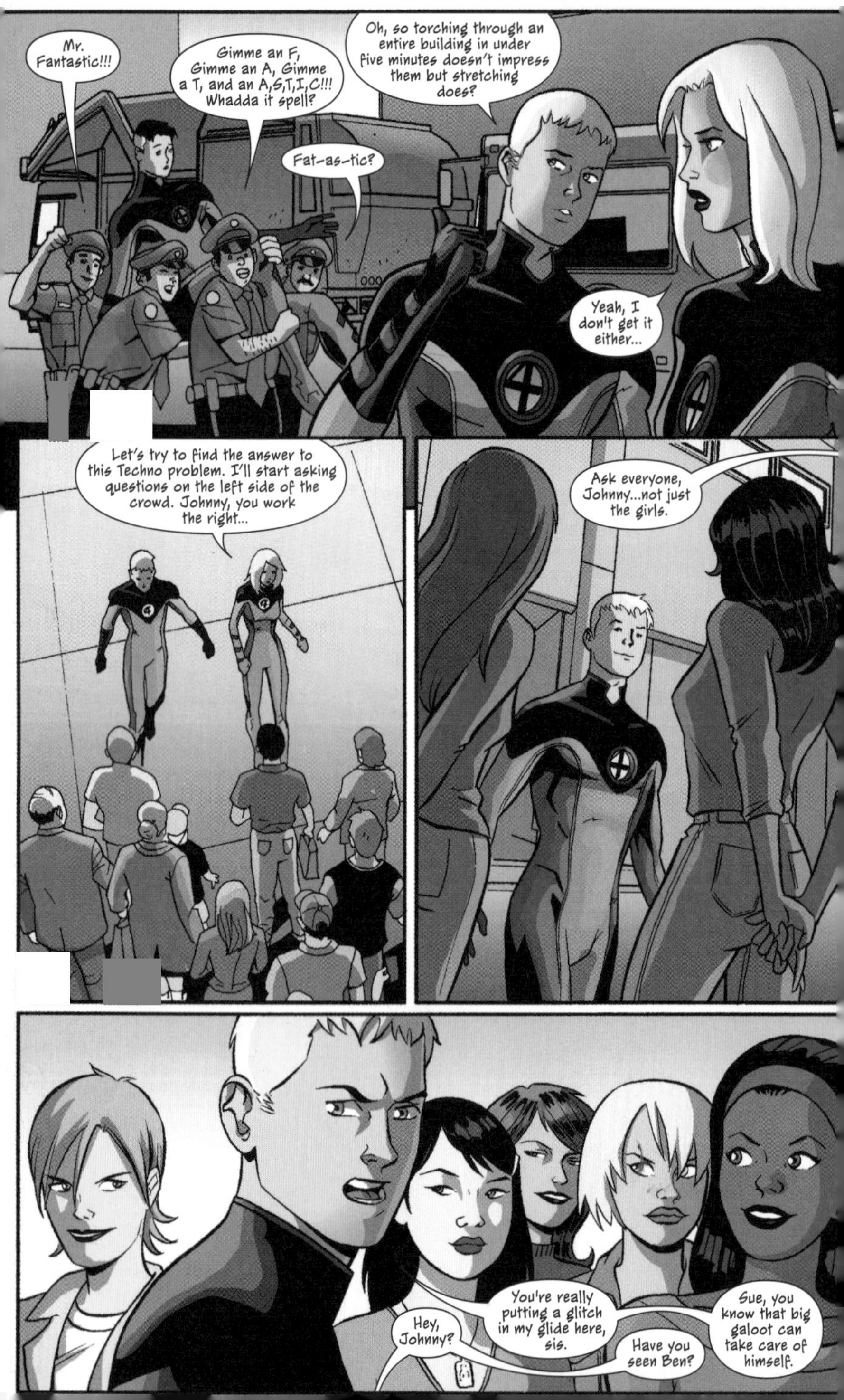
Mr. Fantastic!!!
Gimme an F, Gimme an A, Gimme a T, and an A,S,T,I,C!!! Whadda it spell?
Fat-as-tic?
Oh, so torching through an entire building in under five minutes doesn't impress them but stretching does?
Yeah, I don't get it either...
Let's try to find the answer to this Techno problem. I'll start asking questions on the left side of the crowd. Johnny, you work the right...
Ask everyone, Johnny...not just the girls.
Hey, Johnny?
You're really putting a glitch in my glide here, sis.
Have you seen Ben?
Sue, you know that big galoot can take care of himself.

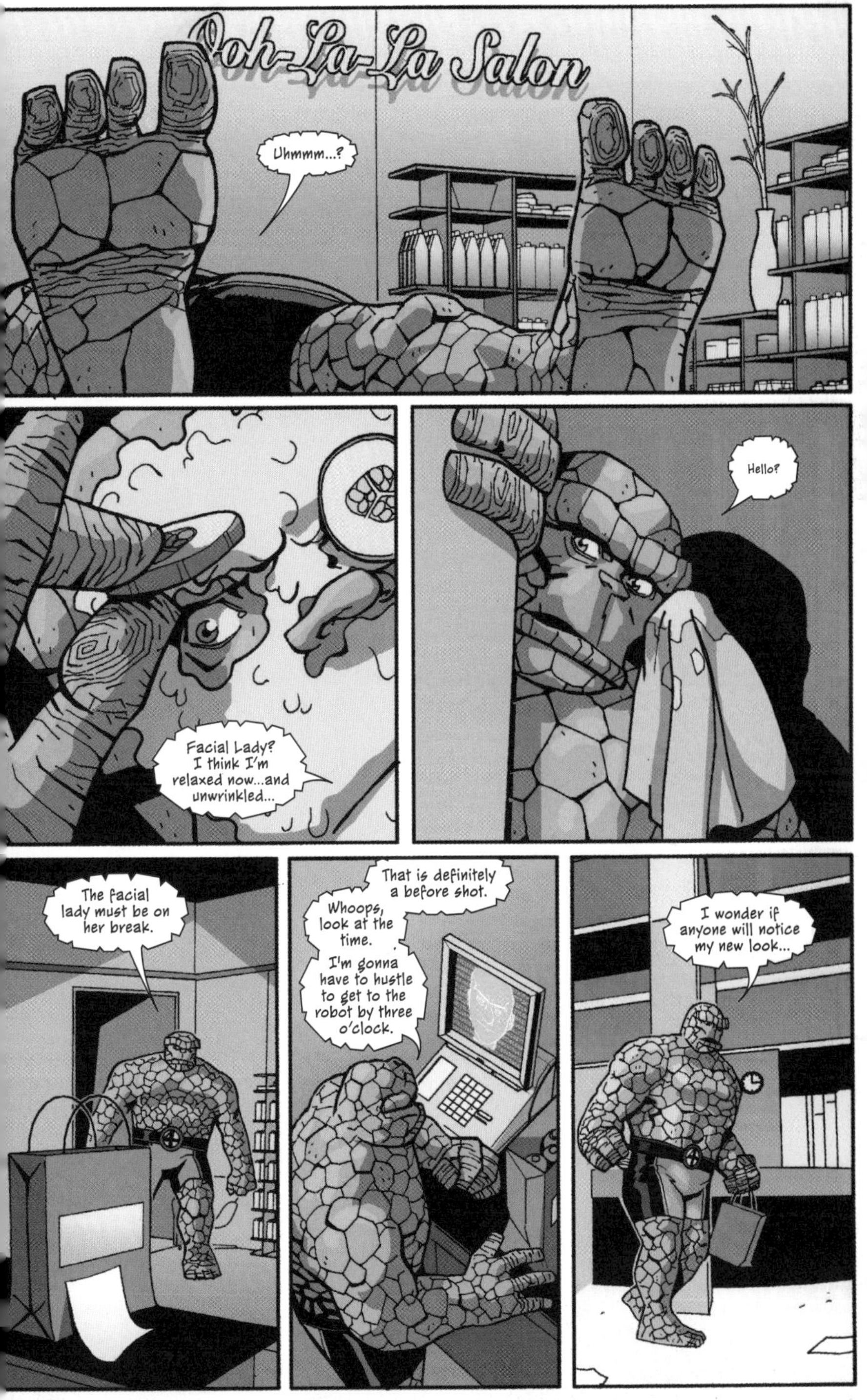
Ooh-La-La Salon
Uhmmm...?
Facial Lady? I think I'm relaxed now...and unwrinkled...
Hello?
The facial lady must be on her break.
That is definitely a before shot.
Whoops, look at the time.
I'm gonna have to hustle to get to the robot by three o'clock.
I wonder if anyone will notice my new look...

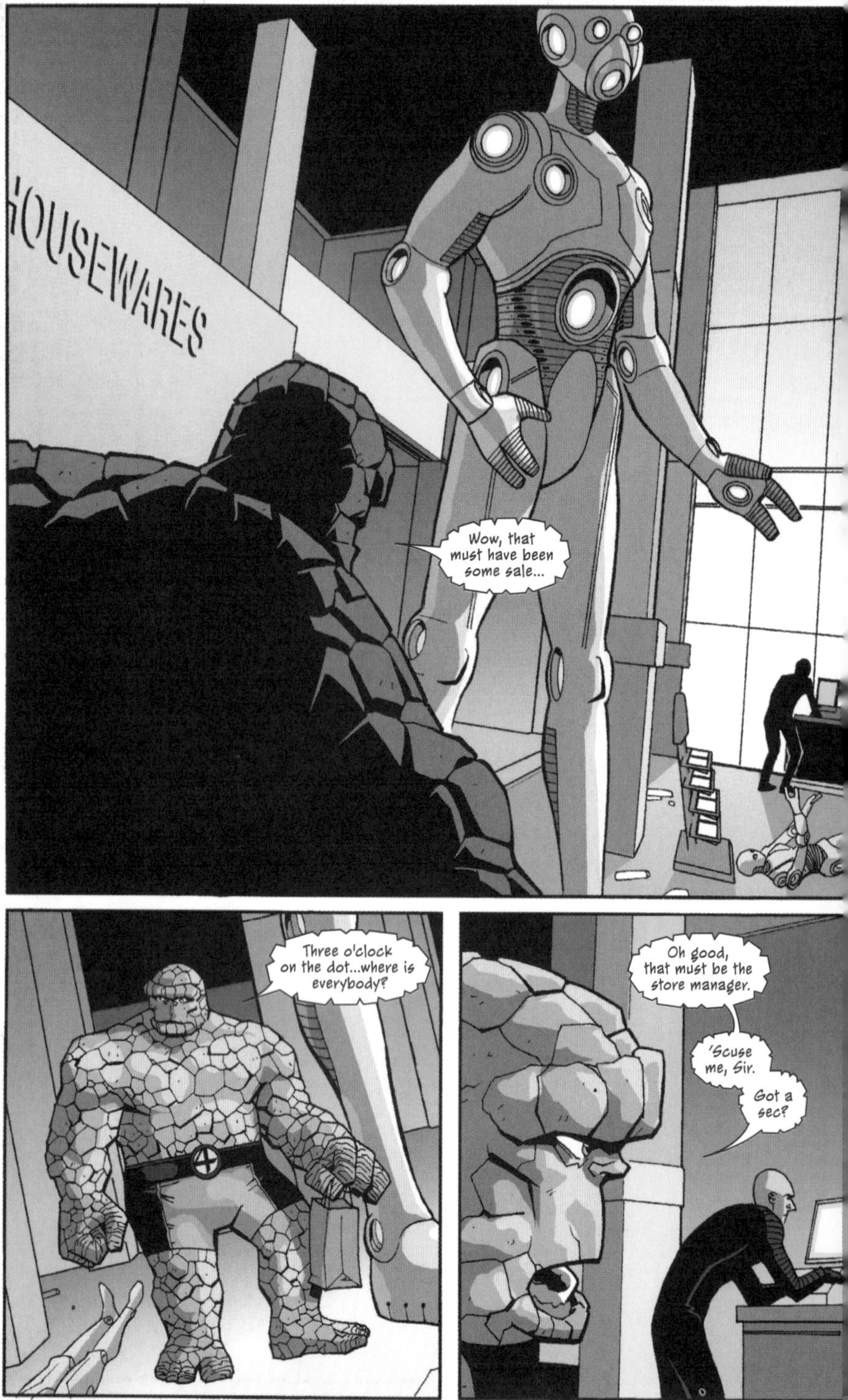
HOUSEWARES
Wow, that must have been some sale...
Three o'clock on the dot...where is everybody?
Oh good, that must be the store manager.
'Scuse me, Sir.
Got a sec?

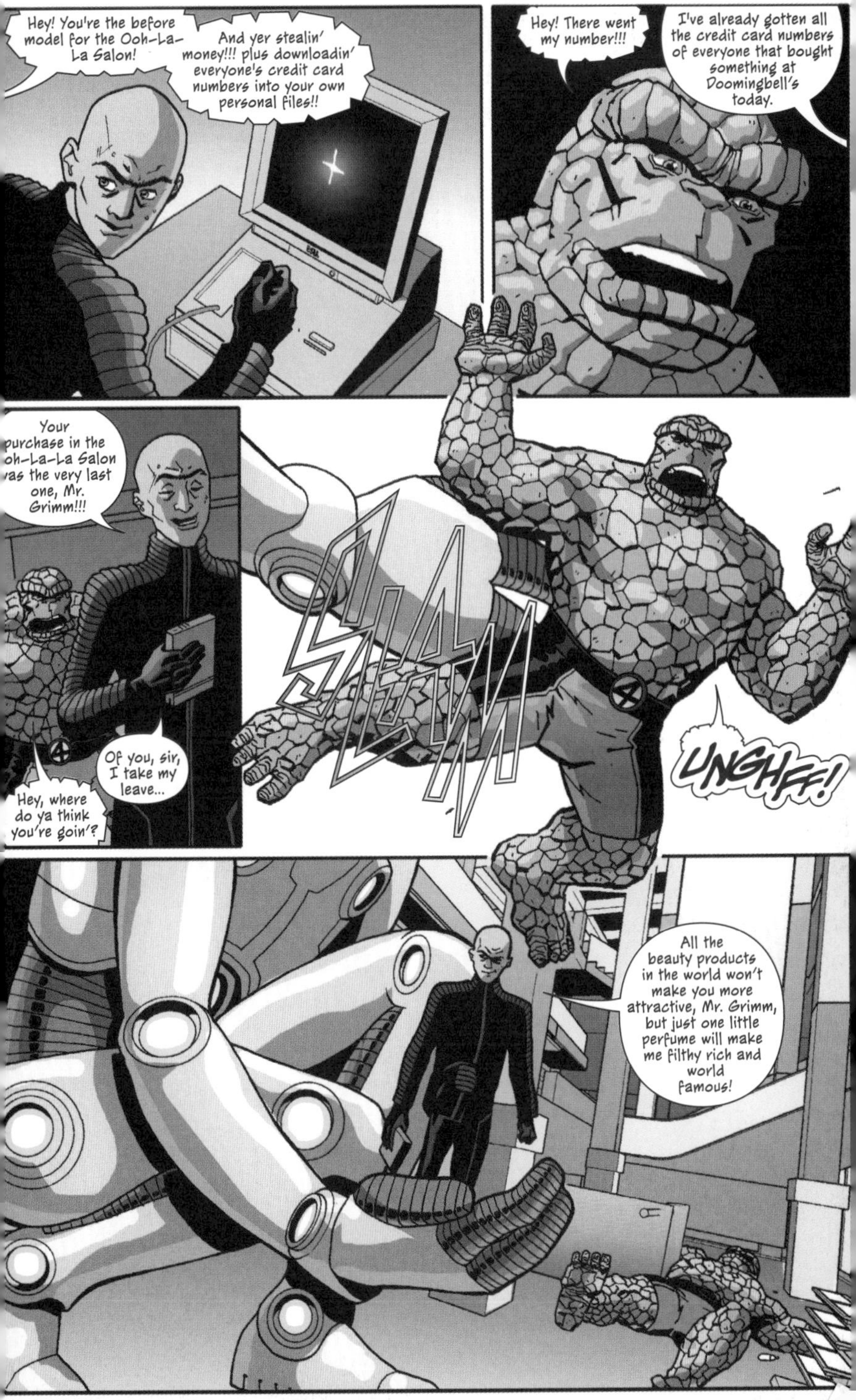

Hey! You're the before model for the Ooh-La-La Salon!
And yer stealin' money!!! plus downloadin' everyone's credit card numbers into your own personal files!!
Hey! There went my number!!!
I've already gotten all the credit card numbers of everyone that bought something at Doomingbell's today.
Your purchase in the Ooh-La-La Salon was the very last one, Mr. Grimm!!!
Hey, where do ya think you're goin'?
Of you, sir, I take my leave...
SLAM
UNGHFF!
All the beauty products in the world won't make you more attractive, Mr. Grimm, but just one little perfume will make me filthy rich and world famous!

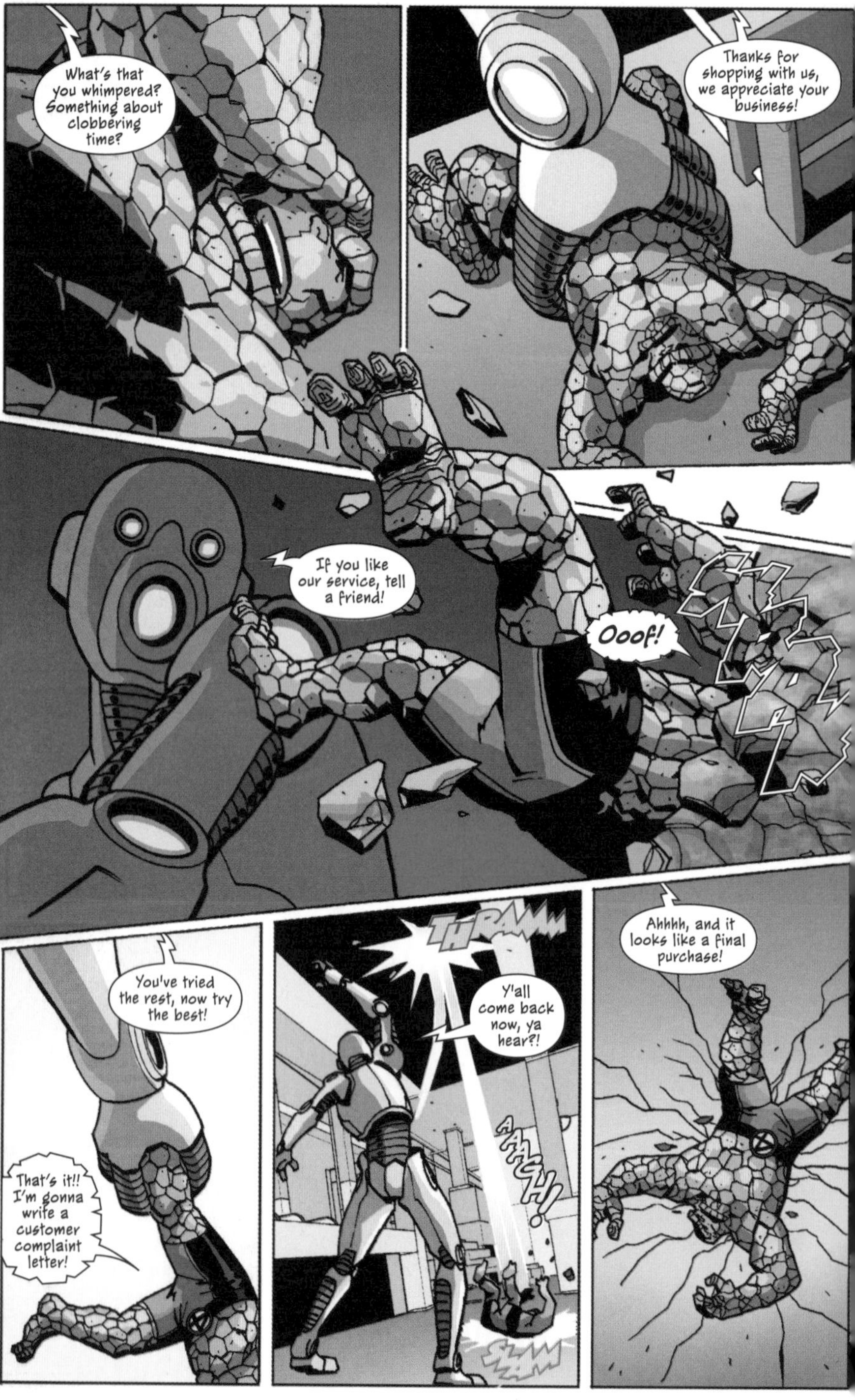

What's that you whimpered? Something about clobbering time?
Thanks for shopping with us, we appreciate your business!
If you like our service, tell a friend!
Ooof!
You've tried the rest, now try the best!
That's it!! I'm gonna write a customer complaint letter!
THRAMMM
Y'all come back now, ya hear?!
AAAGH!
SLAM
Ahhhh, and it looks like a final purchase!

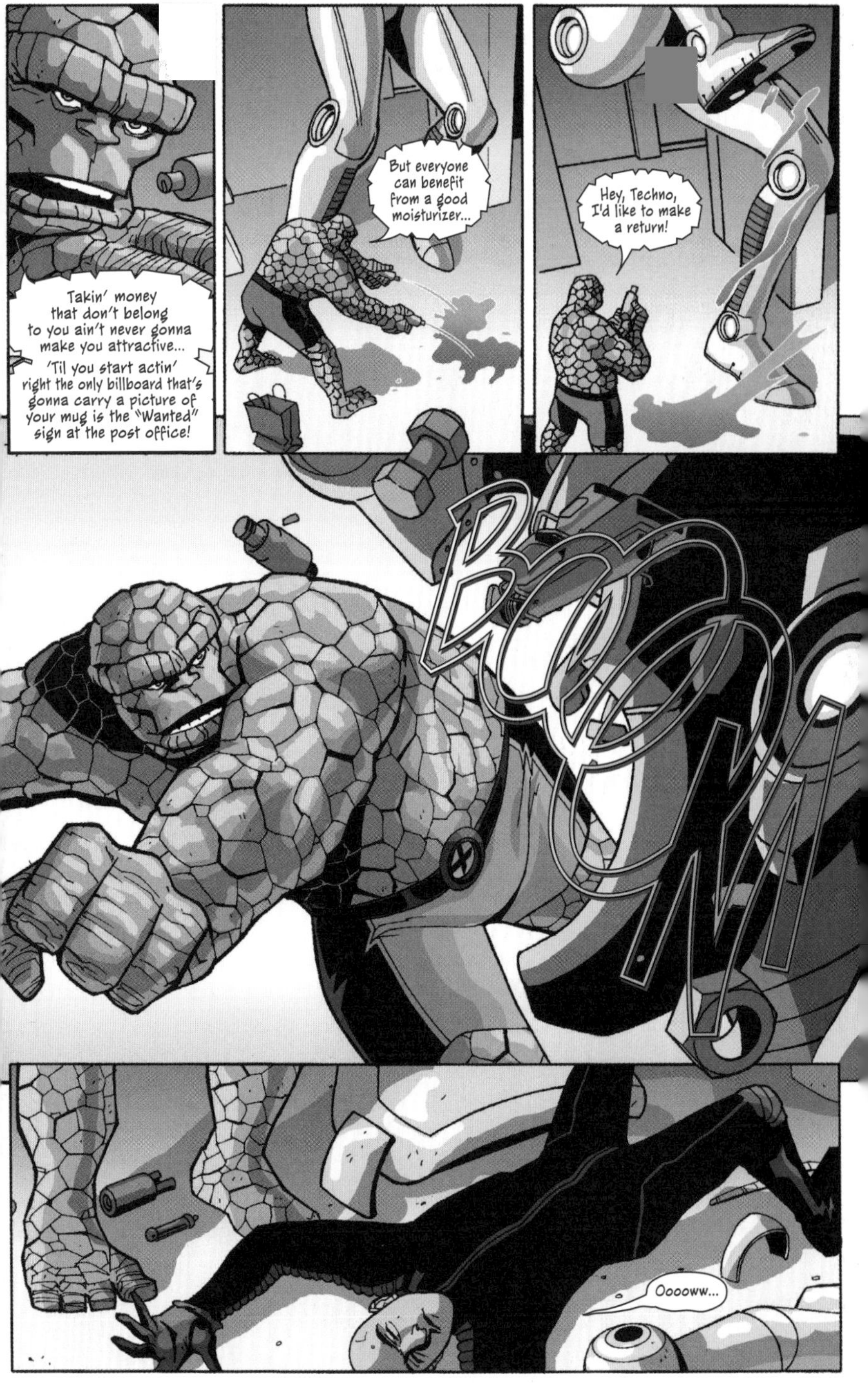

Takin' money that don't belong to you ain't never gonna make you attractive...
'Til you start actin' right the only billboard that's gonna carry a picture of your mug is the "Wanted" sign at the post office!
But everyone can benefit from a good moisturizer...
Hey, Techno, I'd like to make a return!
BOOOM
Oooow...

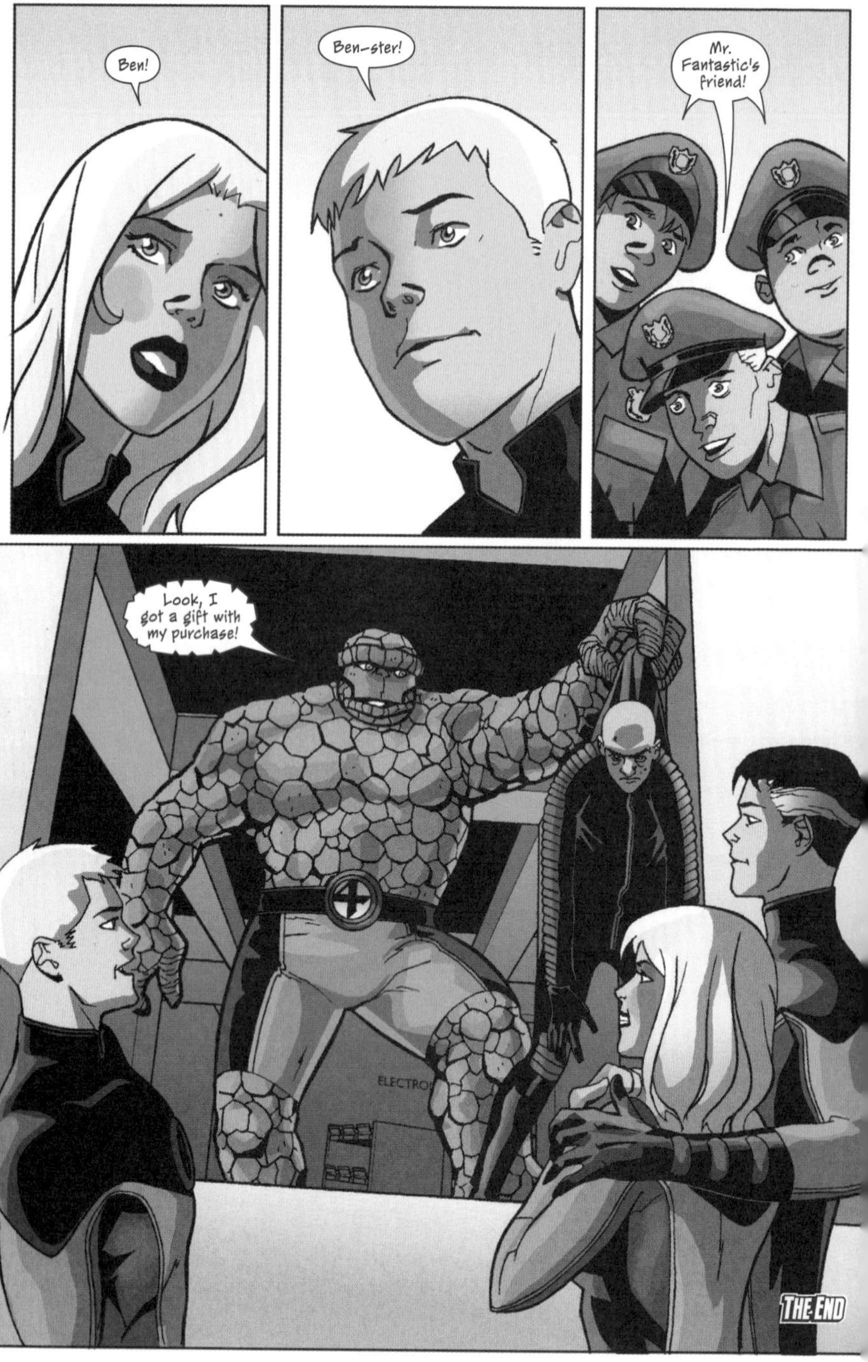
Ben!
Ben-ster!
Mr. Fantastic's friend!
Look, I got a gift with my purchase!
ELECTRO
THE END

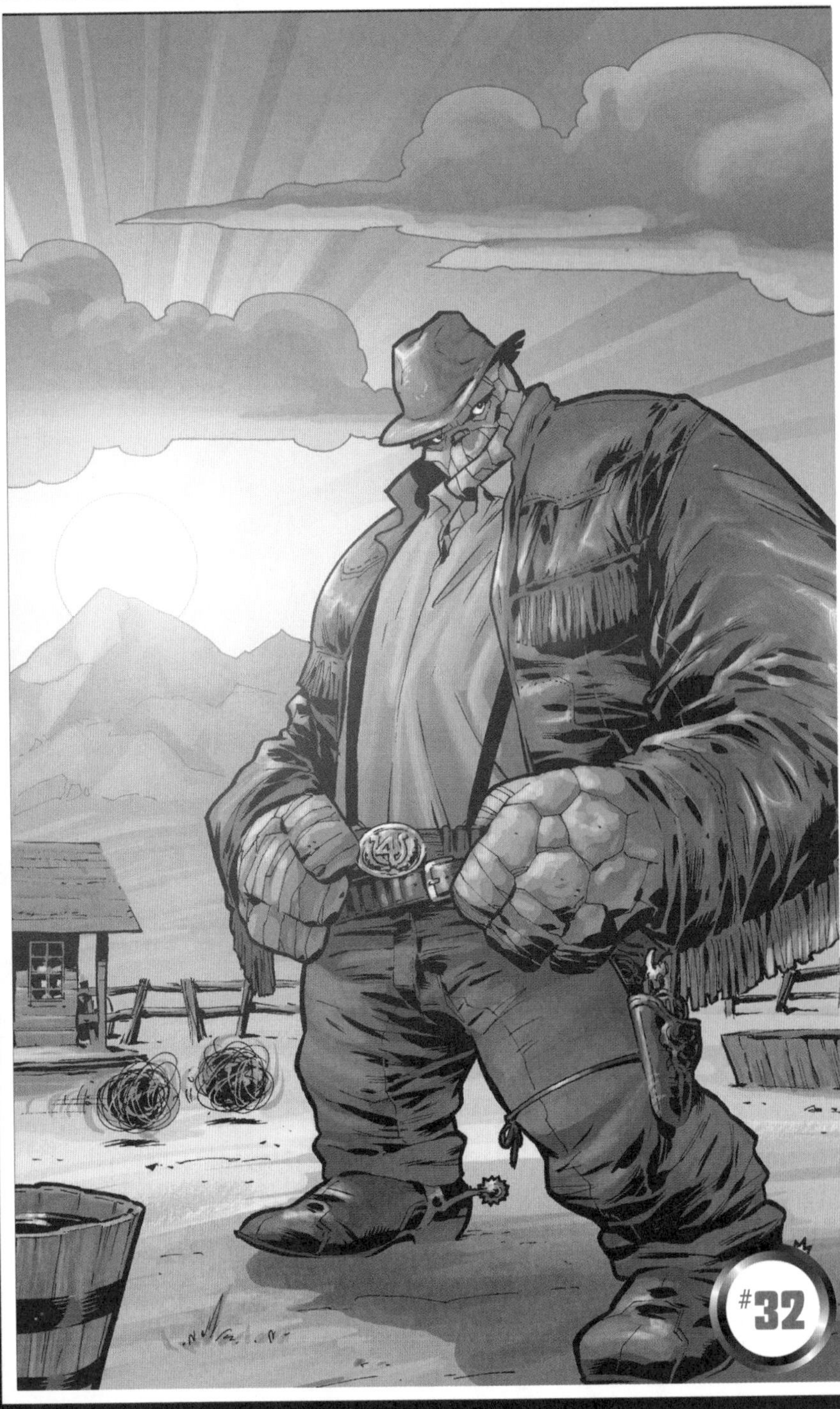
#32

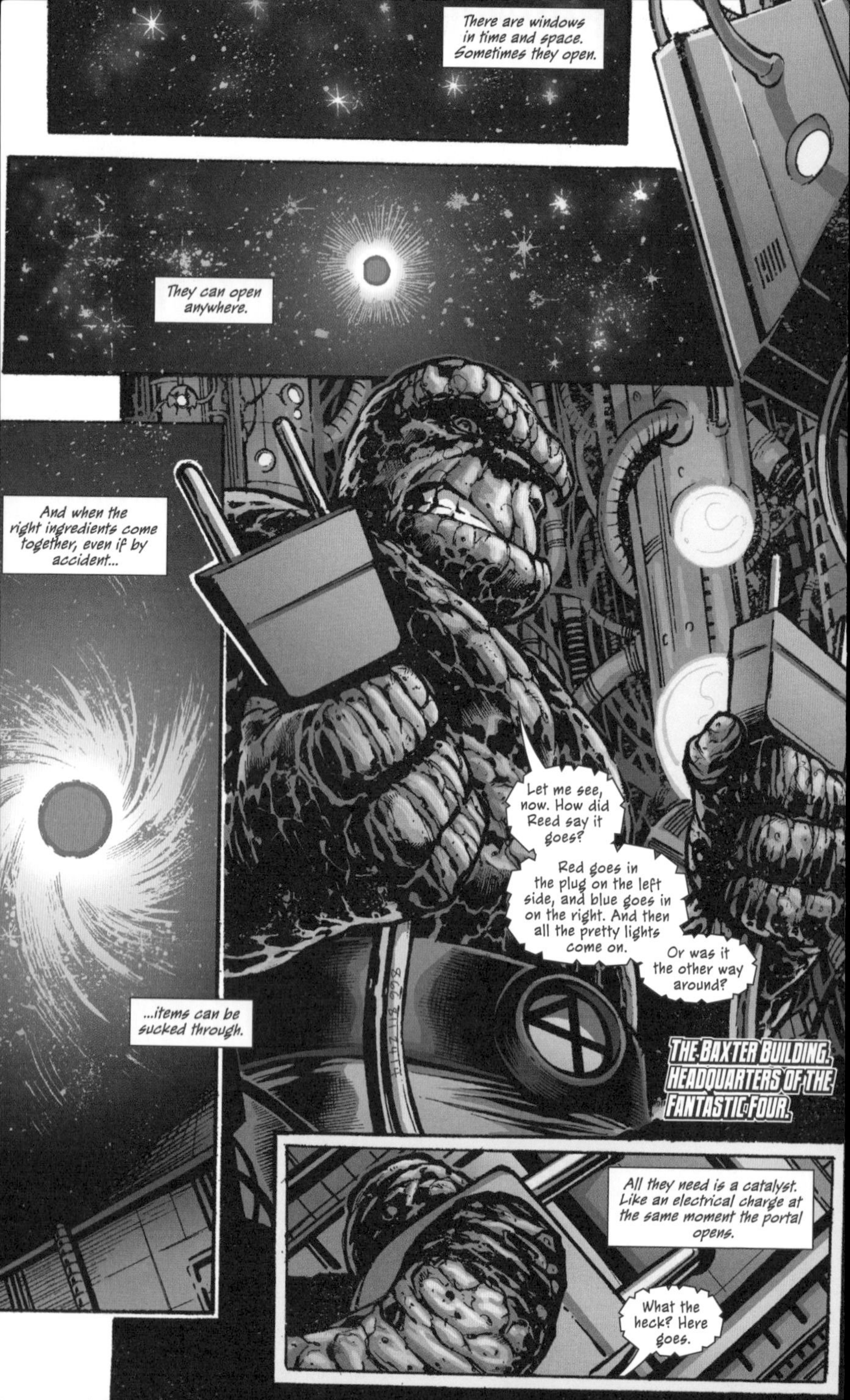
There are windows in time and space. Sometimes they open.
They can open anywhere.
And when the right ingredients come together, even if by accident...
...items can be sucked through.
Let me see, now. How did Reed say it goes?
Red goes in the plug on the left side, and blue goes in on the right. And then all the pretty lights come on.
Or was it the other way around?
THE BAXTER BUILDING. HEADQUARTERS OF THE FANTASTIC FOUR.
All they need is a catalyst. Like an electrical charge at the same moment the portal opens.
What the heck? Here goes.

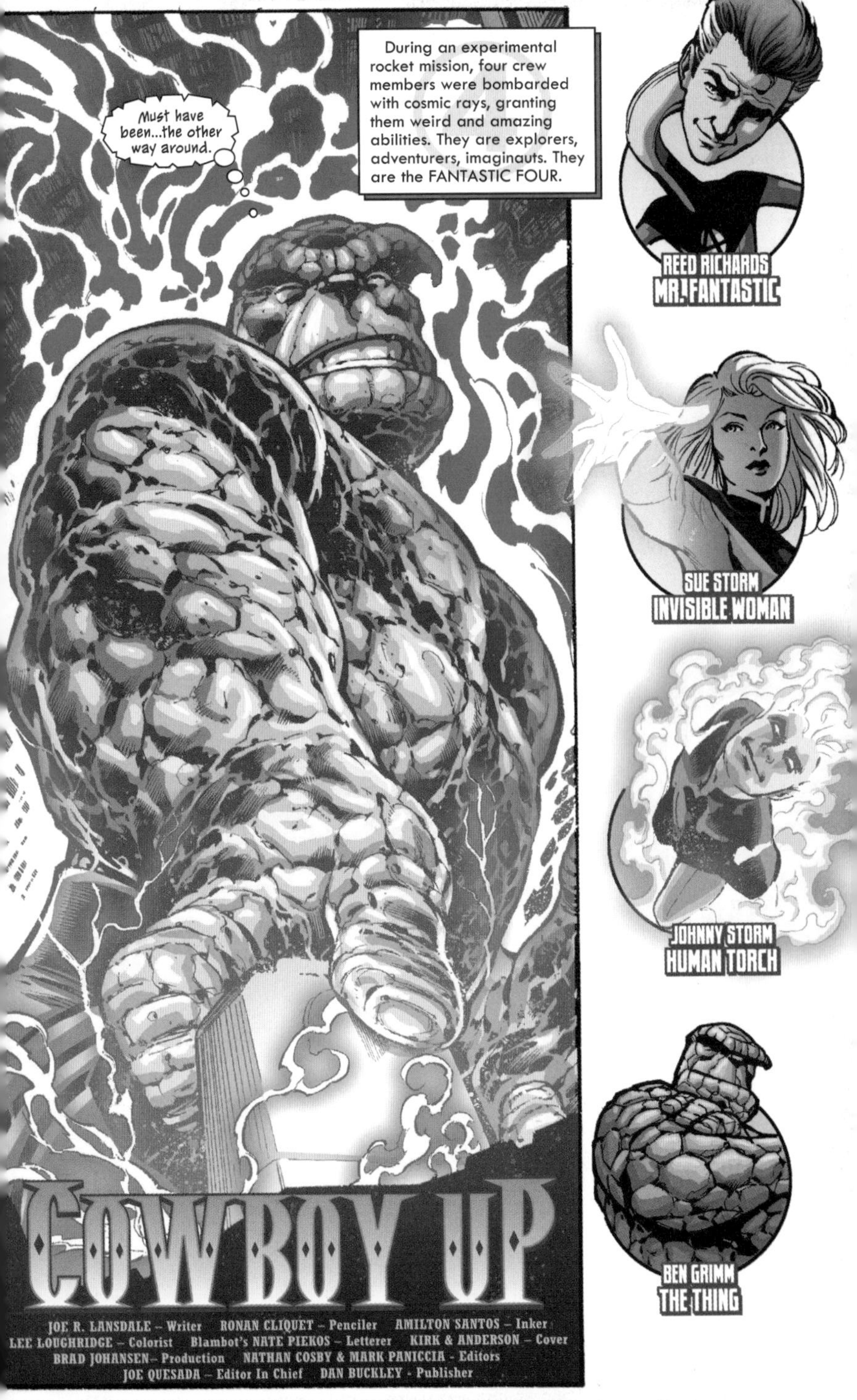
During an experimental rocket mission, four crew members were bombarded with cosmic rays, granting them weird and amazing abilities. They are explorers, adventurers, imaginauts. They are the FANTASTIC FOUR.
Must have been...the other way around.
REED RICHARDS MR. FANTASTIC
SUE STORM INVISIBLE WOMAN
JOHNNY STORM HUMAN TORCH
BEN GRIMM THE THING
COWBOY UP
JOE R. LANSDALE – Writer RONAN CLIQUET – Penciler AMILTON SANTOS – Inker
LEE LOUGHRIDGE – Colorist Blambot's NATE PIEKOS – Letterer KIRK & ANDERSON – Cover
BRAD JOHANSEN– Production NATHAN COSBY & MARK PANICCIA - Editors
JOE QUESADA – Editor In Chief DAN BUCKLEY - Publisher

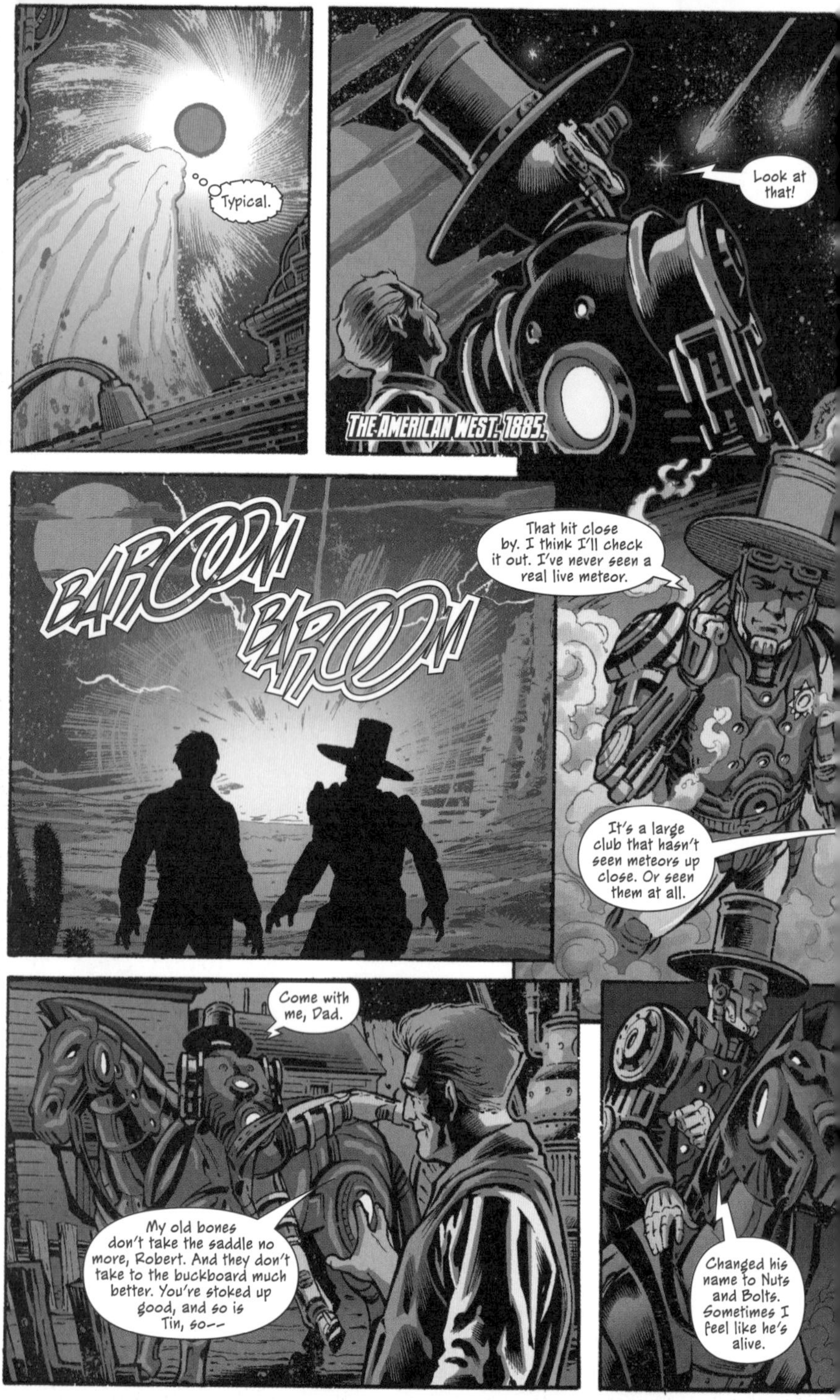
Typical.
Look at that!
THE AMERICAN WEST, 1885.
BAROOM
BAROOM
That hit close by. I think I'll check it out. I've never seen a real live meteor.
It's a large club that hasn't seen meteors up close. Or seen them at all.
Come with me, Dad.
My old bones don't take the saddle no more, Robert. And they don't take to the buckboard much better. You're stoked up good, and so is Tin, so--
Changed his name to Nuts and Bolts. Sometimes I feel like he's alive.

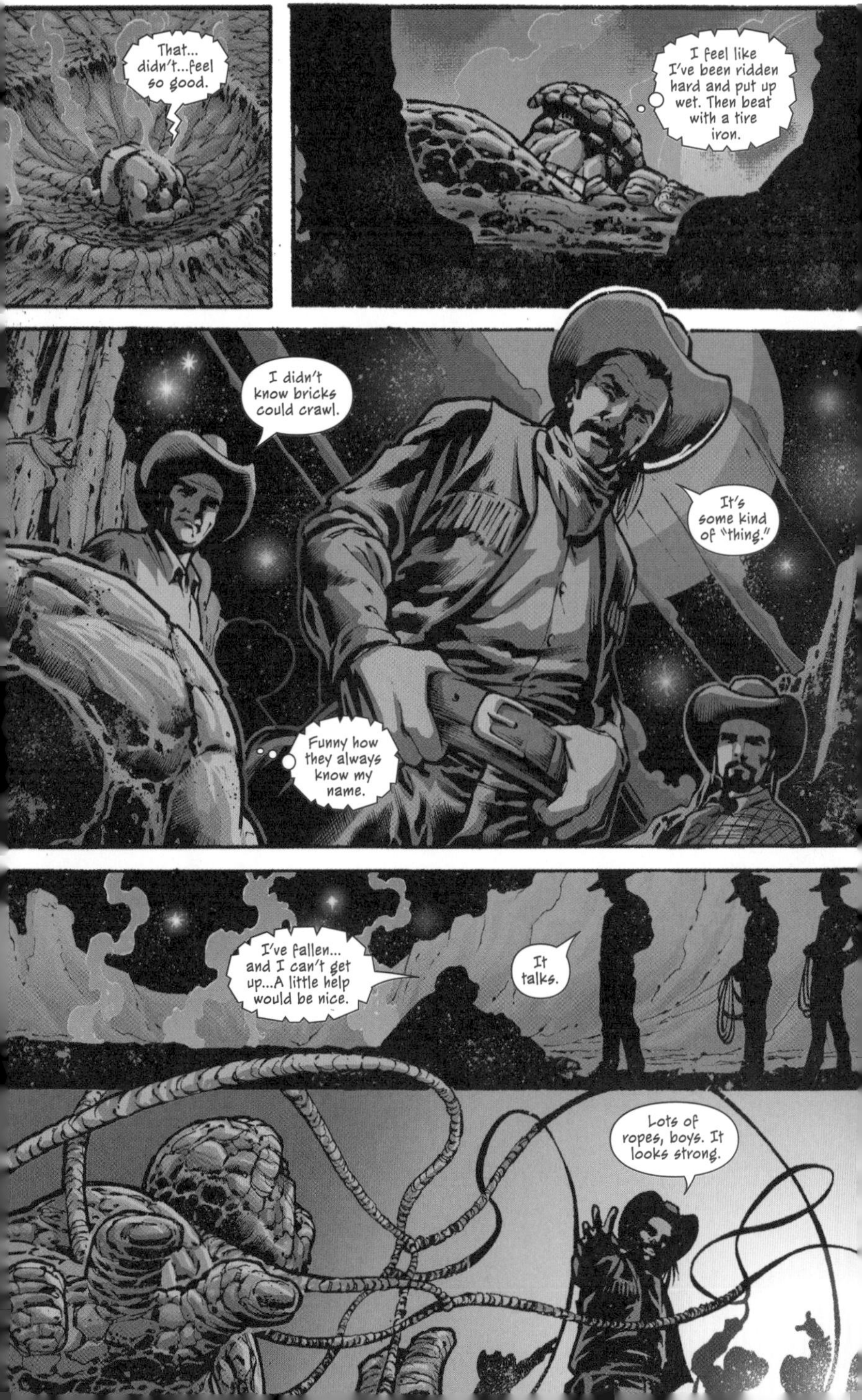
That... didn't...feel so good.
I feel like I've been ridden hard and put up wet. Then beat with a tire iron.
I didn't know bricks could crawl.
It's some kind of "thing."
Funny how they always know my name.
I've fallen... and I can't get up...A little help would be nice.
It talks.
Lots of ropes, boys. It looks strong.

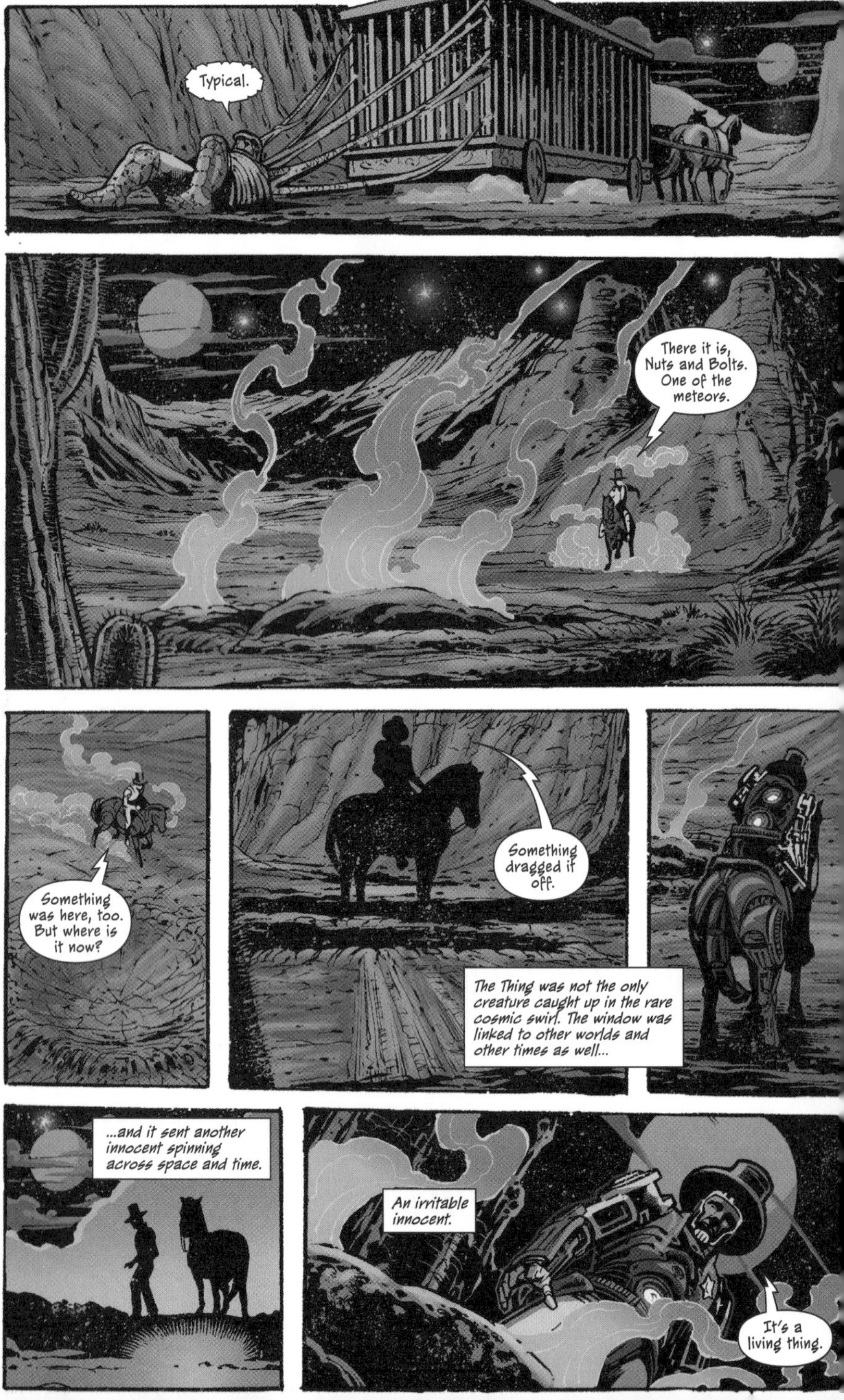
Typical.
There it is, Nuts and Bolts. One of the meteors.
Something was here, too. But where is it now?
Something dragged it off.
The Thing was not the only creature caught up in the rare cosmic swirl. The window was linked to other worlds and other times as well...
...and it sent another innocent spinning across space and time.
An irritable innocent.
It's a living thing.

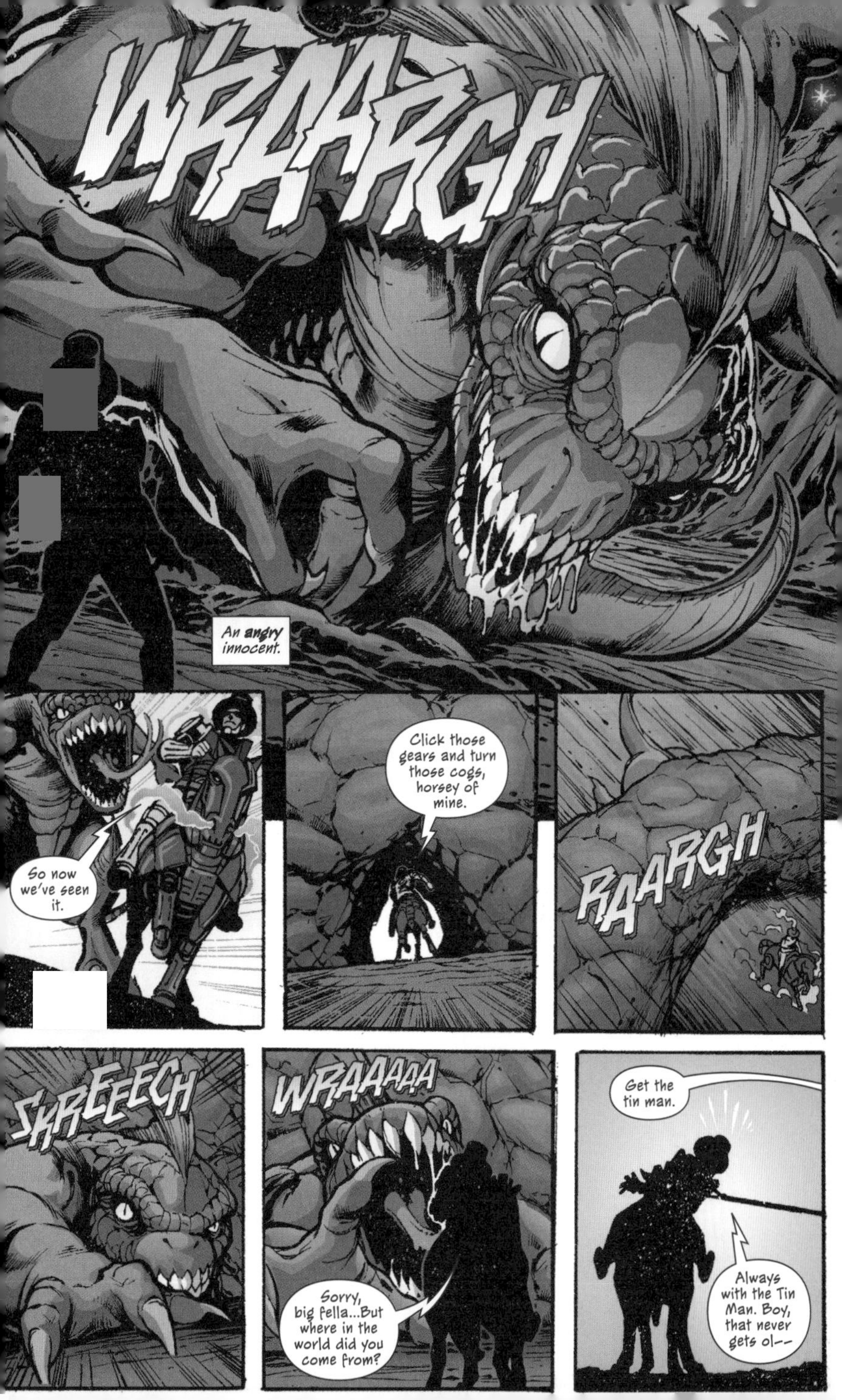
WRAARGH
An angry innocent.
So now we've seen it.
Click those gears and turn those cogs, horsey of mine.
RAARGH
SKREEEECH
WRAAAAAA
Sorry, big fella...But where in the world did you come from?
Get the tin man.
Always with the Tin Man. Boy, that never gets ol--

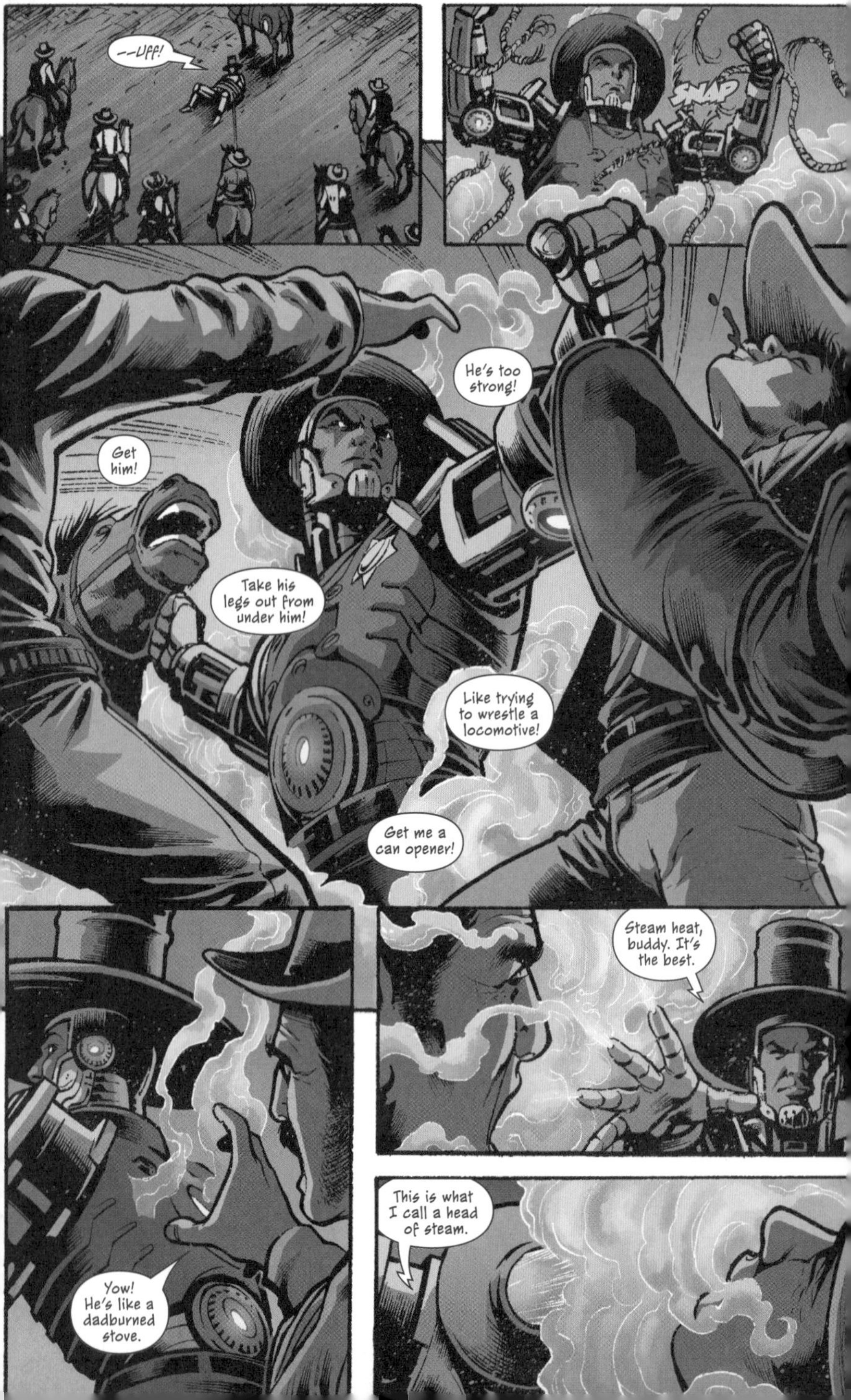
--UFF!
SNAP
He's too strong!
Get him!
Take his legs out from under him!
Like trying to wrestle a locomotive!
Get me a can opener!
Yow! He's like a dadburned stove.
Steam heat, buddy. It's the best.
This is what I call a head of steam.

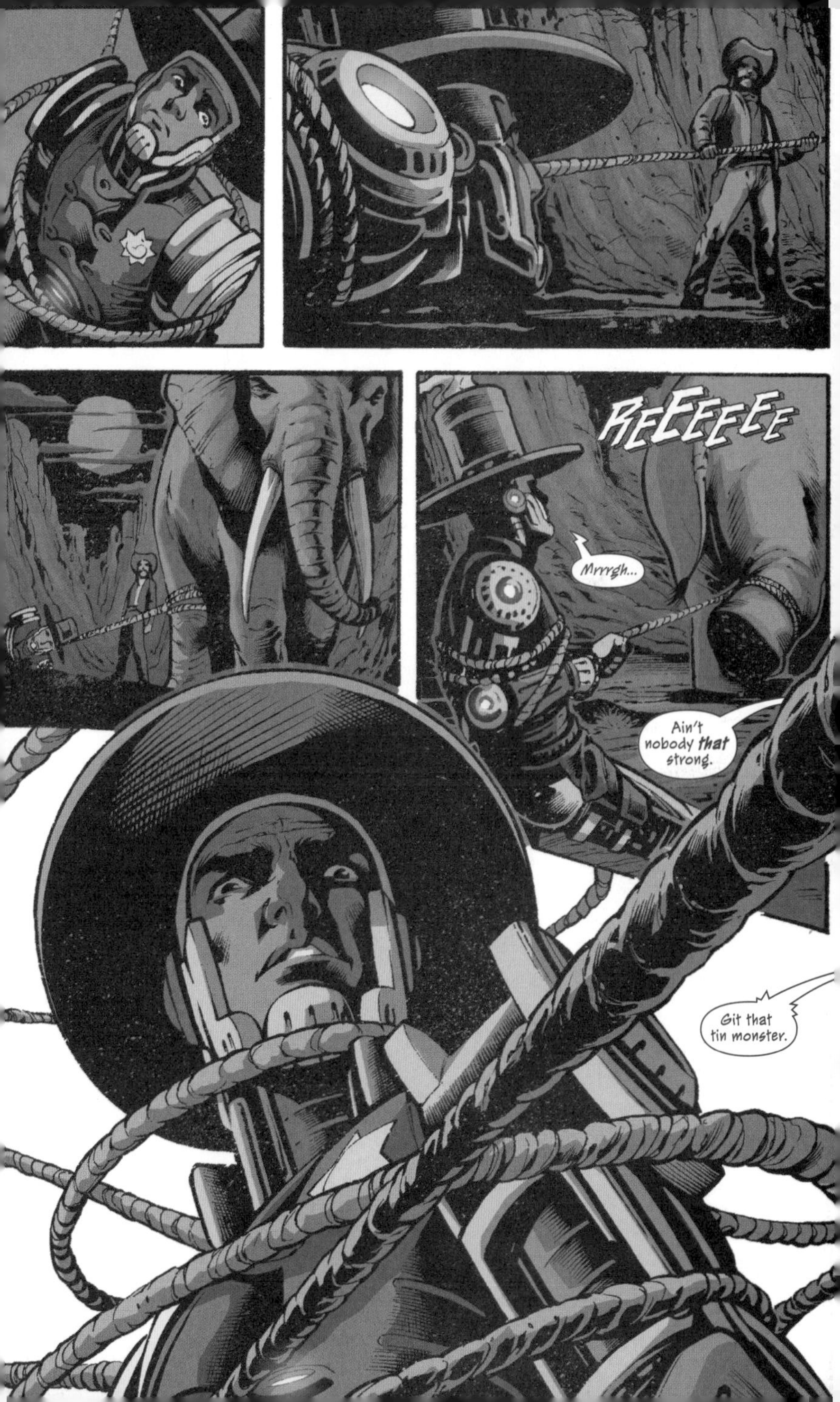
REEEEEEE
Mrrrgh...
Ain't nobody that strong.
Git that tin monster.

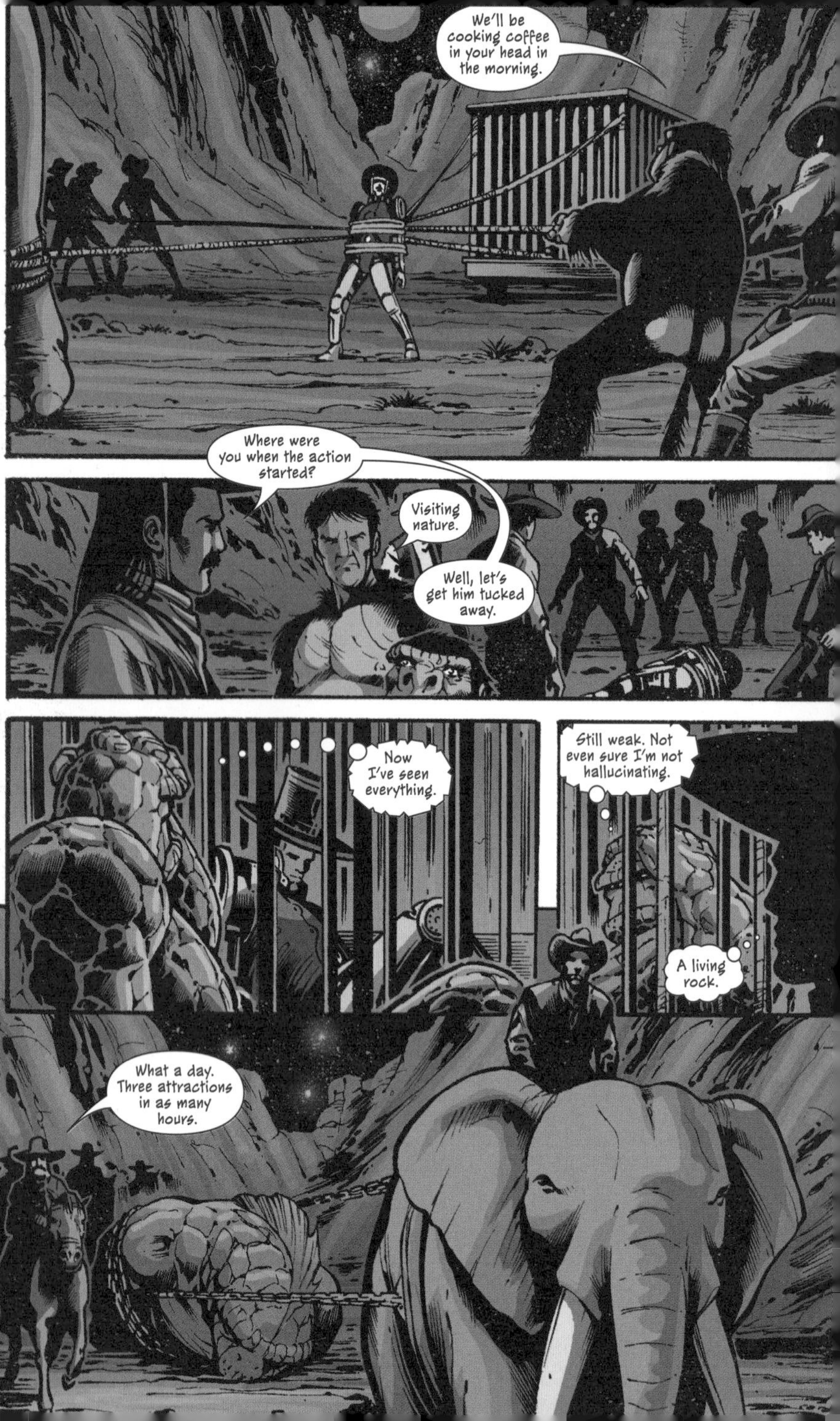
We'll be cooking coffee in your head in the morning.
Where were you when the action started?
Visiting nature.
Well, let's get him tucked away.
Now I've seen everything.
Still weak. Not even sure I'm not hallucinating.
A living rock.
What a day. Three attractions in as many hours.

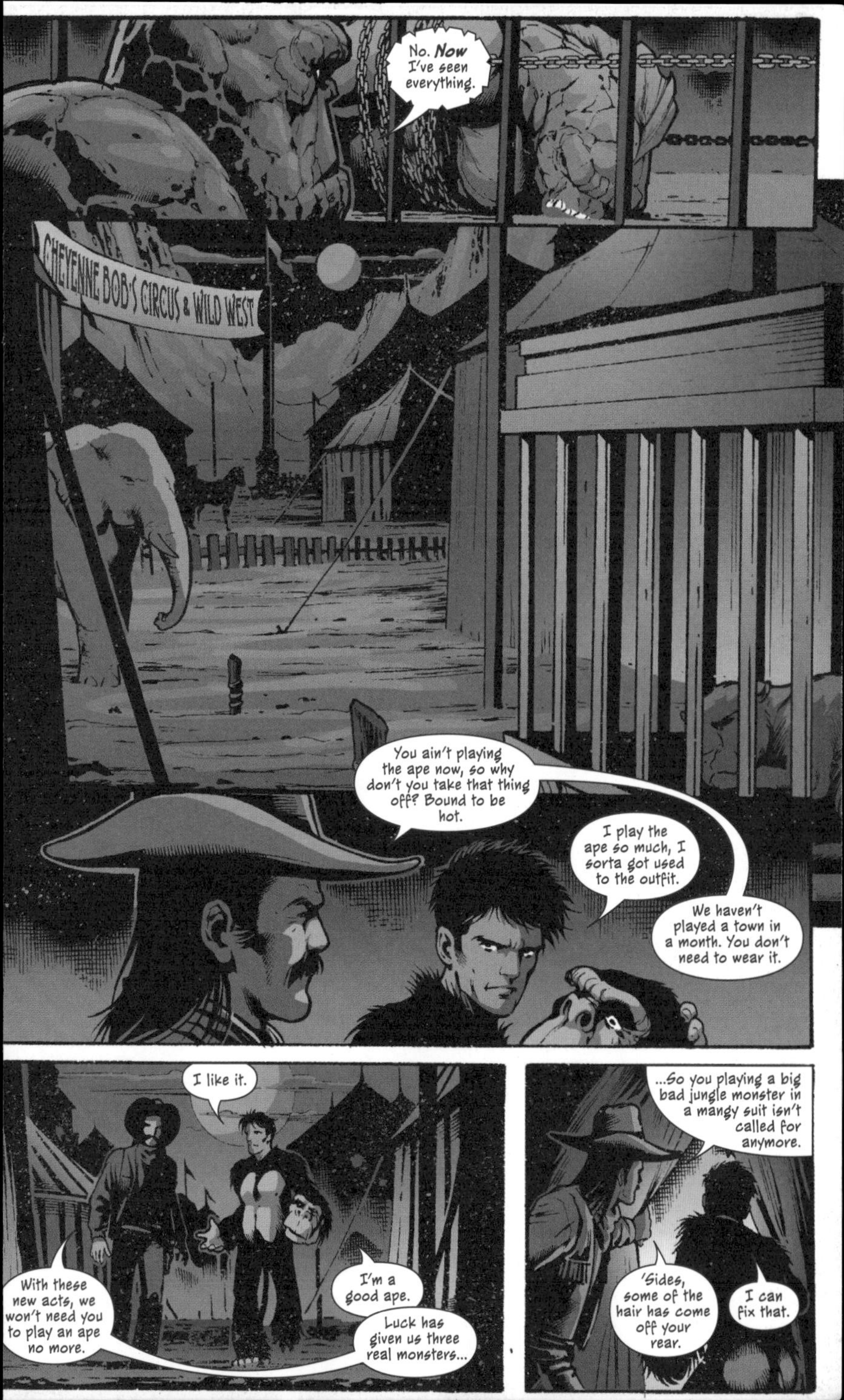
No. *Now* I've seen everything.
CHEYENNE BOB'S CIRCUS & WILD WEST
You ain't playing the ape now, so why don't you take that thing off? Bound to be hot.
I play the ape so much, I sorta got used to the outfit.
We haven't played a town in a month. You don't need to wear it.
I like it.
With these new acts, we won't need you to play an ape no more.
I'm a good ape.
Luck has given us three real monsters...
...So you playing a big bad jungle monster in a mangy suit isn't called for anymore.
'Sides, some of the hair has come off your rear.
I can fix that.

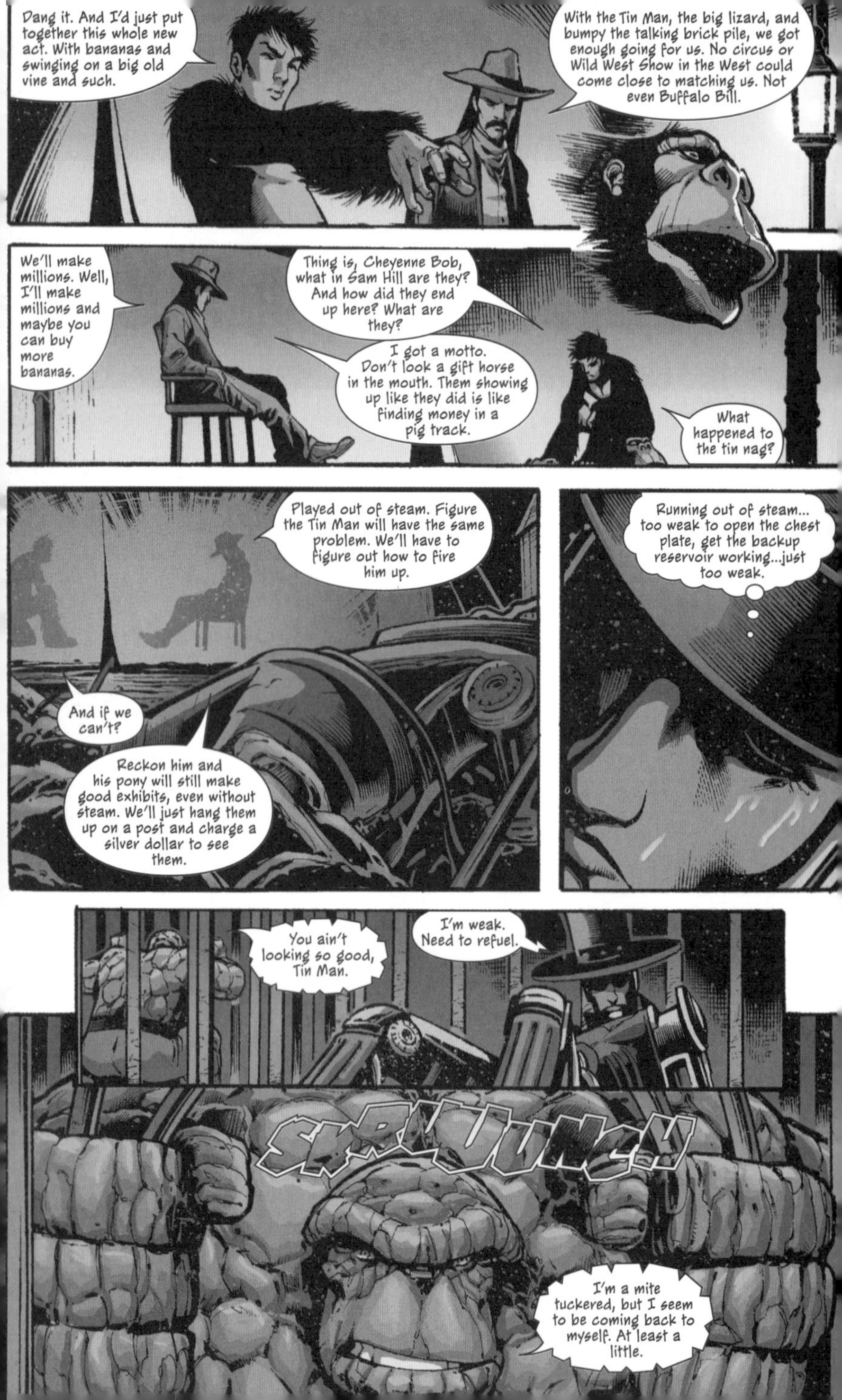

Dang it. And I'd just put together this whole new act. With bananas and swinging on a big old vine and such.
With the Tin Man, the big lizard, and bumpy the talking brick pile, we got enough going for us. No circus or Wild West Show in the West could come close to matching us. Not even Buffalo Bill.
We'll make millions. Well, I'll make millions and maybe you can buy more bananas.
Thing is, Cheyenne Bob, what in Sam Hill are they? And how did they end up here? What are they?
I got a motto. Don't look a gift horse in the mouth. Them showing up like they did is like finding money in a pig track.
What happened to the tin nag?
Played out of steam. Figure the Tin Man will have the same problem. We'll have to figure out how to fire him up.
And if we can't?
Reckon him and his pony will still make good exhibits, even without steam. We'll just hang them up on a post and charge a silver dollar to see them.
Running out of steam... too weak to open the chest plate, get the backup reservoir working...just too weak.
You ain't looking so good, Tin Man.
I'm weak. Need to refuel.
SKRUUNCH!
I'm a mite tuckered, but I seem to be coming back to myself. At least a little.

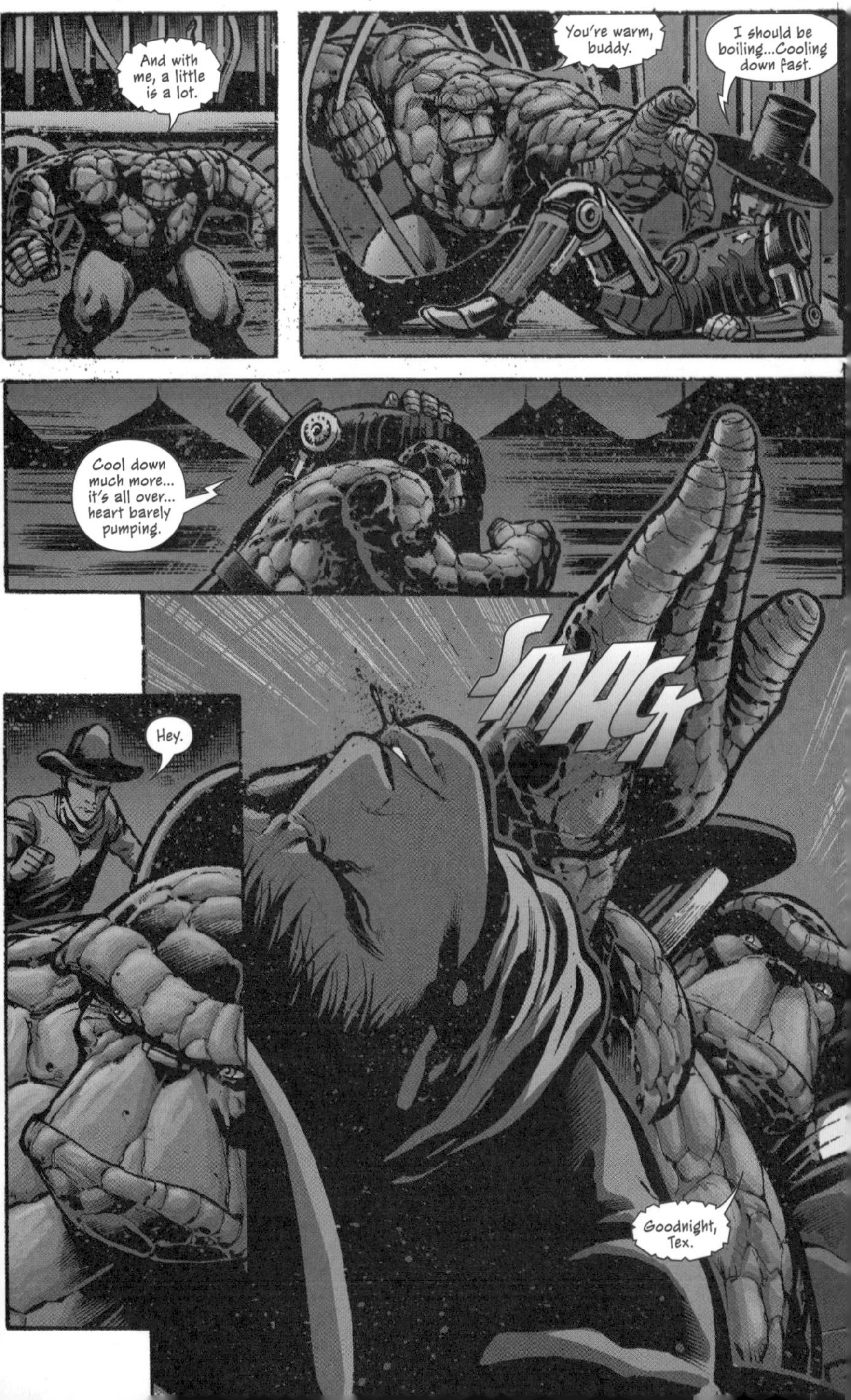
And with me, a little is a lot.
You're warm, buddy.
I should be boiling...Cooling down fast.
Cool down much more... it's all over... heart barely pumping.
Hey.
SMACK
Goodnight, Tex.

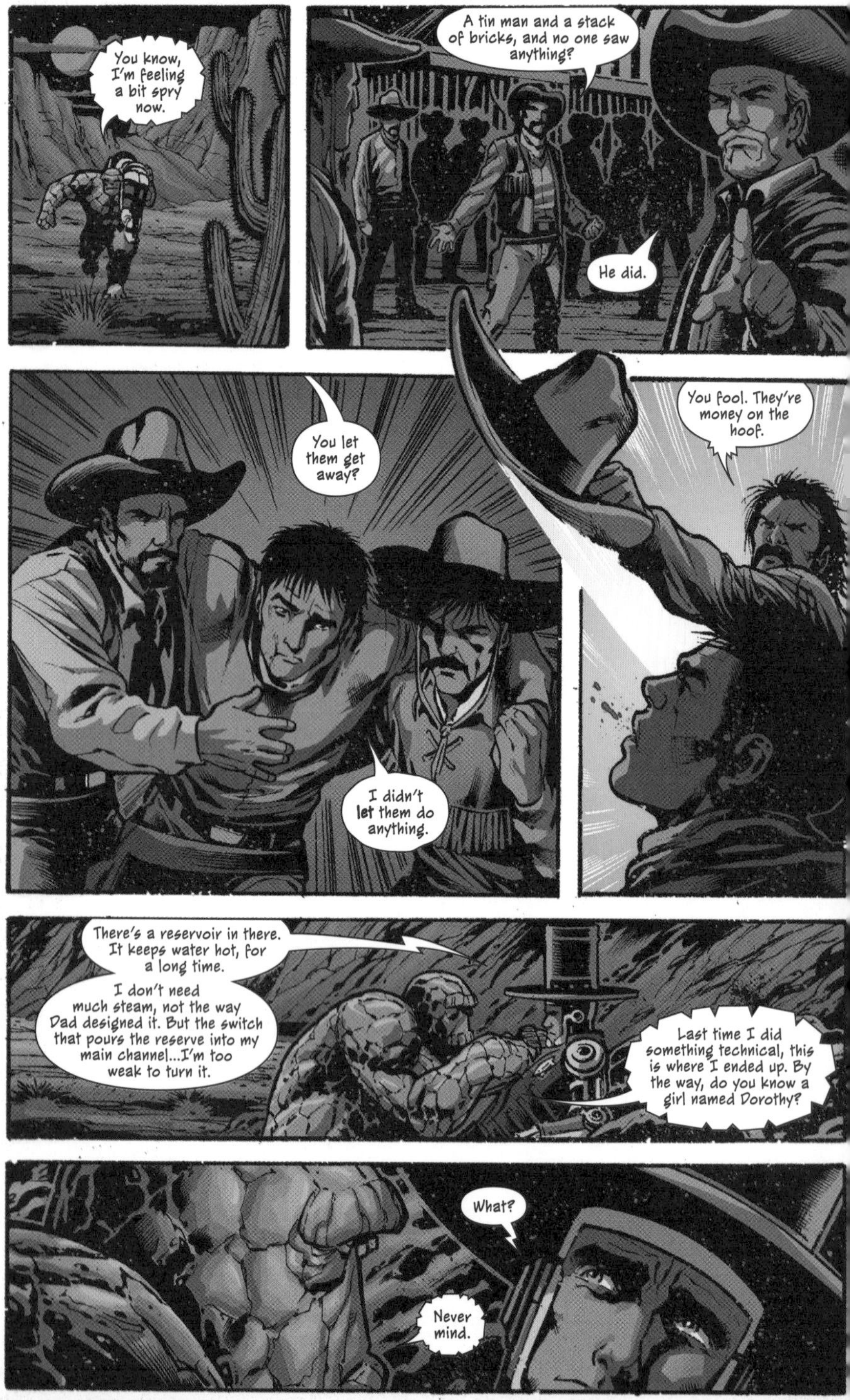
You know, I'm feeling a bit spry now.
A tin man and a stack of bricks, and no one saw anything?
He did.
You let them get away?
I didn't **let** them do anything.
You fool. They're money on the hoof.
There's a reservoir in there. It keeps water hot, for a long time.
I don't need much steam, not the way Dad designed it. But the switch that pours the reserve into my main channel...I'm too weak to turn it.
Last time I did something technical, this is where I ended up. By the way, do you know a girl named Dorothy?
What?
Never mind.

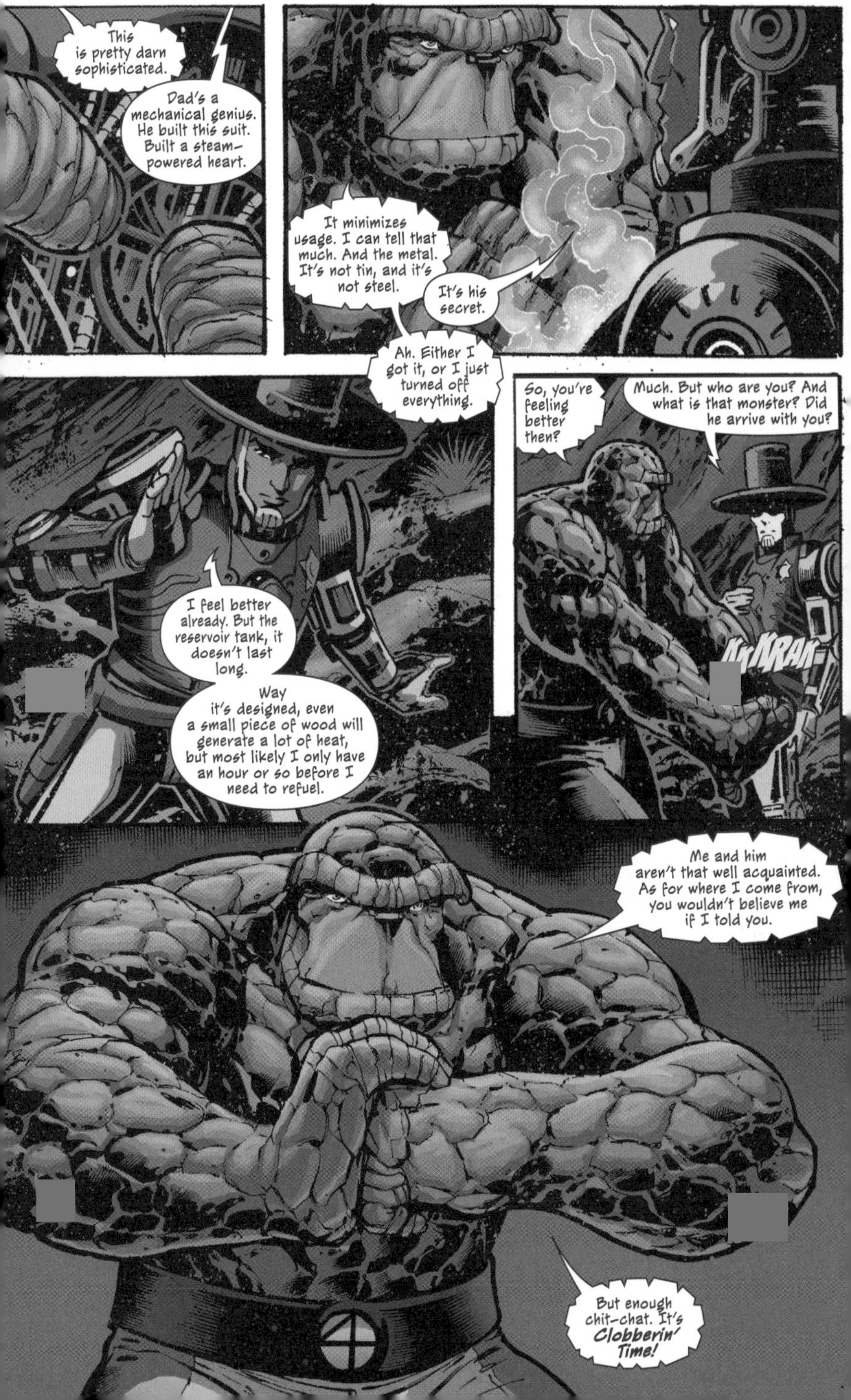

This is pretty darn sophisticated.
Dad's a mechanical genius. He built this suit. Built a steam-powered heart.
It minimizes usage. I can tell that much. And the metal. It's not tin, and it's not steel.
It's his secret.
Ah. Either I got it, or I just turned off everything.
I feel better already. But the reservoir tank, it doesn't last long.
Way it's designed, even a small piece of wood will generate a lot of heat, but most likely I only have an hour or so before I need to refuel.
So, you're feeling better then?
Much. But who are you? And what is that monster? Did he arrive with you?
KKKRAK
Me and him aren't that well acquainted. As for where I come from, you wouldn't believe me if I told you.
But enough chit-chat. It's *Clobberin' Time!*

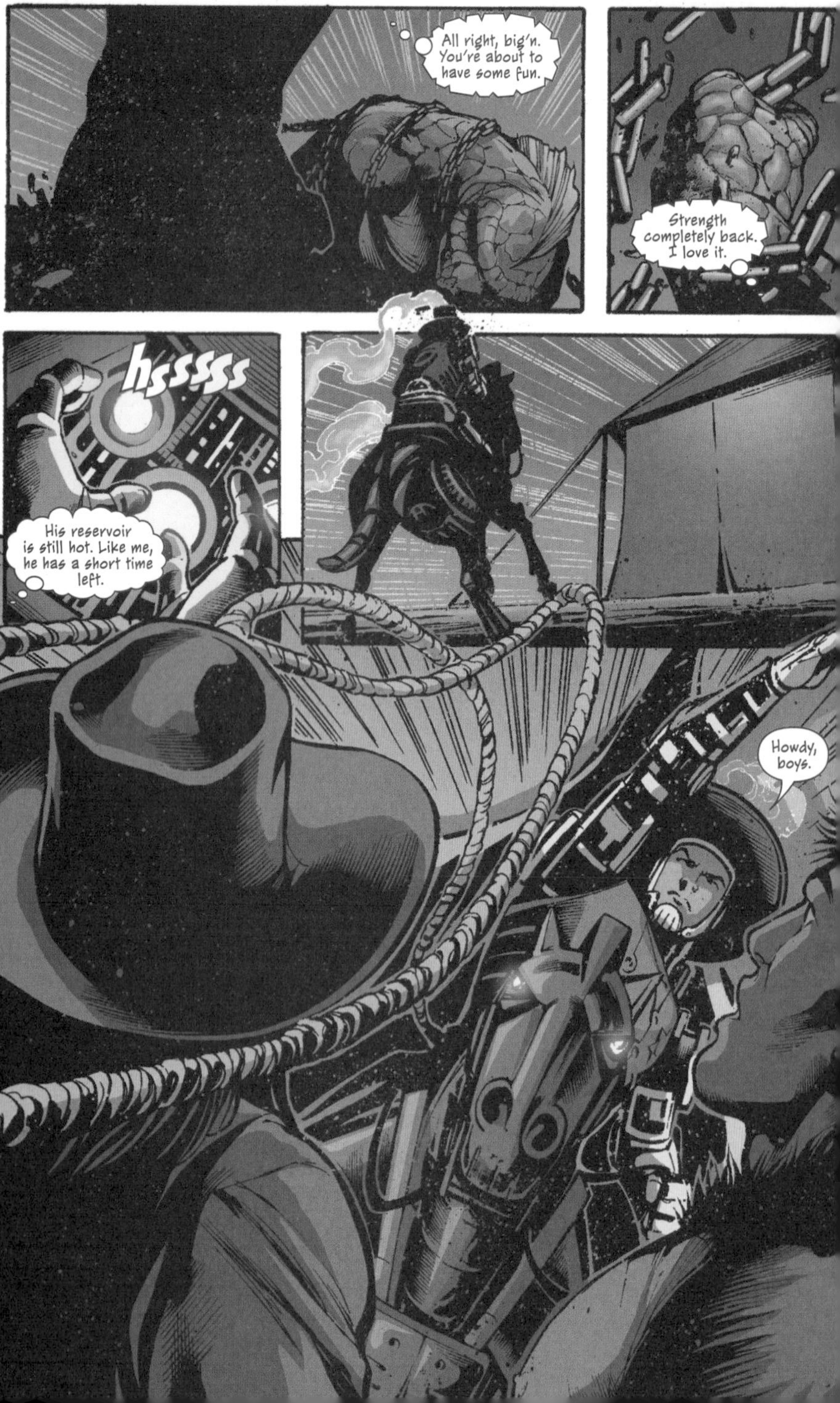
All right, big'n. You're about to have some fun.
Strength completely back. I love it.
hsssss
His reservoir is still hot. Like me, he has a short time left.
Howdy, boys.

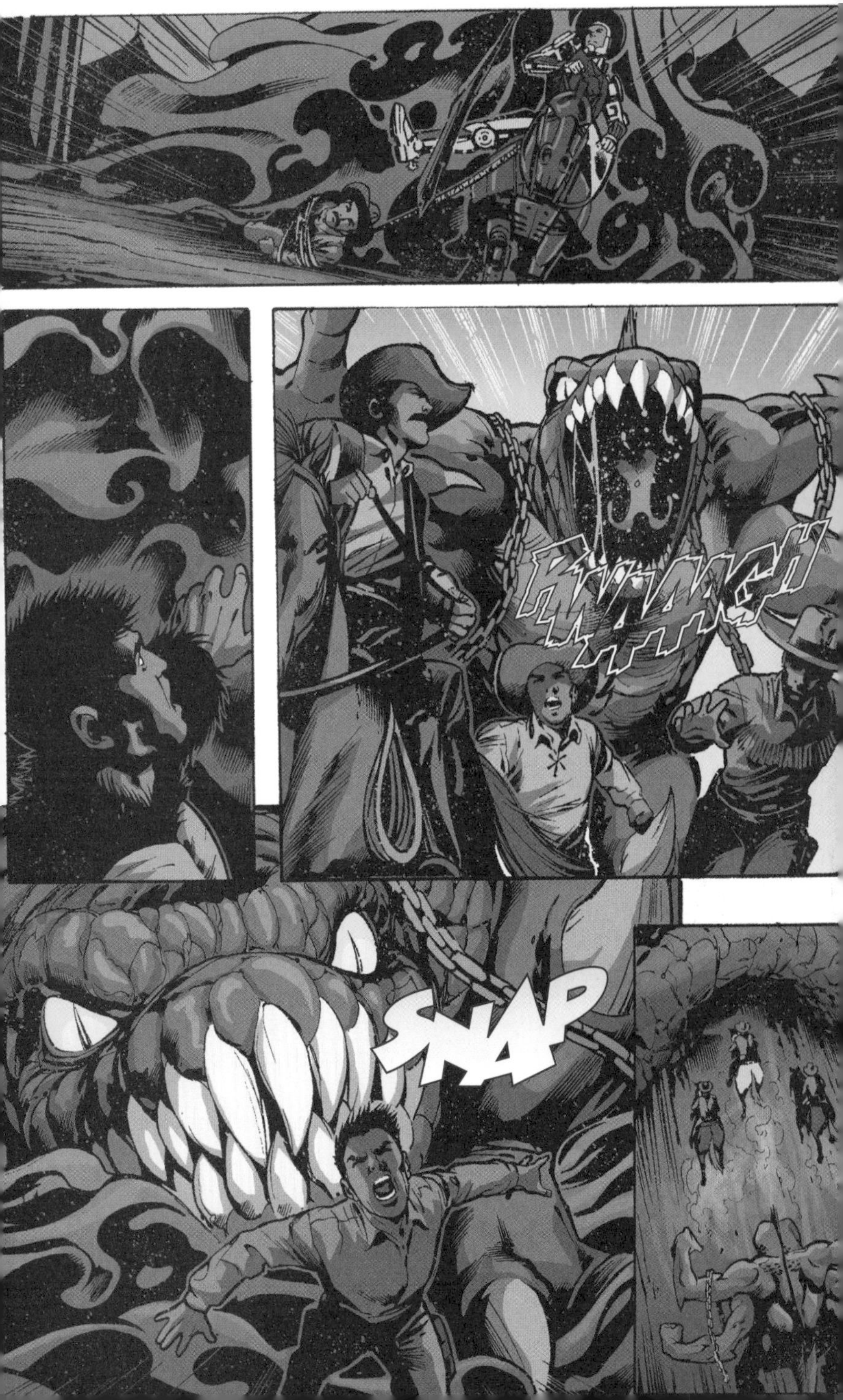
RWAAGH
SNAP

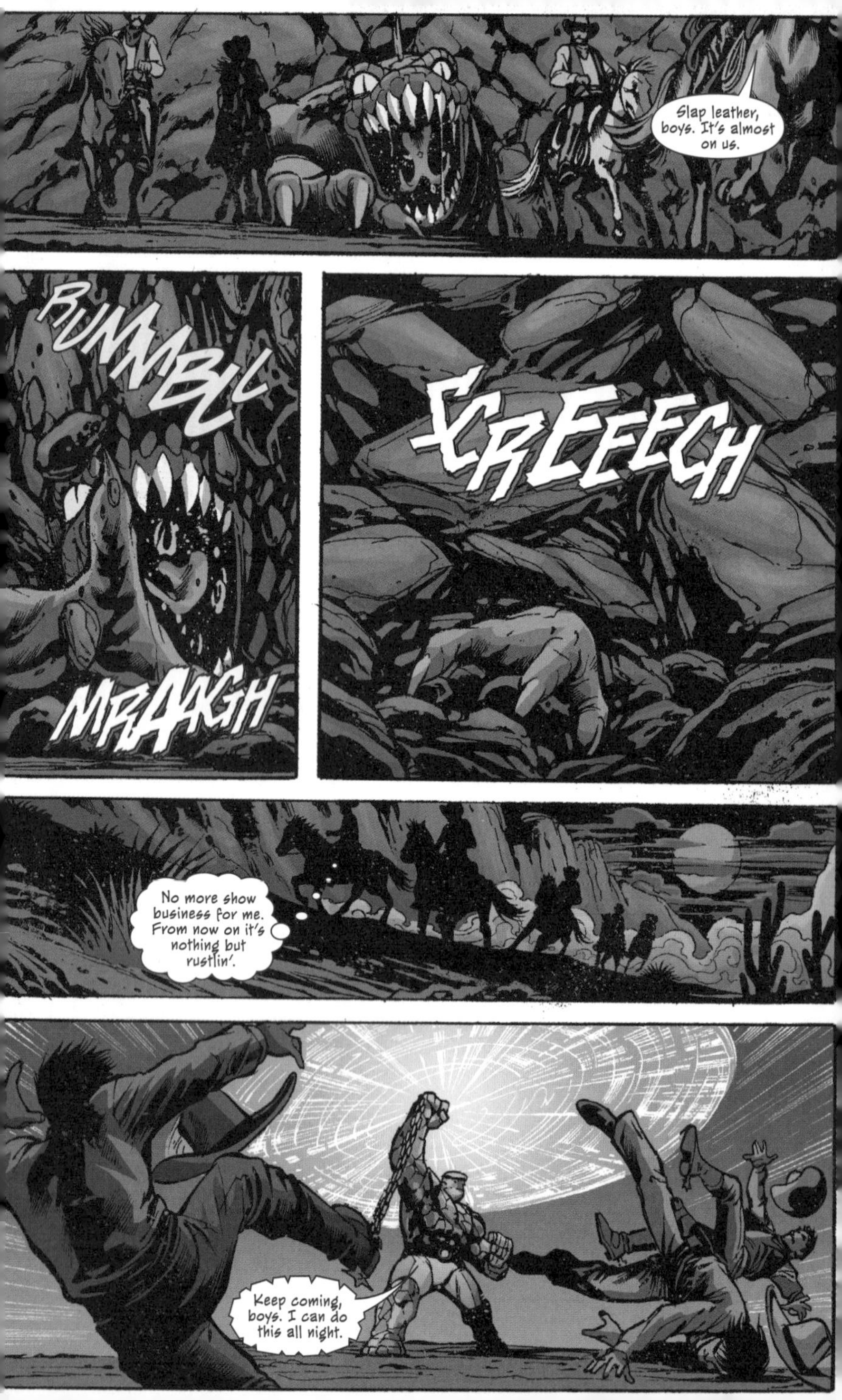
Slap leather, boys. It's almost on us.
RUMMBLL
MRAAAGH
SCREEECH
No more show business for me. From now on it's nothing but rustlin'.
Keep coming, boys. I can do this all night.

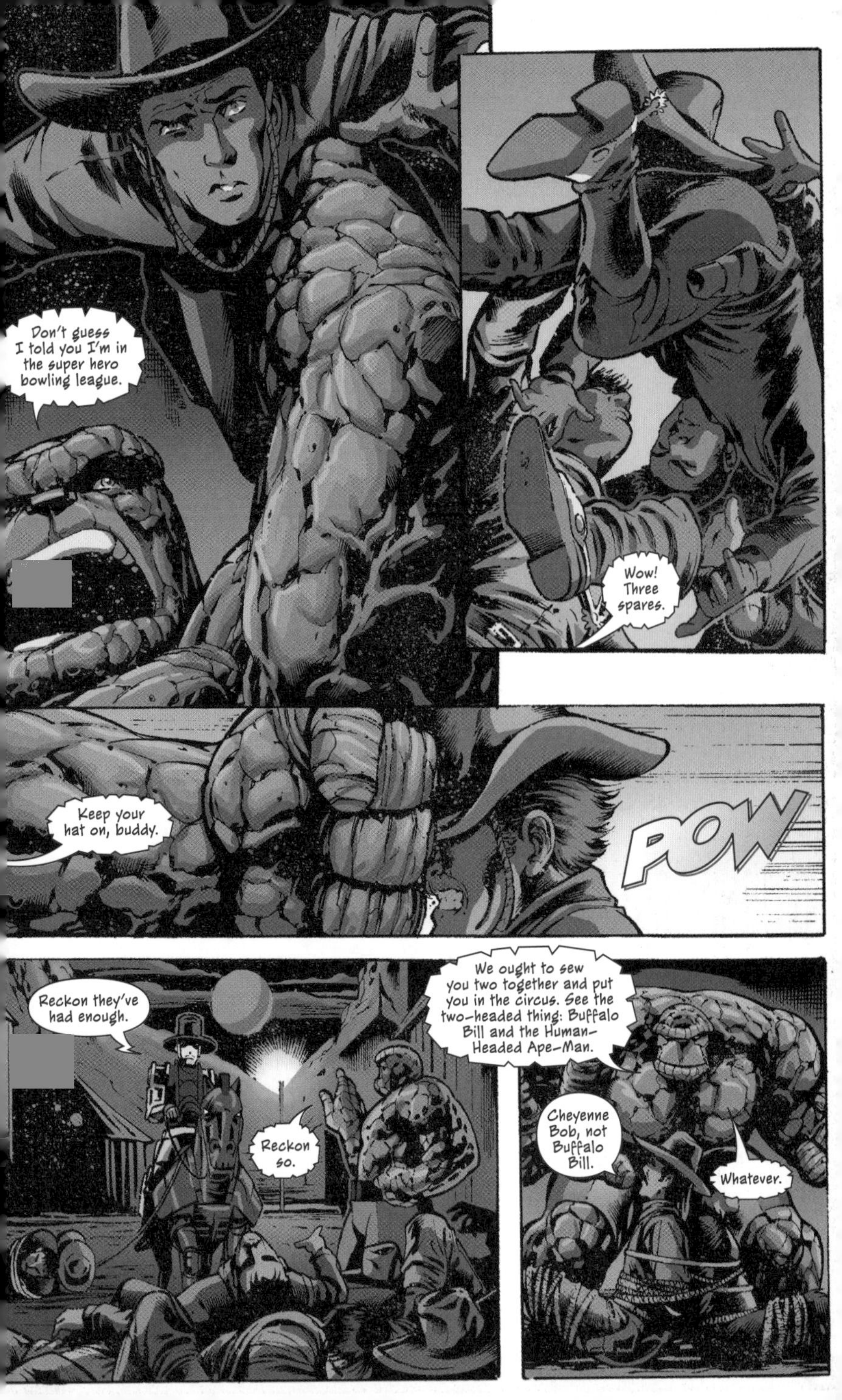
Don't guess I told you I'm in the super hero bowling league.
Wow! Three spares.
Keep your hat on, buddy.
POW
Reckon they've had enough.
Reckon so.
We ought to sew you two together and put you in the circus. See the two-headed thing: Buffalo Bill and the Human-Headed Ape-Man.
Cheyenne Bob, not Buffalo Bill.
Whatever.

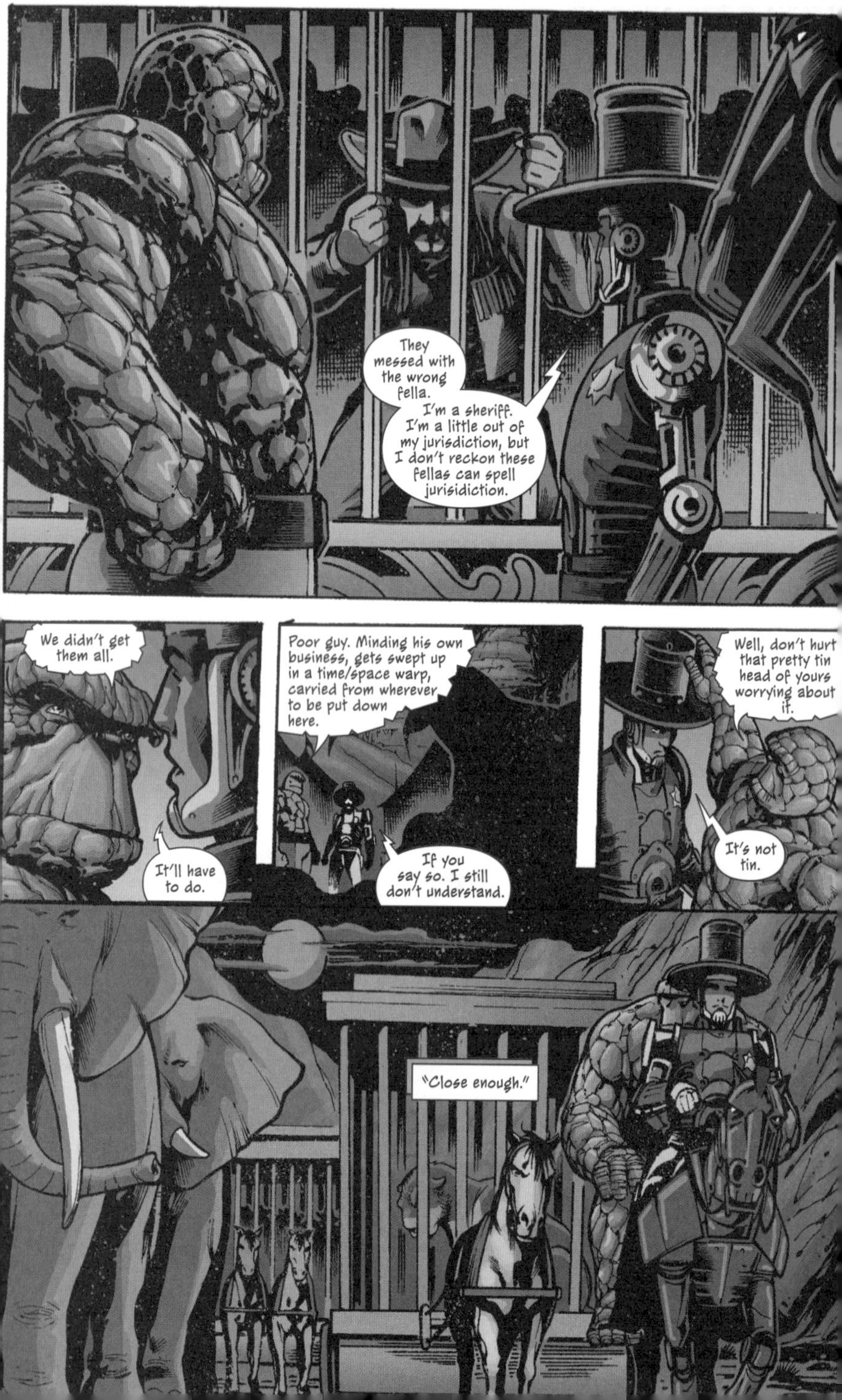

They messed with the wrong fella.
I'm a sheriff. I'm a little out of my jurisidiction, but I don't reckon these fellas can spell jurisidiction.
We didn't get them all.
It'll have to do.
Poor guy. Minding his own business, gets swept up in a time/space warp, carried from wherever to be put down here.
If you say so. I still don't understand.
Well, don't hurt that pretty tin head of yours worrying about it.
It's not tin.
"Close enough."

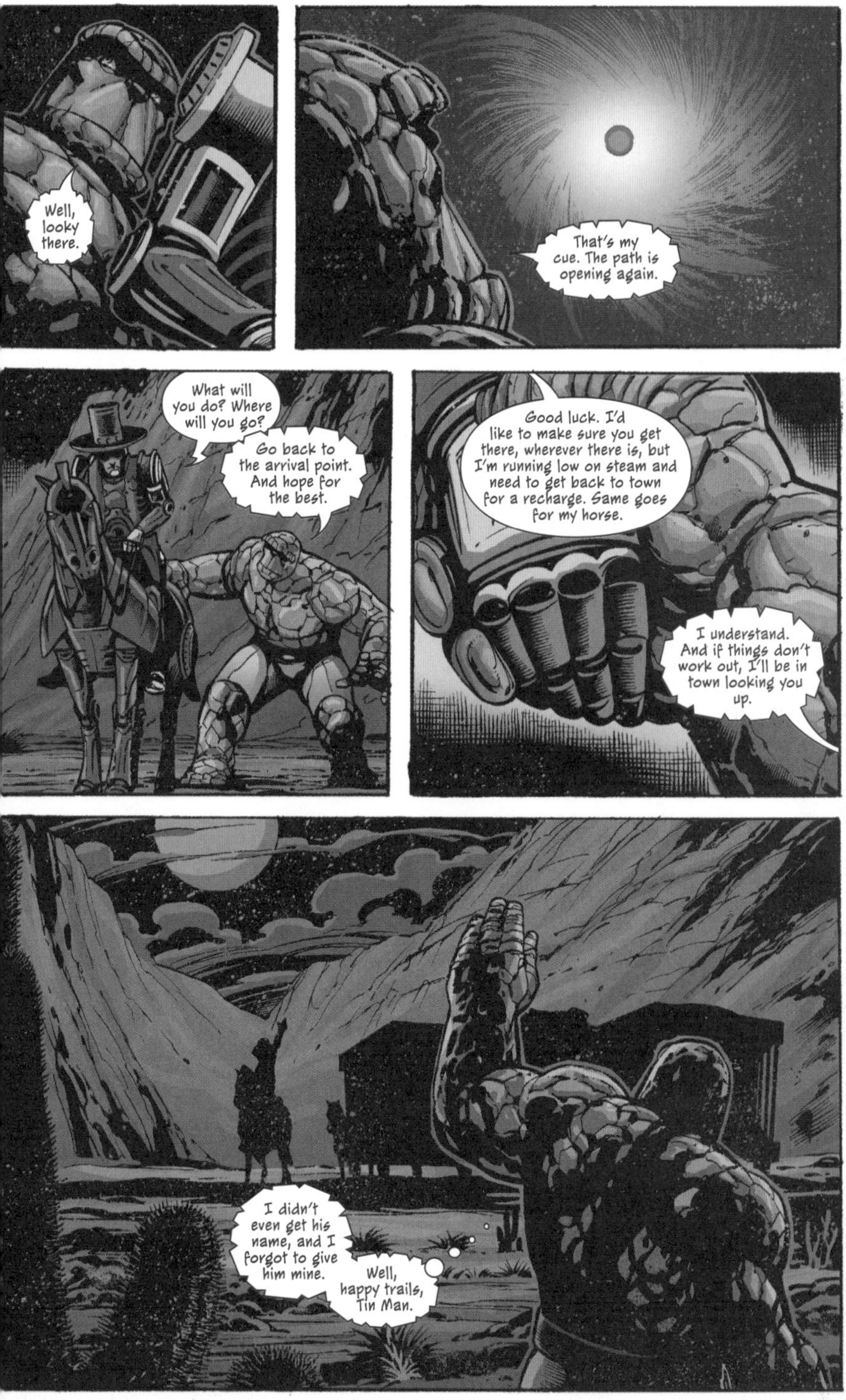
Well, looky there.
That's my cue. The path is opening again.
What will you do? Where will you go?
Go back to the arrival point. And hope for the best.
Good luck. I'd like to make sure you get there, wherever there is, but I'm running low on steam and need to get back to town for a recharge. Same goes for my horse.
I understand. And if things don't work out, I'll be in town looking you up.
I didn't even get his name, and I forgot to give him mine.
Well, happy trails, Tin Man.

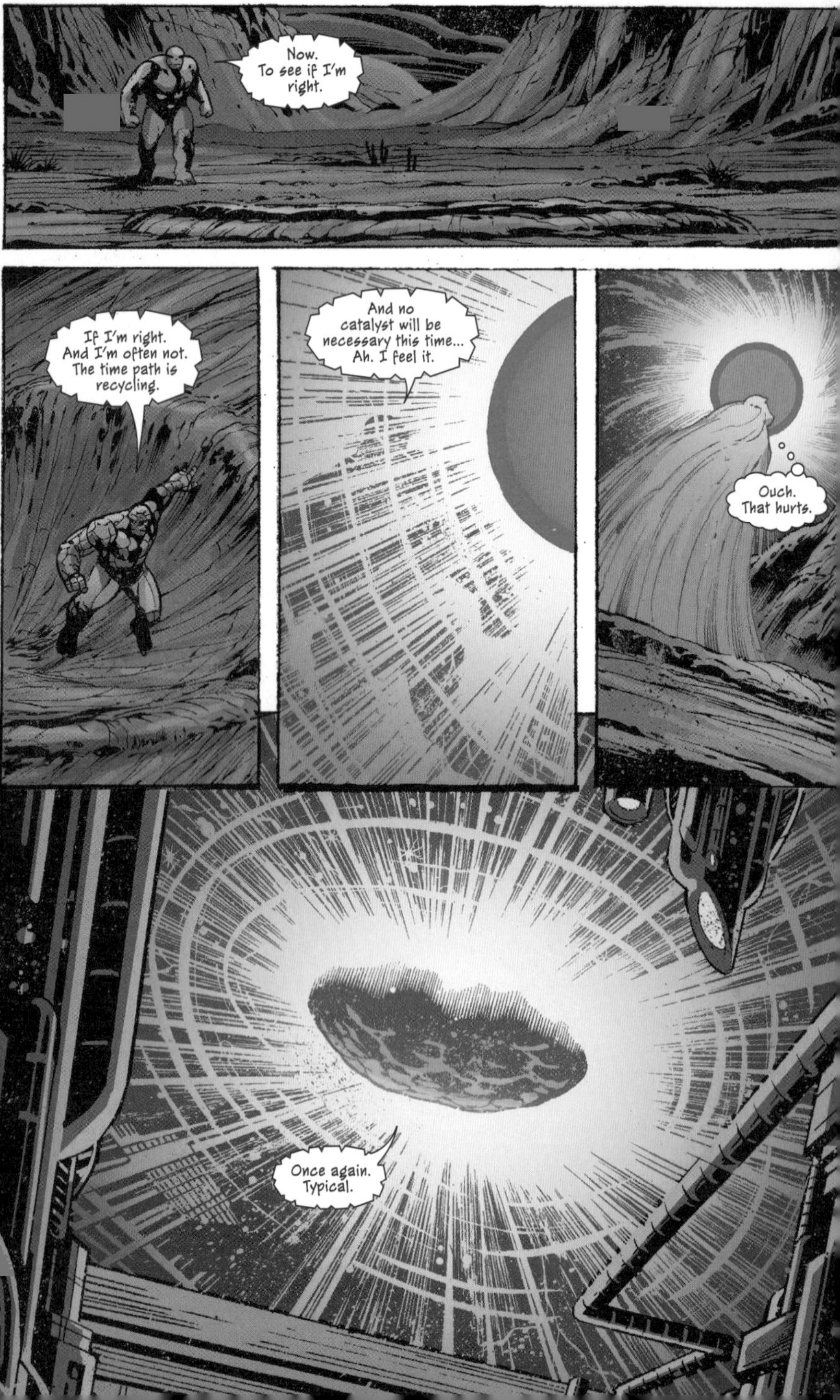
Now. To see if I'm right.
If I'm right. And I'm often not. The time path is recycling.
And no catalyst will be necessary this time... Ah. I feel it.
Ouch. That hurts.
Once again. Typical.

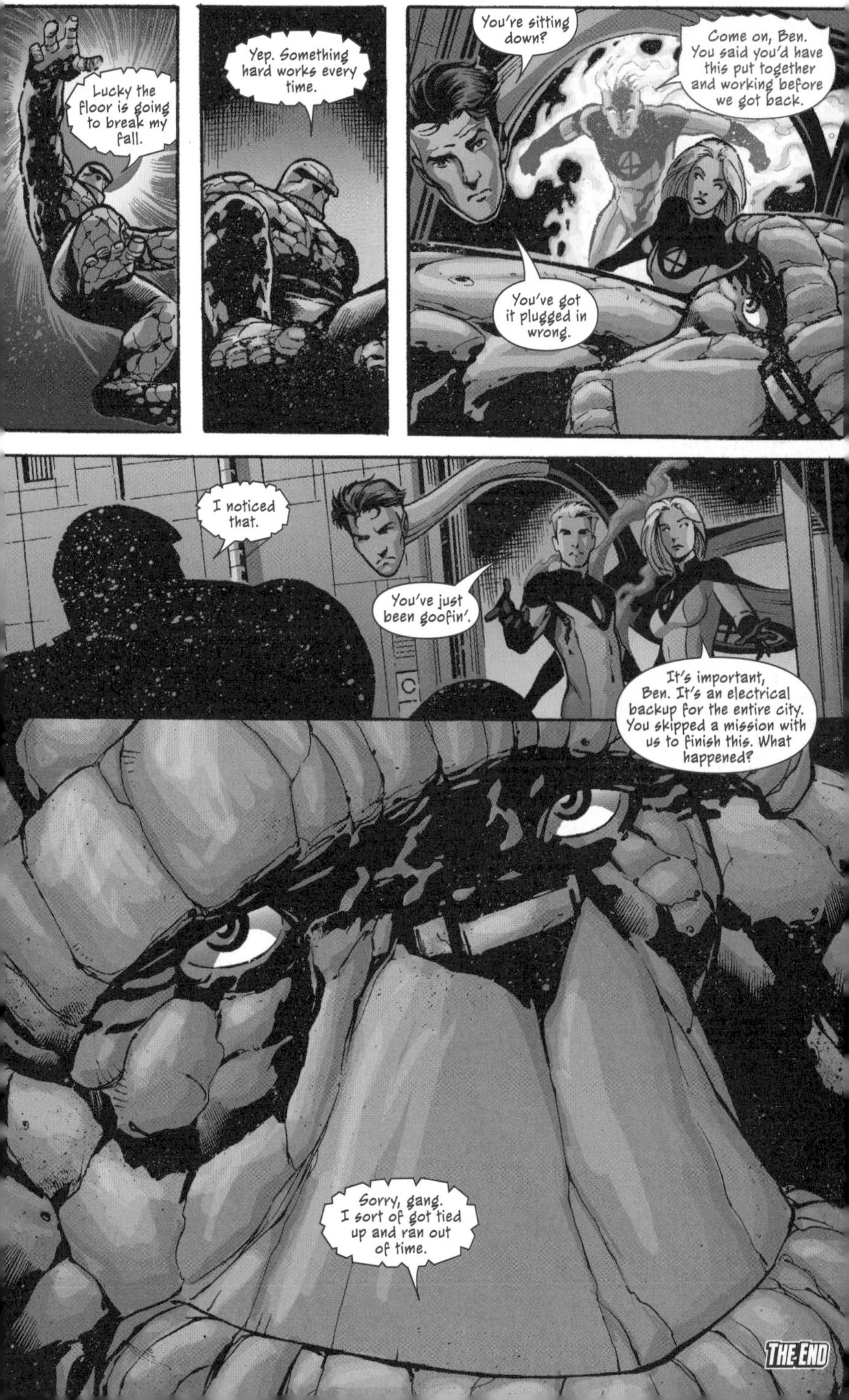

Lucky the floor is going to break my fall.
Yep. Something hard works every time.
You're sitting down?
Come on, Ben. You said you'd have this put together and working before we got back.
You've got it plugged in wrong.
I noticed that.
You've just been goofin'.
It's important, Ben. It's an electrical backup for the entire city. You skipped a mission with us to finish this. What happened?
Sorry, gang. I sort of got tied up and ran out of time.
THE END